A GLEAM OF LIGHT

BOOK ONE

THE SURVIVAL TRILOGY

BY

T.J. & M.L. WOLF

COPYRIGHT

The characters portrayed in
this book are fictitious. Any
similarity to real persons,
living or dead, is coincidental
and not intended by the authors.

The events surrounding
America West Flight 564,
which occurred on the night
of May 25, 1995
are well documented.

Cover illustration
by Rebekah Sather

Copyright © 2016 T. J. & M. L. Wolf
All Rights Reserved

ISBN: 1541055632
ISBN-13: 978-1541055636

CONTENTS

PART ONE – THE UNEXPECTED

1	Two Worlds	1
2	Departure	9
3	Cactus 564	19
4	Hawk 85	29
5	Bigfoot	38

PART TWO – ANCIENT VOICES 47

6	Bus Trip	48
7	Home Again	57
8	Intruders	67
9	Spirit Woman	78
10	Flashback	90
11	Proof	100
12	Prankster	110

CONTENTS

13	The Skeptic	120
	PART THREE – FOUR CORNERS	131
14	Balance	132
15	Deep-Seated	141
16	Aftermath	151
17	Reason	160
18	Heart-to-Heart	169
19	The Return	177
20	Invasion	187
21	Arm-in-Arm	197
22	Respect	206
	PART FOUR -- AWAKENING	214
23	Echoes	215

CONTENTS

24	Skinwalker	224
25	Just a Feeling	233
26	Forever	243
27	Illusion	251
28	Revelation	259
29	The Vow	268
30	Nexus	278
	PART FIVE – THE LONELY ROAD	285
31	The Search	286
32	Authenticity	294
33	Reluctance	302
34	Loose Ends	310
35	Field Report	321
36	Keepsake	328

PART ONE

THE UNEXPECTED

*"You have to believe in gods
to see them."*

--Hopi Proverb

1

TWO WORLDS

On a cloudy afternoon in late May, 1995, eight-year old Una Waters waited patiently in line beside her parents at the America West terminal of Dallas-Fort Worth International to board their flight. On layover from its starting point in Tampa, Florida, the giant B-757 airliner would only be here for an hour, to pick up a few passengers before heading to its final destination, Las Vegas, Nevada. It was the first time she and her mother had been asked to accompany her father, a missionary who had devoted his entire life to the betterment of U.S./Native American relations. It was how he met her mother on the Hopi reservation she called home, and the reason for this trip.

Una did not understand much about the Indian *problem*, as some people put it, though she thought she knew what it meant to be a Hopi. All her teachers at the Mission School in Arizona taught her to respect tribal elders, obey the law, and work hard at her lessons. Good grades were the key to a brighter future. People with good grades could grow up to be decision makers, and that could make the world a better place--for *everyone*.

The airport made her head spin! So many people everywhere with luggage, and all the announcements of flight times. There were families with children, youths in uniform with duffle bags, and older men in business suits, clinging to briefcases. Whatever they kept inside must be awfully important, because they never let them go, except to light a cigarette or make calls from airport telephones lined up along one wall. Most of them seemed tired and cranky, without much to smile about. Una decided she would not like to walk in their shoes. By the looks on their faces, it seemed that black leather must make their feet hurt.

"How much longer, Mummy?" she asked.

Lenmana Waters tried to smile. Their arrival flight from Flagstaff had given them just enough time to wait in long lines for the Ladies room and a quick lunch from *Urban Taco*. The food reminded her of hominy and beans back home, but more spicy with plenty of hot peppers. Texans seemed to eat a lot like Mexicans, even though they lived in America. It was like two worlds overlapped. That also reminded her of life as a Hopi.

Una gazed up at her father, white-haired, tall and lean like an actor she'd seen on TV reruns of *Barnaby Jones*. Simon Waters smiled pleasantly at everyone they met. He seemed out of place here. His genuine, easy-going style enabled him to connect with people of other cultures, because they did not feel intimidated.

"The eyes are the window to the soul," he once told her, "People know when you're not sincere."

Everyone who worked in the airport smiled a lot. People at the ticket counter, baggage handlers, even people who emptied trash cans or swept up the endless stream of wrappers and styrofoam cups left by weary travelers. Una sensed pain in their eyes. Of course, this was only her second time entering an airport since leaving her home on the Reservation. Dallas had more runways, more planes...more everything! The bigger the city, the more smiling workers. But it had nothing to do with happiness. Behind those smiles, they weren't happy at all.

"Why, Papa, why?" she'd asked him only a few days before.

"It's a National Conference on Indian Affairs. I've been graciously invited to present a paper on my work. Many people will be there who share our values. They understand the importance of preserving ancient lands. Some even have friends in high places. We need those kinds of friends...to protect our way of life. Without them, everything we cherish might one day disappear."

Already most of Una's friends spoke English, but had little understanding of Hopi words used in traditional ceremonies. Her mother once told her the people of their village had grown blue corn for a thousand generations, long before Columbus came to America. It was getting harder to grow all the time. Without it they could not make Piki bread--one of her favorites!

Just the thought of it made her mouth water. It seemed like ages since their last home meal. *One week*, her father said. One week and it would all be over. This was still only the first day! She was getting tired of airports. Tired of waiting. Tired of bright lights and loud noise. Tired of smells repeating themselves every 50 feet no matter which way they turned. Smells like McDonalds, floor wax, upholstery and stale coffee.

"It's not time yet," said the woman at the boarding desk. "Your flight has been delayed."

Her father sighed.

The woman smiled at Una. "I'll bet you can't wait to see *Pocahontas*. My daughter can't stop talking about it."

Lenmana took Una by the hand. They'd seen all the hoopla on TV. All the picture books and toys. One of her classmates even told her about a shopping mall display in Phoenix, complete with a huge model of a sailing ship. The movie release was still weeks or months away. It might as well be an *eternity*.

They sat in a row of blue cushioned seats that made it easy to read the lighted monitors overhead. The nearest screen displayed their flight number and destination as part of a list that seemed to flicker every few seconds.

One of the destinations that caught her eye was Venezuela, because it was the home of the Andes mountains. She recognized it from a book she had read in school. During a class visit to the library, while all the other children looked for age-appropriate books, she wandered over to the adult section, browsing until she came across one called *Alive*, a true story about a plane crash in the Andes and how they had to resort to cannibalism to survive. "But you're only in the third grade!" her teacher said. That didn't matter to Una. She wanted to read books about the real world. And she wasn't afraid of the truth.

Feeling restless, she climbed up on both knees, peering back over the edge of her seat. A huge picture window revealed the shiny silver, red and white tail of their America West airliner. It was so big! It reminded her of a rocketship. Birds flittered by. *When the Red, Red Robin Comes Bob, Bob Bobbin'* sang someone in white robes not far away. People called them Moonies. Una smiled. That plane could probably take her anywhere. Even the moon.

More and more passengers came to fill the seats beside them. A nervous little man in blue jeans and cowboy boots reached up, adjusting the black brim of his stetson, which seemed too big for his head. A big breasted blonde, pouting in red lipstick came marching out of the Ladies room to join him. "Dammit, Earle, I thought we'd be there by now. It's nearly sundown. I had big plans!"

The nervous man laughed. "Honey, we're not missin' a thing. Casino's open all night. You'll see. Vegas is for night owls. Hell, that's when all the fun begins. Have a couple drinks in the air, and we'll be there before you know it! Now just get over here and keep me company."

Apparently their destination had more going on than a National Conference. Una didn't know much about gambling, except what she heard in the news. Several Arizona tribes apparently had slot machines, hoping more money would solve the problem of Indian poverty. Without jobs, life for many Native Americans meant surviving on government handouts with little hope for the future.

As a child growing up, Una's grandmother told her tales about life in the old days. For many centuries, Hopi lands stretched across almost all of northern Arizona, from California to parts of Southern Nevada. They planted corn, beans and squash, hunting deer, antelope and small game. With villages on desert mesas for defense purposes, Hopi culture developed elaborate ceremonies and enjoyed trade throughout the Southwest.

First came the Spaniards to Hopi territory, seeking the legendary Seven Cities of Gold. Then Europeans moved in, pressuring the Navajo, who fought with the Hopi for survival over land and water, until both were forced onto reservations in 1864. Her grandmother was not yet born when all of this happened, but the stories were passed down. Her only memories as a child were formed on the Hopi Reservation in Black Mesa. It was all that remained of their native lands.

The Indian *problem* had evolved over time,

making life complicated for Una's family and everyone that she had ever known. To find a solution might take many years, many votes and many marches to achieve. It was all too much for an eight year old girl to absorb, but she hoped one day to understand.

Maybe even to help.

The Governor of Arizona wasn't too happy about slot machines, so he sent FBI agents to raid five Indian casinos and shut them all down. People always fought over money. Sometimes fighting seemed like a bad idea, especially against the United States government.

"Attention passengers. America West Flight 564 will begin boarding soon. Please check your bags and have tickets ready. Thank you."

People stood up all around them, forming a line to the departure gate. Beyond it, a narrow carpeted opening curved out of sight. A smiling stewardess in blue uniform, ready to greet them, brushed dark bangs away from her eyes. One family came rushing over with two small children and a baby stroller from the nearest McDonalds. She waved them to the front of the line. A woman grumbled. Una turned to see it was the blonde, standing nearly a head taller than the cowboy, without his hat.

Outside, the gray desert sky began to turn bright orange. No doubt it was much warmer than the air conditioned comfort inside. Soon they would be high above the cactus and sage brush, practically invisible to anyone on the ground. Closer to heaven than

Earth.

Before leaving the reservation, one of her friends asked Una if they were going to see the Sky People.

She did not know what to say.

According to legend, once a great flood was about to engulf a Hopi village and people fled from destruction. A little boy and girl, twins, were somehow left behind. They decided to try to find their parents and escape. So they went out across the desert. While they camped over night, a 'flying shield' came down right before them.

Emerging from it, one of the Sky People came to the children and said, "Do not be afraid. We're going to fly above the desert to search for them." And so they flew many miles, until the children were delivered to their parents. Then he told them, "In the future, I will come to you in your dreams and teach you the proper way to live."

Una grasped her mother's hand. Life beyond the reservation could be scary at times. It was full of surprises. So much had happened already that she did not expect. It was impossible to know what might happen next.

At least she did not have to face it alone.

For now, it was enough to stay right here, between her parents, protecting her like Guardian Angels. She only hoped that when it was over, they would all return home, safe and sound, to the world she knew best.

2

DEPARTURE

The boarding bridge from the airline terminal bounced and creaked beneath their feet as passengers made their way toward Flight 564. Though at first appearing half empty, a traffic jam of people with carry-ons filled the narrow space from wall to wall as the plane's open hatch came into view.

Audio from a recent ad campaign played softly in the background:

> *R - E - S - P - E - C - T,*
> *Find out when you fly with me,*
> At America West,
> we respect your need to save money...

Yet muffled voices ahead made it clear there was some commotion that prevented the line from moving forward. Una craned her neck from side to side, unable to see beyond the assortment of bags and adult legs blocking her view.

"Patience, dear," her father said, "It won't be

long now."

"Nooo!" a woman complained. "This is no joke. I'm telling you I won't go...because it's not *safe*."

The bridge suddenly fell silent.

"Ma'am, please lower your voice, and step aside. Other passengers are waiting to board."

"But you don't understand. It's not about the plane. It's your destination. I...*see* things. It's...hard to explain!"

As more and more people joined those already in line, tempers flared. Una could hear whispers all around her.

"Maybe it's not her fault," said a man in long sleeved dress shirt and tie. "I fly this route all the time. Going to Vegas can be a real head trip. Some people lose it. Happened on a flight from Denver, once. Passenger swore there were demons under the runway. Relax. They know how to handle it."

Sure enough, moments later the poor woman walked calmly past them, head down, escorted by airport security.

Again the line began to move, shuffling toward the hatch.

A white-haired grandma in pink shawl with pearl earrings and thick glasses, accompanied by her grandson, paused, reaching into her purse. "Damn," she said, "I *thought* I recognized her. Get rid of this for me, dear. Psychic nonsense. I should've known better."

He accepted a small tattered paperback, entitled

Beyond the Veil, with a cover photo of the woman they escorted away, a woman who once appeared on Carson and Sally Jesse Raphael--and tossed it into a trash can.

Simon Waters seemed surprised when a young stewardess reached out to shake his hand. Lenmana smiled, clinging to her husband. "Welcome to America West," she said as they stepped onto the plane. "Enjoy your flight."

Una breathed a sigh of relief.

She gazed up in awe as they moved down the lighted center aisle. It seemed to go on *forever*. Every row contained three seats to either side. A few people in First Class reached up, stuffing bags into sleek overhead storage compartments that closed with a click.

"When do we sit, Papa?" she asked.

"Not yet. We're Economy Class. Further to the back. Row 39."

The seats became smaller, more cramped together. But still plenty big. At the end of each row was a window seat with its own little shade that moved up and down. Una decided to pick one if she could, and keep hers open all the time.

She saw mostly adults, many wearing sunglasses and bright-colored t-shirts except for ladies with big hair, like the blonde in blue jeans and high heels, whose plunging neckline revealed her breasts for all to see. A few older women had rain bonnets, just in case. They said it might even storm.

There were plenty of teenagers, too. Girls in halter tops with butterfly tattoos on their shoulders and thighs, skimpy skin-tight dresses and Walkmans to play their favorite tunes. One girl's ankle displayed Mr. Peanut with top hat and cane. They were all giggling and pointing at teen boys who played with buttons, adjusted their seats, and seemed not to notice.

Una kept track of the row numbers, hoping-hoping-hoping her seat would not overlook the wing, because that would make it impossible to see anything.

She passed a young boy her own age dressed in gray shirt, matching pants, white hat, red scarf, black gloves and silver badge. He waved a toy gun resembling a six shooter from the Old West.

"Who are you?" she asked.

"I'm the Lone Ranger. Can't you tell? Usually I wear a mask. Better not cause any trouble, or I'll have to take you in."

Una's father liked to watch old TV shows on their VCR back home, so she knew all about classic heroes like The Lone Ranger and Superman. Sometimes they even watched Wonder Woman. Una liked her about the best.

"So where's Tonto?"

"Had to shoot 'im," the boy said, taking aim at Una, "He was an Indian. That's how we won the West. Everybody knows that."

A big man in green Army uniform beside the boy

turned abruptly, taking the gun from his hand. "*Colin*! How many times must I tell you? Never point this at anyone. Or I'll take it away for good. Don't be a brat!"

The boy only grinned, with a clever look in his eye.

"Come along," her father said, pulling her hand.

The rows went on and on. They had to keep stopping while people took their seats. Her eyes brightened as they finally passed the wings. Somehow, as they neared the back of the plane, it seemed to be getting dark. Maybe those older women were right. If only she had a rain bonnet.

Finally they came to row 39. Clicking sounds made her turn until she found the source: another boy a few years older, with a camera in his hand. He seemed to take pictures of everything; the plane, its passengers, even the distant runway outside his window. She thought he might be alone, until the woman beside him cautioned him to slow down. "You'll be out of film before we get there."

"No way!" he grinned. His open backpack revealed boxes and boxes of it.

"It's for the High School paper. A journalist is always prepared. I'm the first frosh in my class to see Vegas. They're countin' on me to deliver!"

The boy looked over at Una just as she turned away. It wasn't polite to stare and she knew that. It's just that he seemed so mature. Boys like him were full of ideas and high hopes for the future.

The window seat suited her just fine. Orange

sunlight bathed all sorts of smaller service vehicles roving about on the tarmac. One carried a long line of luggage, stacked in neat rows. Another said EMERGENCY in big red letters, but the driver was standing outside, talking into a car phone.

After all the seats were filled, two airline employees closed the boarding hatch. Several stewardesses positioned themselves in the center aisle as red and white lights flashed overhead, accompanied by a male voice:

> "Ladies and Gentlemen, this is your captain speaking. Please fasten yourseat belts. If you need assistance, raise a hand. We'll be moving out onto the runway momentarily. Weather radar indicates a major storm currently tracking toward our flight path with winds and rain. Arrival is expected in Las Vegas around 10:40 PM. Thanks again for choosing America West, and have a pleasant flight."

Una fastened her seat belt. Another voice reviewed passenger safety instructions in case anything should go wrong, but no one paid much attention. As the aircraft began to shake, she realized it was backing slowly away from the terminal, then swinging around. Outside her window, the scene turned to wide open space. Next, the giant craft taxied up to a specific point and stopped, waiting for instruction from the airport control tower.

Another plane lifted off before her eyes. One minute it was touching the ground, the next it was airborne. She read somewhere that a B-757 weighed over *one hundred tons*. It seemed miraculous, and yet, there was the proof of something that ought not to be possible.

Already high above, faintly, she could see stars, and wondered if her parents ever felt this way about going to the moon. Her teacher said there was a race in the 1960s, between the United States and the Soviet Union. President Kennedy challenged the nation. Later it became the mission of Apollo 11 to make the historic landing. *One small step for man, one giant leap for mankind*, an astronaut said. They spent just over two hours on the moon's surface, collecting rocks, before returning to Earth. Everyone was real happy about it except for Kennedy. He was already dead.

Of course, it all happened long ago, before Una was even born. These days nobody went to the moon. Astronauts flew in the Space Shuttle to fix the Hubble Telescope, but it never left Earth orbit.

"What's the hold up?" a man said.

"You heard the captain," a woman in the seat beside him replied. "*Major Storm*. Sounds like trouble.

Oh, god! Why did he have to say that? Rain would've been one thing. Planes fly over rain clouds all the time. Now I'm worried!"

Una was all ears.

"Oh, it's not *my* fault. Blame my therapist. He said it would be good for me. Confront my fears and all that. *Bullshit!* I'm just not ready."

"Sure. Sure you are," the man said.

The woman shook her head. "I keep having the same dream...on a plane, in Economy Class, by a window seat...in a storm."

"So? What's it mean?"

"*He* says it's all about my journey in life, to higher awareness. *Economy* because I feel ordinary, *window seat* because I'm seeking 'the big picture', *storm* because I'm feeling insecure. A journey into the unknown."

"Makes sense to me. Okay," as if he was losing interest. "Let's cut to the chase. Does it crash? Are we all gonna die?"

"N-nooo."

"Not to worry, then! Lady, all you need is a drink. When the lights go off, I'll get one for each of us."

Lenmana patted her daughter's hand. Other children played with toys, but Una was always so inquisitive, absorbing the world around her. Unfortunately, adult conversations were not always appropriate for the ears of an eight-year-old.

"Don't be afraid. It's nearly past your bedtime. Try to sleep. It will make the trip go faster."

But the thought of a storm did not frighten her.

Every summer, from July to August, as hot air off the desert came east to meet cool air of high mountains, thunderstorms came to the reservation. Farming without irrigation, Hopis had learned to utilize every drop of moisture, planting crops in the mouths of washes, to catch any runoff. Each storm might only deposit a little rain, but two to three in a week was just enough to water their corn.

She remembered her first glimpse of desert lightning. They called the storm a 'monsoon'. Stepping outside, she spied an approaching wall of gray clouds, everything in motion from high winds. A streak of light, from cloud-to-ground, split a huge tree in half, with a scar burned right down the middle.

To the people of her village, rain was everything. They would sing and dance--not to bring rain, but to welcome it.

Una tried to imagine what it would be like to see the storm up close, as lightning danced all around them.

She wondered if *Kachinas*, known as spirits who bring rain, might be watching them. Once, long ago, they danced for the Hopis, and taught them powerful ceremonies. Some said these spirits still came to her village every spring, to help with daily activities. To help them survive.

Suddenly, there was movement. The runway

scene outside her window began sliding by, slowly at first, then faster. Everything started to vibrate, including the arm rests, the floor beneath her feet, and overhead doors on the storage compartments. She could hear the roar of engines. Any moment, they would depart from the Earth, and leap toward the sky.

Sleep was the *last* thing on her mind.

3

CACTUS 564

It all happened so fast. Una felt her seat tipping back, everything tilted and suddenly they were looking *up* toward the front of the aircraft. It was exhilarating and scary, all at once. She could hear a few gasps, followed by nervous laughter. Turning side to side against her headrest, she could see people with their eyes closed.

"How long, Papa?" she asked.

"Three hours. Try not to think about it. We'll be there in no time."

She already knew that. She meant *how long till we level out?* Sitting back like an astronaut, too many questions like *what if we go too high* or *how can they see through the clouds* came to mind.

Though it probably lasted only a few minutes, it seemed like a really long time. A hush came over just about everyone, except for the pair of gamblers who kept right on talking. The man gave advice on 'Games of Chance', while the woman pretended to listen.

Finally the plane's nose began to drop and Una

could feel her feet touching the floor again. Lighted SEAT BELT signs went off, and everyone started to move around. A stewardess came slowly down the aisle with a cart of refreshments.

Outside her window, Una could see thick, white cumulous clouds, against a darkening sky. Somewhere below lay New Mexico and her home state of Arizona, including the Grand Canyon. Rocks and sand stretched to the horizon, with no end in sight. She guessed a few straight lines with moving dots to be desert roads. There were no more buildings or lights on the ground. Just miles and miles of sage brush, and empty wilderness.

The thought of flying at night had not occurred to her. She sighed, placing one hand to the glass. Soon perhaps there would be nothing to see at all, beyond her own reflection.

The gamblers opened a new deck of cards to practice. Every time the woman said "Hit me!" seemed to be wrong, until finally, she started to cry and didn't want to play any more. But the man said it would be all right, because he was the real gambler anyway, and she could be his good luck charm.

The whole concept never made sense to Una. If a charm, like a rabbit's foot could bring good luck, why didn't everyone wear one all the time? Her parents never did. Some people said, "You make your own luck" but 'luck' often seemed to elude hard working people, who simply learned to live without it. In her mind, 'luck' was not something that came to you, but something you already have. She felt lucky to have two loving parents, learning the Hopi Way from her elders, and lucky to be alive.

"Pretzels or peanuts?" repeated the stewardess, stopping a row ahead of them. Her assistant poured soft drinks like Pepsi or Sprite into small plastic cups. Two out of three passengers politely accepted.

"Never mind *him*," said an older woman, pointing discreetly to the window seat beside her. Its long-haired occupant, in headphones and dark rimmed glasses, studied a well-worn copy of *2001*. "Not much company."

The young dude, in his early 20s, seemed oblivious to them, except for a slight shifting of the eyes. Una caught a glimpse of them as she stood up to reach for her snack. He clearly had something to hide.

The stewardess frowned as her cart began to shimmy. The entire cabin suddenly pitched a few degrees to one side, causing drinks to spill. Bags jostled in overhead compartments, raising more than a few eyebrows.

"N-now what the hell?" someone cried.

"Relax!" she said calmly. "Just turbulence. Flights to Vegas always get a little bumpy. It's worse this time of year."

A frequent flyer raised his hand. "Thermal variety, no doubt. Caused by the summer sun. Desert areas heat up more rapidly, creating updrafts. Turbulent air behaves a lot like rough water. It's like hitting a speed bump."

"C-can it d-damage the plane?"

"Of course not. No more than a pothole will make your car crash. Usually occurs closer to landing, though. We're too far out. Storms can be felt even 20 miles away. There may be one up ahead."

The stewardess rushed over, bending down to hold the shaken man's hand. "You're hyperventilating. Take slow, deep breaths. Loosen your grip on the arm rest. Try closing your eyes."

Una pictured their plane as a tiny boat, trapped in a stormy sea. Though she had never been to the coast, she had seen TV news reports on Hurricane Gordon, back in November. After landfalls in Jamaica and Cuba, it crossed the Florida Keys as a Tropical Storm. There it caused eight fatalities and 43 injuries, with total damages of $400 million. Boats could be capsized or dashed into rocky shores. Why not a plane? If air turbulence was like that, the danger *must* be real.

Only Captain Tollefson, in the cockpit, could tell how many feet the plane was actually moving up and down, or side to side. He kept a close watch on the altimeter, which showed a variance of less than forty feet--more like twenty, most of the time. Any change in the plane's direction was undetectable. Passengers saw it differently, no doubt. It was like riding in the back seat of a car. Even the slightest shift felt magnified.

"Slow to TPS," he said to his copilot, meaning

'turbulence penetration speed', a safety measure to stabilize the ride and prevent damage to the airframe. It was so close to normal cruising speed that most passengers would not detect the change from their seats.

When all the excitement was over, Una found herself yawning, and soon drifted off to sleep. She dreamed of a perfect sunrise on the Hopi Reservation with her favorite uncle, Lapu. He dipped a green measuring cup into a large bag, and filled it with 12 seeds, dropping them down a long tube into sandy soil. Scoop after scoop, row after row, they traveled together across a huge field on a blustery day, until all the blue corn was planted.

A little after 9 PM, she stretched and opened her eyes. "Are we there yet?"

"Almost," her father replied.

Moments later, the call of Mother Nature pulled Una from her seat. With the nearest bathroom occupied, she found another toward the front of the plane, and emerged a few moments later. There, an anxious-looking stewardess shuffled by. As she opened a small door, Una could hear the captain's voice:

> "Cactus 564 going direct crow,
> Crow 6 arrival Las Vegas,"
> then a brief pause, followed
> by "564 at 39000."

She almost giggled. *Cactus* for a call sign? Tall, tree-like saguaros and flat padded prickly pears were familiar sights in the Arizona desert. Some tribes, like the Pima, would harvest wild fruit to make syrup. Hopis sometimes used the fleshy pads like medicine for snake bites and more. Last summer, her mother made a poultice to treat a particularly nasty sunburn.

She sat wide-eyed upon returning to her seat. *39,000 feet!* Could they really be that high? She hoped the plane would not run out of fuel, because that seemed like an awfully long way to fall.

A light flashed, outside her window.

"See?" one woman whispered in front of them. "Thunderstorm, I'll bet. Just as I thought."

"No, that can't be!" her friend said, "Pilots avoid them, at all cost. We must be miles away."

Una listened for thunder. That was the *real* test. It always came after lightning, because light travelled faster than sound. She looked carefully at everyone's hair, including her own. Standing on end would precede a lightning strike. She quickly bent over, face tucked into her lap.

"What are you doing?" her mother asked.

And there it went--a rumble in the distance.

Again she watched and waited. Counting the number of seconds between the flash and the rumble, then dividing it by five, would tell how many miles between her and the storm. When it flashed again, she counted. Only three! It was much too close for comfort.

Others faced their windows. The light display was spectacular, considering their point of view. The sky came alive, inspiring others to act. She could hear repeated clicks of a camera and knew its source. From first class came the pops of a revolving cap gun. Each person on board, in their own unique way, responded to what was happening outside the airliner.

A stewardess raced up the aisle toward the cockpit. "The lights!" she cried, opening that same small door. "In a row. Can you see them?"

That's when it *really* got interesting.

Anyone outside the craft would have observed the captain, leaving his seat to peer out the windshield as they were passing near Bovina, Texas, across the state line from Clovis, New Mexico around 9:25 MST (Mountain Standard Time).

"Cactus 564," he said to Albuquerque Air Traffic Control (ABQ), "Off to our 3:00, got some strobes out there. Could you tell us what it is?"

ABQ: "Uh, Uh...I'll tell you what, that's some, uh...right now...I don't know what it is right now. That is a restricted area that is used by the military out there during the day time."

"Yeah...it's pretty odd."

ABQ: "Hold on...let me see if anybody else knows around here."

The headphones dude seemed to perk up, tossing his book aside. Una could tell he was no longer indifferent. Holding his face to the window, he searched the night sky.

"What *is* that?" said the woman beside him.

A row of bright lights, some distance below their line of flight, hovered in the darkness, flashing in sequence from left to right.

"I dunno...exactly," he replied. "But I don't think it's...one of *ours*."

She glanced around the cabin, at other passengers. "What does he mean? Not American? Russian? Chinese? What?"

He slowly shook his head, eyes rolling upward.

No one else dared to speak, for fear of sounding foolish.

Una thought she understood. The secret he was trying to hide. He knew something that no one else did. At least no one sitting around him. But how? He might be a psychic, but that was unlikely.

She had to think.

What set him apart from everyone else? Not the long hair or the glasses. Not his book. Lots of people read to pass the time.

His headphones!

That buzzing in his ears...*must* hold the answer. Not just music. More like a radio, a portable CB scanner. Truck drivers came through Black Mesa all the time. One even broke down once, driving a sixteen wheeler, right out there on State Route 264. He used his CB to call for help. Maybe *that* was it.

Maybe he could hear the captain--and knew they

were in trouble.

Reaching over, Una pulled the plug on his headphones. Suddenly, *everyone* could hear the captain's voice, speaking to Air Traffic Control:

"Cactus 564...can you paint that object at all on your radar?"

ABQ: "No I don't, and in talkin' to 3 or 4 guys around here no one knows what that is, never heard about that."

"Cactus 564...nobody's painting it at all?"

ABQ: "Say again?"

"I said there's nothing on their radars on the other centers at all on that *kssshhhh...* clear area...that object that's up in the air?"

ABQ: "Huh?...it's up in the air?"

"A-FFIRMATIVE!!"

ABQ: "No...no one knows anything about it. What's the altitude about?"

"I don't know, probably right around 30,000 or so. And it's uh...there's a strobe that starts...um, going on counter-clockwise, and uh...the length is unbelievable."

For three rows on either side, people sat in disbelief, staring at the dude's Bearcat scanner radio. No one seemed to know for sure what it meant, but they kept pointing out their windows. By now, at least, it seemed clear that Flight 564 was not alone.

A stewardess had tried to intervene only once,

telling him to *shut the thing off*, but that just wasn't happening. She resigned herself to the galley, seated behind a curtain, and remained quiet.

Una's parents had no time to react to their daughter's impertinence. After all, it was apparently her insight that uncovered the mystery surrounding their flight. She appeared to have everyone's blessing.

Lightning and thunder continued to fill the sky. Minor turbulence shook the aircraft. People closed their window blinds, afraid to look outside. More than a few fastened their seat belts.

There were no more formal announcements from the cockpit. Passengers felt completely on their own. But it wasn't due to lack of R-E-S-P-E-C-T or because no one cared.

Clearly the crew was preoccupied.

4

HAWK 85

In spite of all the commotion, only a few passengers on Flight 564 regarded the light show as anything more than a thunderstorm. If there was another aircraft, so be it. Lots of people flew to Vegas this time of year.

For those clustered near row 39, however, it was a completely different story. They had every reason to believe an unknown threat was lurking amongst the clouds. In spite of every precaution taken by the crew, an unauthorized craft had invaded their airspace--and no one knew what to do.

Suddenly a new voice entered the radio transmissions between the captain and Albuquerque Center. It came from Cannon Air Force Base (CAFB):

"Cannon 121?"

CAFB: "Cannon...go ahead."

ABQ: "Do you guys know if there was anything like a tethered balloon released that should be above 'tieband'?"

CAFB: "Uh, no, we haven't heard nothin' about it."

ABQ: "A guy at 39,000 says he sees something at 30,000 that's as...the length is unbelievable and it has a strobe on it."

CAFB: "Uh huh...?"

ABQ: "This is NOT good... (chuckling)...okay..."

CAFB: "Uh, wha, wha...what does that mean?"

ABQ: "(laughing)...I don't know, it's a UFO or something, it's that Roswell crap again!"

CAFB: "Where's it at now?"

ABQ: "He says it's right in 'tieband'."

CAFB: "Tieband? That's restricted!"

ABQ: "Yeah!"

CAFB: "No, we haven't seen nothin' like that."

ABQ: "Okay, keep your eyes open."

Briefly, there was nothing but static (*kssshhhh*).

The frequent flyer grinned. "*There's* your answer. Tieband! Must be some military thing. Mystery *solved*!"

"Not so fast," the radio dude replied.

ABQ: "Cactus 564...we checked with Cannon and they don't have any, uh weather balloons or anything up tonight. Nobody up front knows any idea about that. Do you still see it?"

"Negative...back where we initially spotted it, it was between the weather and us and when there's lightning you could see a dark object...and, uh, it was pretty eerie looking. This 'air coptr... *kssshhhh*... right here going eastbound ... maybe he'll see it."

ABQ: "Okay..."

"First time in 15 years I've ever seen anything like this."

More static (*kssshhhh*), followed by a voice from *another* aircraft, an Air Force Hawk 85, breaking in on the conversation:

ABQ: "Aircraft calling...try again!"
HWK85: *"Center...uh...got time for a quick question?"*
ABQ: "Okay...go ahead."
HWK85: *"Kssshhhh...781, what was that Cactus guy talking about he saw?"*
ABQ: "I, I don't know, off your right wing about 15-20 miles. He's saying he saw a large object with a strobe that looked like it was at 30,000 feet."
HWK85: *"Ah...that secret stuff!"*

Una wondered what *kind* of secret he meant. Good or bad? Sometimes secrets were harmless fun to keep and share with her friends--like surprise birthday parties or holiday gifts. Good secrets were always temporary, to be revealed in the near future.

Bad secrets were not fun at all--the kind that parents and teachers said NOT to keep, like if someone does something bad and warns you not to tell, especially if they say you'll get in trouble. Bad secrets were meant to last forever.

She could see by the looks of fear and anxiety on adult faces all around her that *secret stuff* must be very bad.

The captain's voice broke in again, seeking confirmation from Albuquerque regarding the Air Force pilot's position:

"Albuquerque...Cactus 564."
ABQ: "Cactus 564...go ahead."
"*Kssshhhh*...that passed us earlier on the right. He'll be in the area in a few minutes, is that correct?"
ABQ: "Yeah, he'll be there in about 3 to 4 minutes, at 27,000. I'll ask him what he sees."
"...be at his left-hand side between him and the thunderstorm. Thanks a lot, we'll just monitor and listen."
ABQ: "Okay."
"Three of us up here saw it!"
ABQ: "Okay."

Silence gripped those seated around Una, as everyone waited for the next transmission:

ABQ: "I can't find...in the next 2 to 3 minutes. Be looking off your right side, if you see anything about 30,000 feet, we had one aircraft reporting something that wasn't a weather balloon or anything. It was a long white-looking thing with a strobe on. Let me know if you see anything out there."

HWK85: *"I'll be careful...kssshhhh."*
ABQ: "He said it was about 30,000."
HWK85: *"Kssshhhh...I'm looking for ET."*

Everyone's eyes lit up, except for Una's. *ET the Extraterrestrial* hit theaters back in '82, five years before she was born. It told the story of Elliot, a lonely boy who befriended an alien, stranded on Earth. Elliot and his siblings helped ET return home while attempting to hide him from their mother and the government.

It brought back memories for many adults on board. The film dealt with broken families, loneliness, friendship, and love. It touched upon everyday emotions, like fear and mistrust, and the need to be understood. ET seemed to bring out the best and worst in mankind.

With her compassion for all living things and natural curiosity, it was the kind of story Una would love. However, since her parents were not necessarily fans of science fiction, the movie had yet to cross her path.

"This can't be *happening*," said the radio dude. "Not here. Not now. I'm totally unprepared."

"What?" Una asked.

"I figured it would happen *some* day. You know, face-to-face with life from outer space. Not just for me, but everybody. To erase all doubt. This way, it's no good. All we have is a story to tell, with nothing to back it up. No one will ever believe us. Maybe after a while, we won't even believe it ourselves."

Una nodded. Sometimes she could sense things, like danger--but had difficulty putting them into words. Whenever she tried to explain it, adults would simply smile and shake their heads. Kids knew how it felt not to be taken seriously. Even when it was the truth. Instead of being corrected for "making up lies", sometimes it was best not to say anything at all.

Once she heard Uncle Lapu pleading with a government agent to block public access to sacred Hopi sites. "These shrines were set up in ancient times, as a *sign* of the Hopi covenant with Maasaw, the Earth Guardian. Each site holds a sacred life essence...that cannot be replaced."

The agent did not believe him.

"How can you tell?" the man said. "Marked by simple stones that resemble mere rock piles? Even the experts cannot agree. Your 'shrines' just so happen to coincide with ancestral formations of great interest to modern archaeology. Mere coincidence? I think not."

"So you just ignore it?"

"I have no choice. If we back off, valuable scientific knowledge could be lost. Who's blocking *who* here, chief?"

Her uncle of course did not win the argument. But Una could never forget the agent's lack of sensibility. Centuries of Hopi tradition meant nothing to him--as if it did not even exist.

A sense of panic came over the transmissions

between Captain Tollefson and Albuquerque, as if they could not believe their own eyes:

ABQ: "Cactus 564...you still up?"
"Affirmative! 564."
ABQ: "That was south of your position?"
"It was north..."
ABQ: "Hawk 85, let's make it out the left window then..."
"Albuquerque, can we get a chance? Cactus 564."
ABQ: "You know we're all up here huddled up talking about it. When it lightning'd you could see the *dark object*. It was like a cigar shape from the altitude that we could see it...and the length is what got us, a...sort of confused, because it looked like it was about 300 to 400 feet long. So I don't *know* if it's a wire with a strobe on it, but the strobe would start from the left and go right, counter-clock-wise...and it was a pretty eerie looking sight..."

Then came a strange dial tone, followed by a strong transmission, like *another* broadcast trying to cut in again:

HWK85: *"ALBUQUERQUE RADIO? ... ALBUQUERQUE RADIO?"*
"...and it was just in the lightning..."

BEEP-BEEP-BEEP

HWK85: *"ALBUQUERQUE RADIO?"*

ABQ: "Yeah...is this one any better?"

HWK85: *"Yeah."*

ABQ: "Oh good! Ha...hey you guys don't know anything about some kind of weather balloon or a UFO that's out in the vicinity of Fort Sumner tonight do you?"

HWK85: *"I don't think so...standby."*

ABQ: "Okay..."

HWK85: *"At this point the answer to that question is 'no'."*

ABQ: "Okay...yeah, this guy sees it up at Tucumcari, says it looks like it's 300 to 400 foot long, cylindrical, some kind of strobe on it, and everything else."

HWK85: *"Well...I would call it...I don't know what it is...kssshhhh."*

Then nothing but static, as the transmission abruptly ended.

Una could not help but wonder if it was a bad sign, like maybe something happened to the Air Force pilot. It was impossible to know, for sure.

After two minutes, the captain spoke again:

"Albuquerque Center...Cactus 564. Thanks for your help and, uh, could we get your call-sign?"

ABQ: "Cactus 564...mine is 'PP'."

"Was that 'tango golf'?"

ABQ: "P for Pappa."

"Pappa Pappa...thanks a lot."

Una sighed with relief. She decided in her heart that later, once they reached their destination, no matter what people said--or would not say--about Flight 564, that everything that transpired, all that she had witnessed, was *real*--and she would never forget it, as long as she lived.

5

BIGFOOT

With an hour to go before landing, the captain of Flight 564 glanced at his watch: 9:48 PM. Considering their chaotic encounter, they were lucky to still be on course. Carefully he listened to his headset, for any further transmissions from Albuquerque.

He did not have long to wait.

Next, the Air Traffic Controller contacted NORAD (North American Aerospace Command) through the Western Air Defense Sector, using the call sign of *Bigfoot* for air patrol intercepts:

ABQ: "Bigfoot...Albuquerque Sector 87."
BGFT: "Bigfoot's on!"
ABQ: "Yea...I've got a, uh, something unusual and I was wanting to know if y'all happen to know of anything going on out here around Tucumcari, New Mexico...north of Cannon? I had a couple of aircraft reported something 300 to 400 foot long...cylindrical in shape, with a strobe flashing off the end of it."
BGFT: "Oh...?"

ABQ: "At 30,000 feet."

BGFT: "Okay...hang on a second."

ABQ: "Yeah, I didn't know if you happen to know of anything going on out there...no balloons in the area, no nothing reported?"

BGFT: "Okay, where's this at again?"

ABQ: "It's at, uh, well ya know where...it's in Tucumcari, New Mexico, it's about 150 miles to the east of Albuquerque."

BGFT: "Okay, eh...how far from Holloman Air Force Base?"

ABQ: "Eh, Holloman, it looks like it's off the zero-three-zero of Holloman about 220 miles."

BGFT: "Okay...I think, okay...it's kind'a hard for us to see here. Okay, they'll be zero for about 200. Um...we don't have anything going on there that I know of."

ABQ: "Yeah...I didn't know, we've tried everybody else and nobody else is...this guy definitely saw it run all the way down the side of the airplane. Said it was a pretty interesting thing out there."

BGFT: "Okay, it was at 30,000 feet..."

ABQ: "...30,000 feet."

BGFT: "It was like...long...um."

ABQ: "Yeah, it's right out of, right out of the *X-Files*. I mean definite UFO or something like that, I mean."

BGFT: "...and...it...ooohh... y'all are serious about this (laughing)."

ABQ: "Yeah, he's real serious about that, too,

and...uh...he looked at, saw it, no balloons are reported tonight, nothing in the area..."

BGFT: "It was strobing off the front he said?"

ABQ: "Uh...I think the strobe was off the tail end of it."

BGFT: "Okay...strobe tail end."

ABQ: "He said it was kinda, well it was dark but...did he say there was lights in it?"

BGFT: "How long did he say it was?"

ABQ: "300 to 400 foot long."

BGFT: "Holy smoke!"

ABQ: "...and we don't have any air carriers out here so..."

BGFT: "Um...the only thing that I can do is, I wonder if any of our aerostats cut loose or something, 'cause we don't have any aerostats there."

ABQ: "Yeah...not that far to the north."

BGFT: "I mean...I don't think ours are that big though. *Wait a minute*...found something, stationary, then...*hey*!"

ABQ: "Come again?"

BGFT: "Whatever it is, just accelerated very quickly...and stopped."

ABQ: "How fast?"

BGFT: "...*impossible*...I mean, what does that?"

ABQ: "Does what?"

BGFT: "Darts between 1,000 and 1,400 miles per hour?"

ABQ: "Nothing...that we know of."

The radio dude grinned. "Did you hear *that*? Not an aerostat. They're blimp-shaped helium balloons that rise up to 15,000 feet, tethered by a cable, to provide low-level radar. *Our* UFO was at 30,000. Not even close."

"So it came and went," said the woman beside him, "Now what?"

"Hey, at least we lived to tell about it. But I wouldn't go overboard. Sure, we all heard the radio, but technically, we weren't *supposed* to. Admitting as much could get you in hot water."

The frequent flyer left his seat a few rows back to come closer. "Besides, what did any of us really see? A few flashes of light, in the midst of a thunderstorm? Doesn't mean a thing. Sure, I saw *something*. But you heard the captain. Even he didn't know for sure. Wanna be questioned for hours without end? Be my guest. I plan to keep my mouth shut."

Una spied the young photographer removing film from his camera. Instead of placing it with others in his backpack, he stashed it out of sight, somewhere below the knees. Another woman, with pencil in hand, who'd been frantically sketching only minutes before, ripped a sheet from her notebook, neatly folded it, and placed it inside a tiny, heart-shaped locket around her neck.

Her parents said nothing. Maybe they didn't want to bring it up again. *Out of sight, out of mind.* It was a common practice among adults, she noticed. And it seemed to work fine with her playmates. Most kids had a short attention span, anyway. It didn't take much for them to get bored, and move on.

But Una was more thoughtful than most. She kept track of every name of every person in her class at school. And she'd done it for every grade--including kindergarten. She watched her mother prepare traditional Hopi favorites back home, like hominy and Piki bread, completely from scratch--and learned every recipe by heart, before she even knew how to read.

And somehow she knew that even now, every detail of this flight--including every sight and sound--was being committed to memory, for the sake of future reference. Someday, she might even call upon it for some reason, but that was the extent of her knowledge. She did not know why.

"What'll happen when we land?" someone asked.

"Good point," the radio dude replied. "For starters, we'll get a debriefing of some kind. Of course, they won't call it that. They'll feign concern over our health, offer us counseling if needed, to overcome any troubled state of mind. Officials from the National Transportation Safety Board(NTSB) will go over the B-757 with a fine-tooth comb, and question the crew. It's all standard protocol."

"But what if--"

"You want to know the truth? Do yourself a favor, and don't ask. It's their job to glean information from *you*. Not the other way around."

BIGFOOT

***

And so it came to pass. Their landing at North Las Vegas Airport was uneventful. Less than an hour later, Una found herself deboarding Flight 564 along with her parents and other passengers, through a special gate, into a private 'arrival lounge', blocked off from everything else, without access to phones or any other form of communication.

First, the return of their bags was delayed. Then a "Resource Team" appeared, moving among them slowly, methodically. The Bearcat radio scanner was confiscated, along with any cameras, including film. The team leader explained that it was all part of an 'official investigation' to uncover the truth. Violation of civilian airspace was a serious offense. "We'll do whatever it takes," he said, "to ensure the safety of all future passengers on this airline."

"Where's the captain?" someone asked.

"Doing his part, just like you, to help us determine what happened. Sightings over restricted military areas are not uncommon. It's our job to find out *what* you saw. It's important that nothing we say here today leaves this room."

Suddenly Una felt afraid.

The 'arrival lounge' felt too much like a holding cell. It was getting hard to breathe. They were helpless here, all of them, unable to leave or even call out to friends or family beyond these walls. Hopis knew the feeling well. Once on the reservation her Uncle Lapu accepted a 'ride' with two men from the County Sheriff's office, only to wind up in jail. They held him without questioning for twenty-four hours--then let him go.

"Why Uncle?" she cried.

"Because they *can*," he replied. "Sometimes men overstep their boundaries, trample on people's lives, just to frighten them."

A tear flowed down Una's face as she held Lenmana's hand.

"Stay on the path," her mother said. The *Pathway* was an important part of Hopi belief regarding peace of mind. Failing to stay focused caused people to stray from the path, losing belief in themselves, their sense of purpose and direction. It was the root cause of many afflictions, like helplessness. All she needed was support, to regain her strength.

Una smiled as the fear began to fade. It was a lesson her elders taught over and over again.

Once the team had completed their rounds, their leader took them aside.

"Look at 'em," said the long-haired dude, twirling the useless cord still attached to his headphones. "It's all about damage control. Should they risk it or not? Attempting to cover their ass with a lame story might do more harm than good. Either we saw a real UFO or it was a military secret. But they can't admit that. If they threaten us, the press'll hear about it for sure. Better to--"

"Ladies and gentleman," the team leader's voice

announced, "Your attention please."

Everyone turned at once.

> "We apologize for any inconvenience. At this time, we have no explanation for what happened. Suffice it to say, you've all survived a rocky ride through a thunder storm. The light played tricks on your eyes. It happens. Rest assured that at no time were you ever in real danger. You may proceed to Baggage Claim at this time. And THANK YOU for flying America West."

Most people got up to leave, while a few stragglers stayed behind. Una's parents rose from their lounge seat, waiting patiently for others ahead to vacate the room. The Army brat pointed at her with his six-shooter, passing by. The young photographer, without his camera, winked as if he could not wait to get home and report to the school paper.

Near a window, she sighed with gratitude and looked to the sky. The Great Spirit had guided them safely to their destination.

Still Una had one thought in mind. *Next time, no planes.* She felt more at home on the ground. Hopis loved the Earth with good reason. It gave them everything, from the first breath to the last. It was the Mother of all.

PART TWO

ANCIENT VOICES

*"When the grandmothers speak,
the earth will be healed."*

--Hopi Proverb

6

BUS TRIP

On a dismal day in mid June, 2016, a dingy white minibus pulled up in front of the Greyhound station in Flagstaff, Arizona. The temperature was 84 degrees. It was just after 3 pm on a Thursday afternoon. The only sound came from a steady downpour, dancing in metal gutters and bouncing off hot pavement, where rivulets of steam rose upward.

The driver, a sixty-something silver-haired Navajo, opened his set of double doors and stepped outside, lighting up a cigarette. His name tag read: HO'KEE.

"You waitin' for a bus?" he said.

The only person in sight, a 29 year-old woman in Western boots and blue jeans with arms folded over her carry-on bag, woke with a start, nearly falling off an old wooden bench. Except for the new clothes, judging by her natural red-brown complexion, high cheek-bones and black hair, she did not seem altogether out of place.

"Waters," the woman said, "Una. I'm headed for

the Third Mesa village of Oraibi." She rose to her feet, ticket in hand.

"Relax," he grinned. "Don't need that. You're my only pick-up. Not many come out this time a day. Especially alone. Most take the fancy tour bus. It's nicer, with air conditioning. You...Hopi?"

She nodded. "I used to be, well, what I mean is...it's been a long time, but yeah, it's all pretty familiar. I grew up on the reservation."

The rain stopped, just as suddenly as it began.

"You're lucky," he said, taking a last puff, "Rain'll keep the dust down for a while. Go ahead, take a seat."

She climbed up inside. It was an eight-seater, most of them patched with duct tape. No wonder her ticket was so cheap. The minibus teetered a bit with each step. Pausing, she pulled out a handkerchief, wiped one off, and sat down.

Minutes later, they pulled onto the road beneath a scorching desert sun.

Una sighed. She had nearly forgotten about the heat. It was much worse than she thought. She tried to open the window for some air, but it was no use. All the latches were broken.

They took Highway 879A North to Townsend-Winona street, turned right and proceeded ten miles to Leupp Road.

"Not as scenic as Oak Creek Canyon," the driver said, "Just after a rain, you can see water-falls spilling over cliff tops. But that's only if you come from

Sedona, further South."

She nodded.

Turning left, they continued north for 31 miles. Una reached inside her bag, opened a small purse, and pulled out a handwritten letter. Its arrival at her office in D.C. only a week before had pretty much turned her life upside down.

She never intended to come back here. When her parents died in a freak avalanche only weeks after graduation, she decided it was time to move on. No more struggling to survive without electricity or running water. No more useless prayers offered to desert spirits who either were not listening or just didn't care. She'd had her fill of poverty and hopelessness. Education at a modern university was the answer to her dreams. It would open the doors of opportunity.

Well, sort of.

Executive assistant to Chelmer Hobbs, Secretary of the Interior, wasn't exactly the dream job she had in mind, but it had taken six years to get there, and she was hoping for a promotion soon--something that would merit a rental car, at least. Her reluctance to fly meant this trip would take up all her vacation time.

She turned to the letter at last:

Dear Una,

It has been too long. We miss

BUS TRIP

*your smiling face. So much has
changed in ten years. Once we
were shunned by the white man.
Now tourists keep coming. We
can't afford to turn them away.*

*You left us still barely a child. I
remember the loss of your parents.
Your mother and I were like sisters.
You had to find your own path. No
one can measure another's sorrow.*

*You remember Nuvatukyaovi,
the Sacred Peaks, home to our
Kachina ancestors, whose spirits
become clouds and bring rain to our
corn fields. We invite them to Oraibi
from midwinter to midsummer, as
spirit guides.*

*You remember how we fought
to protect them.*

*There was always a light in your
eyes. The light of understanding.
Your mother spoke of it often. She
said one day it would shine on us all.*

*We don't know what's happening.
Strangers came overnight, with trucks*

and heavy equipment. Digging on south slopes has begun. We do not know why, and cannot get answers.

The Tribal Council has tried to stop it, but men cannot see eye to eye. The Earth is already out of balance. Men cannot fix it alone. They need to hear a woman's voice, one they can all respect—who sees a problem through both Hopi and white man's eyes.

Our ancestors cry out. Can you still hear their voices?

Please help us in this fight. Come home to Oraibi. We welcome you with open arms.

*Your friend,
Kasa*

They passed an old suspension bridge crossing the Little Colorado River. Spanning over 600 feet, its towers rested on the rim of a steep-walled canyon, with concrete deadmen anchoring the suspension cables some way back. Built in 1911 for the Office of Indian Affairs to improve access to the Navajo Nation and the Hopi Reservation, it was closed to highway traffic in '59, replaced by a newer deck truss bridge, but still carried a natural gas pipeline.

"We're just about halfway," the driver said.

Una tried to picture the village in her mind. Perched on the edge of Third Mesa, Old Oraibi dated from 1050 AD and was considered the oldest continuously inhabited settlement in North America. Run by tribal elders, the village did not allow power, gas or water lines, because they tore up the earth. Beneath it were plenty of ruins. It consisted mostly of ramshackle houses, made of stone and concrete. In her childhood, they carried water to town in buckets, heating with piñon wood. She remembered it as a quiet, sort of desolate place.

At least *most* of the time.

From her seat about half-way back, Una moved up a couple rows, toward the driver.

"You need rest stop?" he said. "This road's BIA. There are none."

She understood. The Bureau of Indian Affairs was a separate agency within the U.S. Department of the Interior. For years, Una had resisted assignment there, afraid it would stifle her government career. Plus, BIA had its own controversial history, including a violent confrontation with protestors over treaty rights in '72 and the Wounded Knee Incident of '73 involving a shootout at the Pine Ridge Indian Reservation, in which two FBI agents were killed.

The government's relationship with tribes had wavered for years between respect for tribal rights and attempts to wipe them out altogether. Some described it as a love/hate relationship.

Una sighed. Yet another reminder of the hurdles she faced. Most villagers would find it hard to trust her.

So why the letter? Because these people, who once taught her the meaning of life and opened her heart and mind to the secrets of the universe, needed *someone* to believe in. Someone who shared their values. Someone who understood the Hopi Way and could be counted on to speak for them with a clear voice--where it would be heard.

That's why she *had* to come.

For a moment, she studied the driver's face in his rearview mirror. He must be seventy, at least. The lines of age attested to years of hardship, from land disputes with the Hopi, to intrusion by white corporations, like the one that built Snowbowl, an alpine ski resort on the Sacred Peaks, long before she was born. Did he know about this new dig?

"Ho'kee, *please*," she said. "Have you heard of any trouble...on the mountain?"

The big Navajo frowned. "Trouble? Trouble comes and goes. Between tribes...races...and folks, like you and me. Some say it never ends. I say it depends on your frame of mind. I've heard rumors mostly...tree falls at night, strange smoke, snakes and tarantulas fleeing the slopes. Started weeks ago."

"My friends are worried."

He nodded. "The Sacred Mountain was given to

us by Holy Ones, who came from the sky. They gave us wind and plants, animals and thunders. When any of these elements is desecrated, it throws Navajo Life out of balance."

Una was not surprised.

The developers would no doubt have a great deal of money and many lawyers to fight for them. If only her father were still alive. He'd know what to do. She could feel a lump in her throat.

Maybe they should turn the bus around.

The road to Oraibi road went up, and up, and up. It was too late for that. They climbed straight up the edge of Third Mesa, rising hundreds of feet above the desert floor. A guard rail gave little comfort. Its location protected villagers long ago from invaders.

Now their world was being threatened again.

In the desert, winds began to shift from west to southeast, bringing moisture. Thunderheads darkened the sky. It was the start of monsoon season. Rain could spur growth of wildflowers, food for migrating birds. Beetles, toads, bats and butterflies would appear briefly in abundance.

Before rain, however, such shifts could trigger dust storms known as *haboobs*: loose swirling walls of dust several hundred feet high. Exceeding 40 miles per hour, these storms could be dangerous--especially in the mountains, where flash floods produced mudslides.

Was this the calm before the storm?

Abruptly, before her eyes, the road's narrow

incline flattened, and her childhood home spread out before them.

It was like stepping backward, into the past. Sights, sounds and smells brought a flood of emotion.

And in that moment, she realized there was no place else she'd rather be. The voices were calling, louder than ever.

Una would find a way.

7

HOME AGAIN

The white minibus slowed to a stop, kicking up clouds of dust. There were no hints of familiar geography, except for the Sacred Peaks to the west. The land seemed to fall away all around them, beyond the edge of Third Mesa.

At first glance, there were no signs of life. The village appeared almost invisible. Through dust-covered windows, the distinction between hand built stone houses still standing and those jumbled on the ground blurred beneath desert sun.

Una retrieved her carry-on bag, waiting for the doors to open.

"You be careful," the driver said.

She stepped down, onto a dirt road. Only the crude-looking structure before her, consisting of cement block and painted wooden slats, appeared to be of modern make. A small, hand-written sign read: BUS DEPOT.

It was like a bad dream.

Returning to Oraibi after so many years, her

memory was surprisingly accurate. The village, over 1,000 years old, resembled a run down shanty town surrounded by cliffs, with no electric or telephone lines. There were no house numbers or street names. No lights and no sound.

It felt completely abandoned.

Startled by a moving shadow, she turned abruptly as two feral dogs appeared, wagging their tails. Shepherd cross-breeds, one light the other dark, they seemed healthy enough and well cared for.

"Una?"

A stout woman in a knee-length black cotton dress with braided hair rushed up to embrace her.

"Kasa!" she cried through happy tears.

Vaguely familiar faces stood nearby. Her heart surged. Suddenly the years apart dissolved away.

"You come all this way...on a bus?"

She could not stop smiling. "Oh...I don't fly is all. Anyway, I thought it might help to *feel* the land again, up close. You know?"

Kasa nodded, as well as her two teenage children.

"Tocho?" said Una, squeezing the boy with a hug. "You were knee high the last time I saw you. And now you're a man!"

She turned to his sister. "You! You can't be Sukya! She was just a little girl. So beautiful now! Where did the time go?"

"Come!" said Kasa, winking to the boy. He took hold of her bag, turning to walk toward the sun. "It's not far. Remember? You must be tired and hungry.

It'll be dark soon, and we have so much catching up to do. The food is all prepared, including your favorite!"

Una's mouth watered for Piki bread.

She eyed a familiar site. In the village center, a rectangular structure with a wood-and-rope ladder marked the top of an underground chamber, known as a *kiva*, used for spiritual ceremonies.

It seemed unreal.

They passed a small craft shop with rooftop solar panels, for electric power. The sale of hand made silver jewelry, pottery and Kachina dolls had become the town's primary source of income.

The dogs followed them down an alley to a two story home, constructed of undressed stone bound with mud plaster. Its propane tank sat next to an outhouse. The flat roof's beams rested on top with rod and grass thatching, a layer of gumbo plaster, and a covering of dry earth. Outside ladders reached the second floor.

Inside, it appeared dim at first, with white-washed walls, rooms separated by hanging rugs, and cracked floors with missing tiles. A glass case near the kitchen held pots painted with dyes made from wildflowers, each bearing the symbol of their Roadrunner clan.

The aroma of fresh yeast bread filled the air as Una tried to take it all in. The furnishings were a mixture of new and old; a traditional corner fireplace and handwoven baskets, beside modern windows.

They led her to a modest table laden with home made dishes, like blue corn tamales, white corn and lamb stew, baked sweet corn, beans and roasted green chili peppers and, of course, blue corn Piki bread, thinly layered to melt in one's mouth. There was even sliced watermelon, for dessert.

"Tell us about D.C.!" said Tocho, "Have you seen the Smithsonian?"

"Yes, of course," she replied, "But it's not just one place. It includes 19 museums and galleries, as well as the National Zoological Park. Eleven are on the National Mall, between the Lincoln Memorial and the U.S. Capitol. Collections include millions of artworks, artifacts, and specimens, like the Star-Spangled Banner, or the ruby slippers worn by Judy Garland in the *Wizard of Oz*. Recently, its Air & Space Museum's curators restored the Enterprise from the original *Star Trek* TV series."

"Now *that's* something I'd love to see."

"In your dreams!" taunted Sukya. "Is it really dangerous? My friends say it's filled with political nerds from upstate New York, and thugs roam the streets at night!"

Una shook her head, eyeing Kasa, who simply frowned. "Not here, too. The internet? Don't believe it. Truth and lies are often mixed. There is good and bad all over."

"Well, *you* oughta know," came a voice from the past.

Everyone turned.

A young woman appeared, in blue jeans and cut-off t-shirt, with dark hair pulled back in a pony tail.

Kasa hesitated. "Y-You remember--"

"Chu'si?" Una smiled warily, "Of course!"

The two embraced. Once inseparable in high school, the tension between them was palpable.

"How's the...farming?" she asked, cheerfully.

"Oh, a struggle to be sure. But we're learning new tricks all the time. It's part of survival. No doubt, *you've* learned the same."

Una nodded. The sarcasm was no surprise. Her friends had no way of knowing. She would *not* draw them into this. Not here. Not now. She'd save it for another time.

Kasa's husband, Ahote, opened a bottle of home-made wine, pouring each of them a drink, to celebrate. His face and hands were tanned, like brown leather. Una took a small sip. The pinkish semi-sweet wine had a pleasant fruity tropical aroma. "Made from prickly pear cactus!" he said.

They all laughed.

The meal proceeded without incident. Everyone had tales to tell. The children could not wait to see the outside world. Una cautioned them to mind their parents and slow down. 'Outside' was not all it was cracked up to be.

When they had finished dessert, Chu'si stepped outside for a smoke.

"We're not *all* blind," she said abruptly, as Una came out to join her. "You're not here to save us. In the end, we'll be screwed, like always."

"Why do you say that?"

"Because I know...what it's like to live here, year after year. I stayed. Remember? The government doesn't care about us. They're two-faced, like you. Coming back, pretending like you're going to help. But you won't. You'll get our hopes up, then tell us to accept it. You'll go back to D.C. and forget about us, all over again."

She stamped out her cigarette, and turned to go.

"Wait," said Una. "I'm sorry for what happened. Sorry we threw our friendship away over such a foolish thing. I never meant to 'steal' your boyfriend."

Chu'si wiped a tear from her eye. "It's okay. You weren't the first. He was never 'mine' to steal. Anyway, he left town a long time ago. Sometimes, I wish I'd been more like you. Studied hard in school...to get away, make something of myself. Now, it's too late."

Una hugged her once more beneath the stars.

"You're wrong about me. I'm not two-faced. And...life is full of surprises...it's...*never* too late."

Back inside, she found Kasa making up a guest bed in the living room. Ahote waited for them to join him in the glow of a small lantern at the kitchen table. He poured them each another drink.

"Now we get down to business," he said.

Una was all ears.

"Here's what we know. Commotion on the Peaks, south slopes, for three weeks now. Heavy equipment. Trucks and backhoes. They dig mostly at night, til dawn. Village scouts head out there daily on horseback. So far, no one's gotten close enough."

"Have you gone to the elders?" she asked.

He shrugged. "They know nothing. The BIA does not return our calls. We even sent a police officer to Flagstaff, hoping to turn up something. But he came back empty handed."

"Here's the thing," said Kasa, "People here are not just nervous. They're angry. They want to organize a party with guns. We're afraid. We thought maybe you could get through to those in charge. At least find out what's going on. Prevent violence."

It was enough to make Una cringe. She did not come home to see people die.

"Okay. I'll try. But first, I need to know more. Can you take me there?"

Ahote nodded. "The Sacred Peaks? At first light. It's rough terrain. Our horses can handle it. But...can you still ride?"

Tears welled up in her eyes.

"What's wrong?" said Kasa.

"*Sacred.* That eludes me. I feel so unworthy. It's just that, since I've been away, with all the pressures...I've lost a part of myself, lost touch with, well...you know, the...*Hopi Way.*"

Kasa grinned. "Relax. Not for long. It's all arranged. Tomorrow night, I'll take you to Kuwanyauma."

Una's mouth dropped. "She's...still *alive*? No way!

She was already old when I was a kid. She must be a hundred, at least."

Ahote finished his drink. "One hundred and two."

She sighed. Facing the spirit woman might be harder than just about anything. It would mean coming to grips with all that she loved here as a child, memories of her parents, the struggles they endured. She'd have to immerse herself once more in a world of supernatural belief, where Sky People came down, almost daily. A world where compassion and truth were essential to survive.

It's the world she tried to escape--when her parents died.

But it seems that one does not discard the past so easily. *Stay on the path*, her mom used to say. Despite all her best efforts to leave it behind, adopt a new frame of reference, based on the modern point of view, she wound up back *here*, where her life began.

The voices were calling. She could feel it. And they would not let go.

That night, Una could not sleep. She kept seeing the *Snake Dance*, part of a 16 day celebration every other August.

Hopis regarded snakes as their 'brothers' and relied on them to carry prayers to the underworld. The dance required nine days of preparation. Villagers made prayer sticks, sand paintings, and built an altar with bowls of water from a sacred spring, green corn stalks and trailing vines. They gathered snakes without fear, stroking each with a feather to straighten its coils, then grab it behind the head. They ran a foot race, streaking across the plain, up a steep slope before sunrise, to represent rain-gods bringing rain.

On the last day, they gathered snakes up into a bag, taken to the village plaza. Each priest would carry a snake, first by hand and then by mouth, dancing around the plaza, dropping it inside a large circle, to be scattered with corn meal by the women. Finally, scooped up in armfuls, the snakes were carried to shrines and released to the underworld.

Dark clouds would follow, bringing rain.

"You all right?" said Kasa, coming in to check on her.

She nodded. "Just a lot on my mind. I keep wondering what'll happen. It's not just a question of protecting the Peaks. It's more than that. We're dealing with primeval forces. Good and evil. It scares me."

The way Kasa came over, to sit down beside her, reminded Una of her mother. The two held hands.

"That's partly why you're here," she said, "To learn what matters. See the difference between white man's world and Hopi Land. Some people act as if the past is forgotten. They disregard their elders, rape the Earth, and take whatever they want. Here it remains a part of us, because we keep it alive. Past and present. Light and dark. They must be kept in balance."

Una smiled. "Being home means I have to deal

with all of it. Accept *both* sides. Like the pair of dogs who first greeted me to Oraibi, then followed us from the Bus Depot."

Kasa paused thoughtfully, squinting her eyes. "*What* dogs?"

8

INTRUDERS

As they departed Oraibi on horseback, daybreak was still hours off. Ahote had recruited two local twenty-something-year-olds to escort them to the Sacred Peaks. Pachua, barely out of high school with loads of enthusiasm, seemed well versed on government conspiracies. Shilah, noticeably more mature, had worked part time for the National Park Service as a tour guide. He seemed to know a great deal about wilderness survival. He was also Navajo.

"Try not to hold it against him," said Pachua. "He did get the horses, after all, and he's way better with a knife!"

Ahote grinned. Apparently, they were close friends.

Una sighed. Back in the saddle for the first time in 15 years, she had mixed emotions. She'd apparently overestimated her flexibility and the give in her jeans, for one thing. It seemed like a long way down, for another. Being the only girl in the group, she was determined not to let it show.

Once upon a time, at the age of nine, she loved horses--decorating her room, tracking dirt into the house with her riding boots, reading *The Saddle Club* books endlessly. Then, at the age of fourteen, she found herself in high school. Things like boys and parties and making new friends seemed way more important. And so, after five years of riding, she left the stables behind.

She thought about it for years, wondering what her life might have been like, wondering if her love of horses might have kept her here. "I'd love to go riding again," she would even sometimes say to friends. But it wasn't until this year, making her 29 Things to Do Before 30 list, that it became an actual goal.

Of course, she never thought it would actually *happen*.

Now, here she was, reconnecting with a part of herself that she'd nearly forgotten. And it felt good in many ways. Good to sense familiar smells and hear familiar sounds. Good to feel that tinge of excitement, as if it was something new. Good to finally overcome the fear that held her back. Fears like: *What if I forget how? What if I get thrown off?* or *What if I hate it?*

And somehow, going back to something she used to love brought an unexpected benefit. It made her feel more *present*. She was very conscious of the feeling of the reins in her hands, the horse's body beneath hers, the movement of its ears. It all seemed to heighten her senses, and make her more aware of what was happening--in the *now*.

The trail away from Third Mesa, mostly flat at first, went south and west. The desert landscape changed from grass to dirt to rocks. They crossed vast open plateaus to go up and down hills through ponderosa pine and oak trees, with small amounts of Douglas-fir as they slowly began to climb.

Una looked up to deep Alpine forest ahead. The Peaks soared to heights reaching over 12,000 feet. Collectively, six summits circled the caldera of a now quiet volcano, formed five thousand centuries ago. Somewhere beyond the tree line were tundra like conditions, where it could snow anytime of year. That's how it earned the Hopi name *Nuvatukaovi* (The place of snow on the very top).

"Where are we going?" she asked.

"Patience," Shilah replied. "The place we seek lies beyond that ridge to the east, but we must take a roundabout path, so as not to arouse suspicion."

Ahote brought his horse up from behind. "Surveillance? This far out? You've got to be kidding."

The Navajo shook his head. Pointing to the top of the nearest tree, he passed over a pair of binoculars. His old friend stared through them in disbelief at a tiny camera, hundreds of feet above. One of many, no doubt.

It was a violation of every written agreement between the government and all the native tribes who considered the Peaks as sacred ground, including not just the Hopi and Navajo, but also the Zuni, Havasupai and Yavapai-Apache. Still, they could not say who was to blame.

"We must be getting closer," said Pachua. "Up to now, in the dark, we've been accompanied by the eyes and ears of natural observers: mule deer, elk, the raven and even an occasional turkey vulture. Now listen."

They froze, staring out into tree-covered terrain. The first morning rays of sunlight began to filter downward. Ordinarily this time of day would be filled with the movement of small animals, the chatter of birdsong.

But there was only silence.

Shilah led them along a narrow path through spaces between fallen rock and yet the horses did not protest.

Una noticed their broad foreheads and wide-set eyes. Navajo horses did not have the attributes of size and speed bred into racehorse or rodeo breeds used to compete for human sport. But their gentle disposition and smooth riding gait could not be denied. Even here, on rocky slopes, one could feel a rhythm created by the steady beat of their hooves.

She tried to lose her old habit of pulling on one rein to steer. The others would simply look in the direction they wanted to go and turn their shoulders, which gave just enough of a signal.

Riding was good exercise. Apart from the aerobic benefits, it engaged muscles that were not used much otherwise. She had to use her core muscles and sit really tall, so it helped with posture and balance. Still, she found herself getting more puffed than expected.

"Don't forget to *breathe*," Ahote said.

Finally, they slowed as the trees gave way to a clearing. But it was not the result of a landslide or flash flood racing down the mountain during monsoon season. There were fences up ahead, and a NO TRESPASSING sign.

Quickly they ducked out of sight behind heavy brush.

"*Now* what?" she whispered.

"It's as far as we dare," Shilah replied. "We did not come to fight, just get answers."

"And?"

"You don't understand. Confront and *we* become targets. Wait here. We'll get some photos. They speak louder than words."

She nodded.

Pachua stayed with her, to look after the horses. When he became quiet, seated against a rock, she realized that he was wearing ear buds.

***

Twenty minutes later, the others returned. Pachua realized this only when someone pulled one of his buds, disrupting one of his favorite tunes from *The Night Watchman*.

"Where is she?" Ahote asked.

"She was..right here...a minute ago, but--"

Bright lights came through the brush, blinding them, followed by a loud voice, from behind the fence.

"STOP. DO NOT COME CLOSER. HOLD YOUR HANDS UP."

As the lights dimmed, through the brush, they could see Una, surrounded by three men in black uniforms, pointing MK47s.

"Sorry!" she said, "This is so embarrassing. I was hiking the trail and...must be lost. Serves me right. Next time I'll wait for a tour guide."

"This area is restricted," one officer said. "Off limits to all civilian personnel. How did you find this facility?"

She tried to see their faces, to no avail. So that was it. *Military*. Not some greedy corporation after all.

That changed everything.

Una dropped her hands. "Excuse me? I think you've got it backwards. Last time I checked, this mountain was open to the public. Your 'facility' doesn't appear on any maps. In fact, I'm pretty sure you're not supposed to be here!"

The officer paused to receive instruction through his helmet.

"Ma'am? We'll have to see some ID."

"You first!"

"What the hell is she *doing*?" whispered Ahote.

Pachua grinned. "Getting answers! Obviously, they're not from around here. Did you see their insignia? They're Black Ops. Officially, they don't exist. It's hard to believe they could transport all this equipment across the desert without being detected. Unless--"

He frowned. "Don't get started."

"Hush!" said Shilah, "Before they find us."

"On your knees, Ma'am. We don't have time for this."

"Wait!" said Ahote, stepping into the open.

The guns turned on him.

"We don't mean any harm! We're just Hopi scouts, from...Oraibi. Let us go, and we'll return, the way we came." He thought it best not to say more. The presence of a Navajo would only complicate matters.

"Hold it, right there!" the lead officer said. He seemed to nod as a burst of instructions entered his ear.

"All right. But first...everyone out of hiding."

Shilah walked out slowly, head up high, apparently unafraid. He knew they would not fire unless provoked. Pachua crept out behind him, trembling, a big wet spot across the front of his trousers.

"Careful, commander," said Una. "We have families. They'll come looking for us. It could get worse. You willing to risk that?"

He examined a charm hanging from her bracelet.

It bore the *Tapuat*, an ancient symbol representing the labyrinth of life. "Wait. Did you say...*Hopi?*"

She nodded.

He stepped away. "I'm afraid it's worse than you thought."

Directing her with his rifle to stand, he led them all at gunpoint through the gate. Something told her this was not supposed to happen. It was either good news ...or very, very bad.

They followed a gravel path around a steel and concrete bunker, equipped with its own generator and rooftop satellite dish. The only windows were completely dark, painted from the inside. It barely seemed big enough.

"W-we're not fools," said Pachua, trying to sound brave. "My phone's got GPS. We're being tracked right now, by people who sent us. Even if I can't talk to them, they know where we are. You can't keep us. They'll--"

The officer laughed, snatching the cell phone from his breast-pocket. Held up to Pachua's face, two words appeared on the screen:

NO SIGNAL

Una gasped as they rounded the small bunker. The darkened arch of a tunnel appeared in the cliff side, completely smooth, as if created by a machine. The paved road coming out of it might originate anywhere.

A flashing blue light revealed the presence of a County Sheriff's SUV, and a yellow police barrier strung up around two dozers and a backhoe. The hillside in between them was partially collapsed around a narrow opening. Its stones were stained with blood.

They were escorted closer, when the deputy in charge appeared from inside the vehicle. Forty-something, caucasian, with thick side-burns, his face was not at all familiar.

"Officer Tooms, from Flagstaff," he said, shaking hands with Ahote. "Sorry to drag you into this. But it seems like one *hell* of a coincidence. I mean, tragedy strikes out here, in the middle of nowhere...and less than 12 hours later, *you* arrive from the same village?"

"I don't understand."

"Of course, well, it's damn inconvenient, and even harder to explain. This kid appears overnight, sets off all the alarms, and winds up dead. Got in through some cave we didn't even *know* about. Hell's bells! When this gets out, it'll open a real can o' worms. But rules are rules. Can't notify next of kin without an ID on the body. We'd sure like to save time. You mind?"

It seemed fair enough. Ahote followed him inside, while the others waited outside. As the sun rose high in the sky, it was beginning to heat up. They had not planned to be here this long.

Shilah drew a sip from his canteen, sharing it

with Una.

Pachua lit up a cigarette, trying to calm his nerves. "What I tell you? It's all secret. That tunnel's probably part of a network. Ever hear of D-U-M-B's? Deep Underground Military Bases! All over the midwest. People say they're like cities almost. We better hope they don't take us there. We'll never come out alive!"

It wasn't easy to just stand there. They wanted to go home.

Una tried to think. She could not remember much of her childhood, but a legend came to mind, involving the *Ant People*, long ago. According to it, with their help, the Hopi passed from a world of darkness below, to ours above. Though dark at first, through trials and tribulations, it became a world of light.

That much seemed to make sense. Finding light, like finding the truth, always required more effort. The truth about these intruders *must* come out, one way or another. Why were they here? On whose authority? And what were they trying to hide? It must be awfully important, to risk upsetting the balance among native tribes surrounding the Peaks.

So what if the legend were true? she thought. And what if the caves could be found? What might they reveal about the Hopi past? This made her wish the boy was still alive.

A screeching hawk soared suddenly overhead.

Una smiled. This gave her hope. Whatever these

Black Operatives were up to, the tragedy here overnight would force them into the light.

Questions would *have* to be answered.

9

SPIRIT WOMAN

Descending the Peaks proved to be difficult in more ways than one. Rays of afternoon sunlight pierced the forest canopy aimed at their backs, feeling worse as they left trees behind. Soon there would be only desert.

Ahote frowned. This was never part of the plan. The scarcity of shade and water here made such crossings unbearable for most. Una was not prepared for this. He would have to watch her carefully.

"What happens when we get back?" asked Pachua.

No one answered.

Una dared not speak out of turn. The men had enough on their minds. The death of a village member was not to be taken lightly, especially under strange circumstances. A police investigation could drag things out for the family, raising tensions and fears.

Ahote would keep the boy's identity to himself until next of kin were notified, giving them time to grieve. The bigger questions were yet to be answered. How did he wind up here, so far from home? Did he really find the intruders by accident? And what was the military's true reason for being there?

"Okay," said Pachua. "I get it. We're all tired. We've got a death we can't explain... or even talk about. A bunch of goons in uniform just threatened us to keep quiet or else--and we don't even know why!

"Their claims are bogus. Know one needs that kind of equipment for a geological survey. And they're not worried about an extinct volcano coming to life! They *might* be after uranium, used in weapons or to power nuclear subs."

"First things first," said Shilah. "Mind your horses. Don't allow them to trot or canter. The trail has plenty of deep sand and rocky terrain. And stay clear of any cactus or rattlesnakes."

So their return journey began to Oraibi. Una knew that in spite of any threats, there would be no secrecy. The people had a right to know what was happening on the Peaks. But what could they do? No one wanted to confront the U.S. military.

There was also a mystery to be solved--regarding the cave. Hopi legends referred to previous 'worlds' below, from which they emerged into the fourth--our present world--above. What did it mean? Was it just a random discovery, or a doorway to the past?

Some doors were best left unopened.

***

Kasa sighed with relief, racing out to greet them. She could not read Ahote's troubled eyes. One by one she hugged the others, reaching Una last. They all seemed too tired to talk.

"Inside now, quickly," she said, "Food and rest."

Tocho felt overwhelmed by his father's embrace. For a moment, as they stood near the fireplace, he stared at a framed photo, with three boys holding up a trophy. "Your friends, Moki and...and..."

"Kwahu," he replied. "Explorers Club, sophomore year. Dad...Dad...*geez*, enough, already." Ahote released him.

It took almost an hour for them to open up. As usual, Pachua went first.

"They had us pegged before we got there. Security cameras. The works. It was completely fenced in. Black Ops. That's all we know."

Shilah nodded. "No desert tracks to reveal point of origin. There was only one tunnel--straight into the mountain. Could connect anywhere...Luke, Yuma, or secret places we've never heard of."

"Deep Underground Military Bases," nodded Pachua, "Known as D-U-M-B's. They could be anywhere."

Kasa poured them each a glass of wine. "It'll be getting dark soon," she said to Una, "I hope you haven't forgotten."

Kuwanyauma, she thought. Always a grandmother,

it seemed, to just about everyone in the village. She told stories passed on to her by generations long gone. When she spoke, it was like hearing ancient voices. Though she could barely walk and never learned to read or write, she could always see the truth.

***

They reached her doorstep by nightfall, bearing gifts of fresh melon and ground coffee beans. Stepping inside, they found her asleep on a bench between two younger women, who ordinarily took turns caring part-time for the Hopi elder. Living alone, she was remarkably self-reliant, preparing most of her own meals, washing her own clothes, and still attending village ceremonies.

Her eyes opened like a cat, waking from its quiet nap and instantly, there was a big smile of greeting on her face.

With pleasantries aside, an attendant brought freshly brewed Hopi tea, made from a plant called Greenthread. Clean, fresh, and simply delicious. There was no need for sugar or milk or lemon. Like green or jasmine tea, it was perfect straight. Una had nearly forgotten how soothing it could be.

"I know why you are here," the old woman began. "Trouble from the modern world. To find your way through it, you must retrace the Path, by word and song. I tell it to you now, the way it was first told to me by my grandmother:

"Long ago, the Great Spirit came down and gathered the peoples of this world together on an island which is now beneath the water.

"To the Indian people, the red race, he gave Guardianship of the Earth.

"To the South, he gave the yellow race Guardianship of the Wind.

"To the West, he gave the black race Guardianship of the Water.

"To the North, he gave the white race Guardianship of the Fire.

"If you look at the center of many things from the white man, you will find fire. In the light bulb. In the spark at the center of a car, a plane or a train. Fire consumes, and also moves.

"The Hopi settled here in Four Corners, where the state lines of Arizona, New Mexico, Utah, and Colorado meet. This area is the 'heart' of *Turtle Island*, which you call the USA. We have been Keepers of the Earth ever since. The elders know that peace will not come until the circle of humanity is complete, until all four races sit together and share their teachings. We long for that day."

"But now," said Una. "This new trouble on the Peaks. The dig. The cave. It's really happening. What does it all mean?"

Kuwanyauma paused to sip at her tea. Small

wisps of steam rose up around her by candlelight. "Reality is a metaphor in which we seek answers...to find out who we are and why we are here.

"The western world has been lost and lonely for a long time. It has tried to fill a hole in the heart with 'things'--like success, attractiveness, prowess, and power. But these do not satisfy. Greed is a sickness that infects every land. Men do not respect the path of the Great Spirit. They consider old wisdom as useless.

"We have taken a wrong turn, forgetting that we belong to the Earth and we are her caretakers. She is not ours to plunder.

"As Hopi, we must hold the world in balance, in accordance with our first promise to the Creator. We do so with special prayers and rituals, to this day."

Eyes closed, she lifted her face upward, holding hands with those nearby. Humming a familiar tune, she began to chant, as the others joined in:

We all fly like eagles
flying so high
circling the universe
on wings of pure light

Oh ichi chio
Oh ay io

Where we walk is holy
sacred is the ground

*forest mountain river
listen to this sound*

*Oh ichi chio
Oh ay io*

*The earth is our mother
and I am her child
please don't make war
killing meek and mild*

*Oh ichi chio
Oh ay io*

*Circling the universe
on wings of pure light
We all fly like eagles
flying so high*

Una's eyes met with Kasa's. Somehow, they were hoping for more. Something concrete. They needed a course of action.

Her mind raced. Soon, Tooms would arrive, from Flagstaff. The boy's family would be devastated. There would be finger pointing, and rage. It was like waiting for a nightmare to unfold.

And when the questions began to fly, the village would need answers. *Who* was responsible? And *why*? What about the cave?

Finally, when all had finished their tea, the pair

rose, to depart.

But Una lingered. There *had* to be more. Maybe the Hopi elder was too tired to go on, or maybe all she needed was the right sort of question--to open the door, a painful one perhaps, that Kuwanyauma thought best to avoid.

No dammit. That was not it. This whole process was going to be painful, no matter what. Pain was part of life, even necessary, to survive.

"Forgive me," she said at last, resisting a tug from Kasa's hand. "But this is more about the future. We can't just wait for someone else to decide. The Sheriff may drag his feet, meaning endless delays. I used to live here, remember? Authorities don't usually care about justice for Hopis. In D.C., we'd take a different tack. Look for leverage. Apply pressure. The people of Oraibi need to know we have a chance to save the Peaks. A way to focus their *anger*, before it gets out of hand."

The old woman grinned. "I thought you'd never ask!"

She pulled out a piece of paper with a familiar hand-drawn diagram, copied from Prophecy Rock, a petroglyph known to the Hopi as "Life Plan".

> In it, a stick figure,
> representing Maasaw,
> the Great Spirit, pointed
> to a diagonal line,
> representing the 'Plan'.

> At the top of this line, a rectangle formed a dividing bridge.

"There are two paths," she began, "The *fallen path*, with technology but separate from natural and spiritual law--leads to these jagged lines, meaning chaos, and destruction.

"The *divine path* shows tests in the form of gourd rattles that represent three wars. If we return to spiritual harmony and live from our hearts, we can survive--and experience Everlasting Life.

She laid the diagram aside.

"*This land* beneath Four Corners holds the precious organs of Mother Earth. Coal is like the liver, uranium is both heart and lungs. Men try to take them for money. This leads only to chaos.

"This world must be purified. There are signs of coming destruction. The white man will battle against those in other lands. World War III will be started by those peoples who first revealed the light of wisdom: China, India, Africa and Islam. There will be many columns of smoke and fire.

"Messages have already come to us from the *Purifier*, written in living stone, through sacred grains, and even on the waters. Only in ancient teachings can the ability to understand them be found. Those who remember the old ways will not be harmed. We are about to enter 'The Fifth Age', which is called 'The World of Illumination'. Some compare it to the 'Age of Aquarius'."

Una's eyes opened wide. Her best friend in D.C. was sort of a horoscope junkie, always looking for 'signs' in the stars: where to eat, who to date, and so on. The city was full of politicians and political wanna-be's. She never gave it much thought--until now.

Tears flowed. All this talk of "purification" sounded too much like the end of the world. Political types in D.C. worried about that a lot, always blaming it on someone else of course, especially Middle East dictators or Communist rivals who threatened U.S. interests abroad.

"Wait a minute," she said, "War? Meaning death?"

"Yes. Many lives will be lost."

"What then?"

"In the end, ambitious minds will decrease, while the people of *good hearts*, who live in harmony, will increase, until the earth is rid of evil. We will walk again with our Star Brothers, and rebuild this Earth--but not until the Purifier has left his mark upon the universe."

Una sighed once more.

The old woman smiled. "Many people have no idea that things really could be different from the chaos we have witnessed. But I believe that a different future is possible. A new time is coming, when women will change the world. Men have tried for too long and failed. It is up to us now, to bring wisdom and healing, to bring the Earth back into balance."

She grasped Una's hands, holding them up to her breast. "Each of us carry a sacred drop of light. They say it takes nine ancestors to agree before conception can occur. Nine ancestors of the husband and the wife must come together in the Spirit Realm and say, 'We will bring life,' before a woman becomes pregnant. At that time the soul is born.

"The Great Spirit has brought you back to us for a reason. Follow your heart, do what you must to stop those who desecrate the Peaks. Ask yourself: What can we learn from Mother Earth? The cave has been opened. Find out why."

"The boy," added Kasa, hastily, "His death will cause anguish, and turmoil. People will not understand. What can we do?"

"The body must be returned and buried within three days. There can be no delay. Rituals must be performed; the hair washed, the body wrapped, the face covered with a symbolic mask of raw cotton. On the fourth day his spirit will leave the body and begin its journey to the Land of the Dead."

Moments later, Una and Kasa stepped outside, beneath a silver moon.

It was impossible to know precisely what would happen next with the Peaks. Violence could lead to bloodshed.

It would be no surprise to the Spirit Woman.

Hopiland was a sacred battleground, between forces of good and evil. Many had fought and died here to defend their way of life.

It was worth any sacrifice.

10

FLASHBACK

Una woke with a start before dawn, still trembling from a nightmare. In it, she saw her parents, waving from a scenic overlook near a Colorado waterfall, just before the cliff shelf above them collapsed, triggering a massive land slide. They were killed by crashing rocks...before her eyes.

In the dream, she screamed *NO!* again and again at the top of her lungs. The thought of them both being swept away so suddenly was too much to take, their broken bodies found later in a massive debris field.

That's *not* exactly how it happened, of course. Una was nowhere near the hiking trail on that fatal day, over ten years ago. There were no eyewitnesses. But it seemed so real.

At the time, authorities could not explain what happened. Recent rains, combined with freezing temperatures, may have loosened the rock, but no one knew for sure.

It made her feel helpless...then and now.

It also occurred to Una that since the moment of her arrival in Oraibi, she had been thinking of them, but avoiding the idea of death itself. Well, that was no longer possible. The corpse from the Peaks was expected back in the village today. The grieving cycle would begin.

Her own grief, a decade ago, had been unbearable. She could not participate in Hopi rituals, except for the final step on the *talus slope*, a pile of rocks at the base of cliffs leading down to a bench from Third Mesa.

Their bodies, tied up in blankets and carried to the burial ground, were placed, facing west, in a shallow grave, covered with sand, heaped up with stones and marked with a stick to serve "as a ladder for the souls to depart."

Soon, it would happen all over again.

She dressed herself quickly. It was time to revisit their graves, to deal with the guilt she carried for leaving Hopiland--to seek their forgiveness, once and for all.

Only then could she move forward.

***

The graveyard was just as she remembered: no enclosure or tombstones, simply unmarked mounds of stone. A few insignias, indicating the order or clan to which some belonged, were occasionally placed on graves, but that was all. The exact location of her family's remains was unknown. It had been this way for centuries. Thus, Hopi dead were reclaimed by the Earth from which they came.

With eyes closed, she stood silently near the cliff's edge. A sudden gust of desert wind threw her hair back. For an instant, she thought she saw them again: the same pair of feral dogs that first greeted her at the bus depot.

They appeared only briefly, from a distance, coming toward her. It seemed like an odd coincidence. The sound of breathing drew her gaze to the cliff beside her, where both animals reappeared. Up close, the light in their eyes seemed unworldly, more like ghosts or wandering spirits. All at once, they leaped together, in a cloud of dust.

She stumbled backward, feeling faint--into a stranger's arms.

"Hey, watch yourself," he said holding her up, "This is no place to lose your step. Good thing I came along."

Pale-faced, in his early thirties with a dark moustache, wearing a baseball cap and blue jeans, he wasn't from the village. The strap around his neck carried an expensive-looking camera.

"Thanks," said Una, acting disoriented, "But how did you get there? It's just that, well, no offense, but I came here to be alone."

"Don't blame you. I was just...passing by, on my way to--oh, *what the hell*. Truth is, I came to see you. Name's Jack Howser, reporter from Winslow, for the

Arizona Journal. I know you're from D.C. I know...all about you."

She crossed her arms. He seemed familiar, somehow.

"It's nothing bad," he grinned, adjusting his wire-frames. "Word gets around, that's all. The Mesas are part of my 'beat'. Anyway, there's been a lot of rumors, regarding the Peaks. I noticed your return on horseback yesterday, and could really use a scoop. What goes on? I'm sure people want to know."

A *spy*, was her first thought. In D.C. she learned to never take people at face value. Anyone who asked too many questions could be a mole planted by political rivals, or even a lobbyist. She learned not to talk to strangers without a background check. But here, that was impossible.

She'd have to go with her gut.

"Why should I trust you?" she asked.

He grinned. "Savvy. Just as I thought. First of all, here's my Press Pass," he said, waving a laminated I.D. with an old photo, sporting a crew cut and black rimmed glasses. What a geek! It almost reminded her of...no, *couldn't* be.

"And second?"

"I've lived in these parts my whole life. Winslow's not exactly the center of the universe. Population, just over 9,000. Named for a prospector at the turn of the century. Once part of Route 66, but they built I-40 to replace it a few years ago, so we're out of the loop. Our sole claim to fame is a line from the old Eagle's song, you know, *Standin' on a corner in--*"

She cringed. Old music wasn't her thing.

"Anyway, my roots are here. Dad was an old newspaper man. I like dry heat. What else can I say?"

She nodded. Good enough. Anyone looking to make a name for himself would've left long ago. Maybe he actually *cared* about the truth.

It was time for a test.

Most people were out to help themselves. They might pretend otherwise, but usually, it wasn't hard to tell. Every day on the job, she dealt with "information seekers", who had little to exchange in return. The smart ones always made it worth her while.

"What do you know about trouble in Oraibi?"

He moved toward a park bench, inviting her to sit first.

"You grew up here in the 90's," he said. "So did I. I was a few years ahead, so you might not remember. But the Hopi and Navajo have waged plenty of battles over this land. Mostly as rivals, but sometimes together, against the white man. I've seen a few first hand. That whole mess with *Snowbowl* seems never ending. Thanks to their track record in the courts, the bad guys usually win.

"But we've got other troubles. Some down to earth, and some far out. Most folks who follow news online or still read the papers know all about the rise of gangs out here in recent years. We've got problems with drugs, alcohol and violence right here--just like in New York City, or D.C., or any other town in

America. Poverty breeds discontent. We have teens who race around on dirt bikes half the night, spray paint graffiti and steal things. Just because we live in the desert doesn't mean we're exempt from modern woes."

Again, she nodded. So far, so good.

"We've also got unique troubles that mainstreamers don't hear about. They're not reported on CNN or FOX, because, let's face it, unless you're talkin' about a major battle over the Indian name of a sports franchise or its mascot, like *Chief Wahoo* or the *Redskins*, most folks could care less about Native Americans or their struggles. It doesn't hit them where they live."

Una's heart soared. Either this guy had a gift for gab or he was sincere. The latter possibility almost gave her a feeling...akin to *hope*. *What if* she had a friend in the Press who could help them get the word out about these intruders? Someone who might even generate sympathy for the Hopi point of view? *What if* he wasn't afraid to question the status quo? The U.S. military no doubt had a strong grip on the likes of people from Flagstaff and Phoenix. But what happened here might have far-reaching implications. The Four Corners region touched people in four different states, after all.

"We've also got a history of events out here that border on the extreme. Amazing Tales. But they're not reported in papers like the *Journal*. Used to be. Look up stories about desert mummies or UFO sightings 40 years ago--before we were born--and you'll find 'em. In the press, sometimes on local TV. Even national. I've actually seen old video with Rather and Cronkite, the giants of Network News. Not anymore."

"Wait a minute," said Una, shaking her head.

Like any reporter, he no doubt had personal hobbies that were perfectly harmless. Some people liked to participate in Civil War reenactments, or build miniature scale models of everything from old WW-2 battleships to futuristic space-craft, like the *U.S.S. Enterprise* or *Millennium Falcon*. Some people collected things, like baseball cards or comic books. Maybe somewhere at home he had a glass bookcase, complete with every known issue of *Spiderman*.

The camera, she thought. Of course! He must be a photographer, with framed photos on his walls...like prize-winning flowers or dogs, or maybe a favorite sports team, like the *Cardinals*, or the *Suns*, or even the *Wildcats*. Photography was a perfectly natural hobby for anyone, especially a newshound.

"Don't get me wrong," he said. "Some things we *don't* report--simply because no one would believe them. My editor draws the line at tales of urban legends. We don't publish ghost stories or photos of UFO's. That's for the *National Enquirer* or *Weekly World News*. The *Journal* has standards to uphold. We have to maintain our integrity. We owe it to our readership."

Una sighed with relief.

"As a lifelong resident, I've heard a few tales that would knock your socks off. Scary shit, in the middle of the night. But some sources don't hold up in the light of scrutiny, or they don't jive with political correctness. That's the nature of the world we live in. I'm sure the same goes for you, in government. As a holder of the public trust, no doubt you're forced to steer clear of taboos."

She reluctantly nodded.

To disagree even privately with public policy from the Department of the Interior was a big no-no. They did not take lightly to criticism. Over the years, she'd seen communication guidelines revised again and again. It had gotten to the point where they simply advised anyone working for Uncle Sam to avoid posting on social media, like Facebook or Twitter. One careless comment or email was enough to sink your career.

Slyly scanning their surroundings for unwanted bystanders, Jack slid over beside her, making Una nervous.

Not because she feared some abnormal behavior. At this point, she trusted him well enough. His face had sincerity written all over it.

"Confidentially," he whispered, "I'd be remiss if I didn't admit there are a few stories I'd *like* to write. Stuff I'd put in print--*if* I thought I could get away with it. But some things...you *can't* report, even if they're true."

A setup line, if she ever heard one. No doubt it

worked well at cocktail parties or on private dinner dates. She could sense the anticipation in his eyes, waiting for her to ask. Any question at all would open the door.

"Such as...?"

He grinned with genuine delight.

"You may not believe it, but I've discovered an incredible coincidence. Don't ask me how I know, because it just came to me. But I get hunches all the time, that even *I* can't explain. Call 'em flashes of insight. We've met before."

And there it was again. That feeling of *deja vu*. He wasn't kidding. It gave her goose bumps.

"Twenty years ago, our paths crossed...on a flight from Dallas. I remember it, clear as day. Well, not face-to-face, the way we are now. But on the plane our eyes met, briefly, and it stayed with me--"

"Oh, my god," she said. "It's *you*. The boy with the camera on flight--"

"5-6-4," they said in unison.

And that was enough. No need to relive the details of what happened--strange lights at 30,000 feet, the frantic voices of their pilot and air traffic controllers, or reactions from the Air Force--though no doubt every sight and sound from that incredible, unforgettable encounter played over in each of their minds.

Just knowing one other person from that America West incident in 1995 was enough to finally chase away all doubt, to make it *real*, for two people now connected through time--forever.

A moment of silence passed.

"Okay, so...maybe this isn't so weird. Maybe we can help each other. I've got the inside track on most things that've happened here since you left. Just keep me in the loop on this whole...Peaks thing? I'd be forever grateful."

Una nodded.

He was right. It was the only thing she knew with any degree of certainty. The 'why' of it was simply beyond them. Why here? Why now, after all these years? The questions were too big to ask. Answers would come, in time.

No telling where all of this might lead. The old feelings were coming back to her now, the way she used to look at the world, through the eyes of a child. When the spirits of her ancestors seemed to surround her.

Thinking back to that night, she could not help but wonder if, even now, the Sky People were watching.

It almost made her smile.

11

PROOF

Una found Tocho skateboarding on a lonely stretch of road near the edge of the village. Howling winds swept in from the desert, kicking up dust. The Peaks dead body turned out to be *Kwahu*, one of his best friends.

He seemed withdrawn.

Ahote had shown her the framed trophy photo and Kasa tried to explain the whole concept of "Explorers Club". Open to boys and girls aged 14 and up, the idea was to promote cultural diversity, focused on the future. It fostered traits of "vision, courage and tenacity" according to their motto. Besides weekly meetings during the school year, club activities included free trips to local concerts, museums, nearby historical towns and even the Grand Canyon.

But Una also knew that teen boys had a way of taking things to extremes, beyond anything their parents or teachers had in mind.

It was impossible to reach the boy's family right now, but Tocho probably knew more anyway. The problem was how to approach him. Kids didn't like to be interrogated. If she came on too strong, he might shut down, altogether.

"Been at it long?" she asked.

Tocho pretended not to see her at first. Patiently she watched him skate, cruise, turn and roll through a variety of trick maneuvers that she could not begin to name, though she had seen them before in public parks. He never lost his balance or fell. Thinking back to her younger days, she almost envied him.

Finally, he stopped, taking his board in hand. "I usually stay 'til 5:30," he said. "What's the rush?"

She glanced at her watch. It was ten after four. "Oh, we don't have to leave. I just wanted to catch up--if you have a minute. Well, what I mean is--"

"You wanna know about Kwahu."

She simply nodded.

"It's not fair. Our whole lives, we've heard stories...from *everyone*...our parents, teachers and elders. About the Hopi past. How our ancestors lived in an underworld beneath the Grand Canyon. How the city from which they came was called *Palitkwapi*, meaning 'Red City of the South.'

"Well, it's a great mystery. Some people say it was the center of the Mayan Old Empire in Mexico. Others say we're descended from Pueblos, who ruled an underworld kingdom. That we were once 'Star Warriors' who fought against 'Children of the Serpent'.

"The Hopi, 'people of one heart', escaped the

'people of two hearts'--those who say one thing, but think another...and speak with a 'forked tongue'. They say those who live out of balance with nature will eventually die out, while honest people, who make personal sacrifice, will survive. Modern man could learn from us, to see why their 'advanced society' is falling apart.

"But they also tell us not to go there. 'Be wary of the canyon at night,' they say, 'For the light coming down toward you may be the Hopi God, Maasaw, coming to take you away.' They say it's dangerous. A place where people experience strange accidents, severe vomiting, and anxiety.

"That was the *whole point* of Explorers Club: to overcome fear and learn from the past. Kwahu wasn't lookin' for trouble. The cave was his discovery. It went on and on for miles. It was so amazing. That compound was a total surprise. You wouldn't believe what we--"

"We?"

He stared at the ground. "You can't tell my parents."

"Tell them what?"

"I didn't want them to worry is all. We thought we had time. Time to really explore. Figure out what it meant. *Then* tell the elders. It wasn't just any cave, you see. I don't know how to say it. There were...*signs*."

Una felt a lump in her throat. "You haven't told anyone?"

He shook his head.

"Okay. For now, let's keep it that way. Come with me. I've got a friend who can help."

***

"We have ten days," said Jack, as the waitress poured him more coffee. He paused to sip at his cup, waiting for her to leave.

Una stared in disbelief. "I thought there was an injunction."

He nodded. "It's only temporary. The judge in Flagstaff's an ex-marine. It was the best they could get, for now. We need a reason to make it stick."

"What do you mean?"

"It all depends on proof. We must show the site qualifies for protection under the Archaeological Resources Protection Act. That requires human remains of 'archeological interest' over a hundred years old, including things like pottery, tools, rock paintings or graves."

"But we'd need an expert to authenticate our findings...on short notice, and a way to get inside."

Jack smiled. "I've already got someone in mind. An old professor who still teaches archaeology at North Arizona University. He's also a part-time consultant for *Antiques Road Show* whenever they come around."

The two of them suddenly turned to Tocho.

The Hopi teen had been sitting there, listening

intently the whole time, sipping his Coke and eating french fries. Sooner or later, they'd have to come to him, and he knew it. Without access to the cave, any plans were meaningless. He grinned with complete satisfaction, realizing that his moment had arrived.

"No problem," he said, "When do we go?"

***

"No can do," said investigator Tooms. "I'm bound by police protocol. We've got the Coroner's report, plus affidavits from Black Ops personnel. It doesn't meet the criteria for a homicide. Technically, there's been no crime committed."

He leaned against the badge-like insignia on his Sherriff's SUV, with broad arms in short sleeves folded across his massive chest. The sideburns reminded her of WWE's the 'Rock', with tattoos to match.

She frowned at the setting sun. "So you can't even accompany us? With you along as an eyewitness, we'd at least have someone to back us up, just in case."

"You expectin' trouble?"

Now this was a sticking point. Since no one else supposedly knew about the cave's secret entrance, they shouldn't encounter opposition. But it was impossible to guess what was happening inside the compound. If Black Ops went in to explore, they'd probably deny it, which would only make her believe it even more. In any case, they'd have to take their chances.

Una shrugged.

"My advice? Take a good camera. Document whatever you see. That way, even if there's sabotage later, you'll have something to show the judge. Without it, you've not nothing but hearsay--and that'll never hold up."

She entered the house with a heavy heart as the SUV drove away.

"So?" asked Kasa, trembling as she closed the heavy door. "What did he say?"

"It's all on us," she sighed. "Officially, he can do nothing."

Kasa peeked out the front window with a scowl on her face. "*Chicken shit*, if you ask me! All those tattoos! All that weight-lifting...for *nothing*! If he were my son, I'd set him straight."

"Speaking of which," replied Tocho, emerging from the nearest arch to stand proudly before them. With a thick bundle of rope over one shoulder, tool-laden utility belt, and leather fedora, he resembled a young Indiana Jones.

"Perfect," said Una, "But not yet. We still need our expert, remember?"

His face dropped.

Tomorrow, she thought, or the next day. The sooner the better--if Jack's source would only come through. Meanwhile, she'd have to confront the other side. No sense in pretending they faced no enemy.

One death already--even if "accidental"--was one too many.

Thinking back to their encounter on the Peaks, she wondered. Who was the SOB in charge? There *had* to be a Black Ops Commander, even if he refused to show his face. Did that make him a coward, or just shrewd?

Una decided to find out.

From the window, Kasa returned to her side. "I'm afraid for you," she said. "Even as a little girl, you were always so fearless. Climbing up rocks where no one else dared. Killing a rattlesnake to save your dog. Venturing out on horseback to find a lost pony in the middle of a heat wave. But this is *different*--like nothing you've ever tried."

"Don't worry," she smiled. "I can *do* this."

***

The next day she set out once more for the Peaks, in a blindfold, seated beside Tooms, who came simply to observe. They took a hidden service road, barred to the public. At least it would save her from the grief of a bad back--if the horses had anything to do with it. She wasn't so sure.

Jack remained hidden, in the back seat, with a camera. For some reason, he didn't have to wear a blindfold, but he wasn't exactly an outsider, either. The *Journal's* standards of 'integrity' probably included a long-standing 'arrangement' with law enforcement.

This would make it tough for him to challenge military authority later--but they couldn't worry about that now.

"You sure about this?" said Tooms. "These folks don't like it when people ask questions. Especially a woman."

"I think they're afraid of me," she said.

"Why?"

"Because I caught them by surprise. They didn't expect me to be there the first time. Women do that to men."

"So?"

"Men don't like it, naturally. And they don't like women who make them look bad. But I already know that. So I won't. In the end, I'll make him feel like a hero, and he'll thank me for it."

Tooms shook his head, but said nothing.

"Besides, we share a common goal. No violence. People from my village are mad as hell. They want something--or someone--to blame. That boy who died was only seventeen. The same age as Tocho.

"This might've been easier if it *had* been a greedy corporation. They tend to be faceless, nameless entities with no soul or conscience. Easy to hate but hard to attack, except in the courtroom.

"Now we've got a fenced in compound full of soldiers in black uniforms, toting guns. They make an ideal target. Half the young men around here grew up playing video games. They're used to shooting at bad guys. Now the bad guys are here, in their own back yard."

"I don't follow," said Tooms.

"Say a group decides to march up there, demanding justice, like a lynch mob. In the end, they wind up dead. The military gets bad press. Nobody wins. Kasa says I'm here for a *reason*. Maybe she's right. All I know is, we've got to prevent that. It's better...for everyone."

Una frowned beneath her blindfold. She kept expecting their vehicle to reach higher ground. The climb on horseback seemed to take hours.

"Something's wrong," she said.

Tooms sighed, as Jack's face appeared in the rear-view mirror.

"There's...been a change in plans," he said from behind her. "It just came in this morning. Something's happened at the school. We thought it best to wait until we were on the road."

She ripped off her blindfold. "Stop the car. NOW!"

Tooms pulled off to the side.

Popping the door, she hopped out. "You can't *do* this to me. I'm not some tourist to be toyed with. This is serious! We have to speak to someone in charge. I thought we agreed on that!"

"We did," said Jack, trying to calm her down, "I mean, we *do*. It's still part of the plan. Just hear me out. We couldn't tell you before, not in town. Someone might overhear and start a panic. They asked for *you*, understand? It's just a delay. But we have to go now."

"Why?" she said.

"It relates to our discussion about 'proof', earlier. To protect the site, it must qualify under ARP. That means it must be considered to have 'religious or cultural importance'. Remember?"

"Yeah. So?"

"Well, it turns out there's *another* boy."

"Don't tell me. The third one in the photograph."

He nodded.

"Well, what *is* it?"

"Better get in. It's...kind a hard to explain."

12

PRANKSTER

Una tried to get more info from Howser to no avail as they entered Keams Canyon, Arizona. Hopi Junior/Senior High School was short-staffed this time of year, for remedial classes only. Tooms set the SUV's dial to KUYI, to eavesdrop on a weekly student-run radio show.

"...nothing like it," said a young DJ, "unless you're coolin' your jets in summer school. Hear the latest? Somethin' *weird's* goin' on...at Hopi High. A dead head has suddenly turned into a brain! They're callin' him the X-man..."

She turned it off.

Tooms chuckled as they pulled into a near-empty gravel parking lot. A Hopi woman waited for them outside, nervously puffing a cigarette. It was Chu'si.

Una hopped out first. "Hey! I didn't know you--"

"Only part time, for extra money. Regular tutor's on vacation. Anyway, thanks for coming."

The women went inside.

For such a large, modern building, it seemed dark

and gloomy. An official-looking red banner above the dimly lit Principal's Office read:

BOARD OF INDIAN EDUCATION

Chu'si never liked school. How'd she wind up here?

"They cut the power to all but a single classroom," she said. "BIA requires us to offer summer classes for any student who fails more than one semester, whether it's twenty or two. It's a second chance to pass. For some kids, it's also the turning point, between getting a diploma or dropping out. This year we started with eight, but there's only one left. He scared the rest off."

Chu'si paused in the hallway before a half-opened door. "I don't know how to say this...but he's not the same kid who came here two weeks ago. And I don't mean just academically. Something has *changed* over the past few days. It's breath taking--and frightening."

They found him writing feverishly on a chalkboard.

Una approached him slowly. He wrote small characters in vertical columns, top to bottom, right to left. The board was practically full of them.

"Moki? Hi. My name is Una. I'm an old friend of Tocho. He told me you were together in Explorer's Club, showed me the trophy photo. I'm sorry about Kwahu. We're...trying to figure out what happened."

The boy continued to write without pausing to look up.

"I guess you know we're all excited to see your new skill. It's rewarding for any teacher when her student...exceeds expectations. But we're also confused, because we don't know what it means. I've never seen writing like that before. Can you tell me--"

"Sure you have," he replied.

Chu'si froze at the sound of his voice. It was perfectly calm, mature, and well enunciated. Not at all like the sarcastic, troubled teen on recordings from two days before. Communication had never been his strong suite. Joining the Club had been a way to bring him out of his shell. It was hoped that forging friendships would help him fend off gangs, who were always trying to recruit new members. She traded glances with Una.

"But--"

"Ever read product labels?" he said. "Or check out the fine print on half the stuff you buy from mega retailers, like Walmart? Electronics, guns, watches and tennis shoes. It's right there."

She sighed. Evidently, a touchy subject. Better to let it go for now, shift gears, until they could find someone to decipher the writing. Press him too hard and cooperation might be lost. She'd try another tack.

"Tell us about Explorer's Club."

He grinned. "Opened my eyes. Everyone talks about the past, but they made it come alive. Took us on trips to museums with real artifacts--even the

Grand Canyon, where human history began, according to Hopi Elders. But there's a lot of unanswered questions."

"Such as?"

His hand slowed, the chalk paused in mid air. Moki turned away from his task to face her.

"I know what you're trying to do. But I'm not an answer machine. I can't explain it. It's like a light went on, inside my head. I don't know where it's from, or how long it'll last. I just--"

Tears formed in his eyes.

Instinctively Una went over, wrapping arms around him. Moki began to sob. She could feel him trembling. His chalk hit the floor.

Chu'si signaled a student aid, flashing a twenty dollar bill. "He's been at it for hours. Get him some food. In fact, I think we all need a break. Something simple. Pizza maybe. Whatever you can find. Don't be long."

Another aid, a junior cheerleader, brought cold drinks from the school cafeteria and fresh popcorn. Moki sat down to open a Coke and chat with the girl. For the moment, he seemed okay.

The two women stepped outside.

"What else?" said Una, "What aren't you telling me?"

Chu'si lit up again. "Look, I'm no psychologist. But kids don't go from delinquents to geniuses overnight."

"Meaning?"

"Something *extraordinary* is going on. I can't even find words to describe it. Either it's some kind of miracle, or he's part of an experiment, or I don't know what. I mean, what's it like...to go from ordinary to *gifted*...just like that? That's just not possible. Right?"

Una shrugged. "The others...he 'scared them off'?"

"You wouldn't believe it. His personality changed, from being reckless, with a devil-may-care attitude, to having this heightened awareness of the 'interconnectedness' and 'sacredness' of all life. It freaked the other kids out and they left."

"How'd he take it?"

"Well, he suffered, obviously. No one wants to be considered 'abnormal'."

"Then what?"

"*That's* when I called for you, remember? We don't know how to handle this. Something's wrong with this kid. I don't know whether to send him home or put him in a hospital."

"You...tell anyone?"

"We sent snapshots of his writing to the Language Department at NAU and local police. So far, nothing. We thought it was a prank at first. You know, a smart ass trying to disrupt things? Now, I'm at a loss."

Tooms left Howser by the SUV, approaching them cautiously. "Not to butt in, but our friend with the camera over there is getting pretty antsy. If you won't let him in, just talk to him, at least? I'm waitin' on a call from Flagstaff. They passed your pics on to Camp Navajo."

Una's mouth dropped. "The Army Base? You gotta be kiddin' me! Who's idea was *that*?"

He shrugged. "Not my call. It's standard procedure in cases like this."

"What the hell do you mean? Standard procedure? This shit doesn't happen every day. Give me a minute. I'll talk to him right now!"

Una marched over to the SUV. Jack's smile fell from his face as she came closer. Suddenly he felt an urge to hop inside, locking all the doors.

"Was it *your* idea?"

"N-n-no," he said, fumbling with the camera, holding it up like a shield, in self defense. "Of course not. I'd never do such a thing. We're a team, remember? It's the *last* thing I'd do!"

She paused with eyes fixed, arms crossed, fuming.

"W-w-what idea?"

"Camp Navajo! You really think they're gonna help us? That's like conspiring with the enemy."

He sighed with relief. "That wasn't me. Apparently--"

The sudden rumble of heavy vehicles came thundering down the road. It looked like a dust storm, racing toward them. In a matter of moments, a convoy of three U.S. Army Hummers roared to a stop near the entrance to Hopi High.

Two officers in desert camo uniforms stepped out of the first one, approaching Investigator Tooms. "Who's in charge here?"

"No administrators," he replied, "But there's a teacher."

The two men moved apart as a third man, in Black Ops uniform wearing a red beret exited the second vehicle, coming to stand between them. Instinctively, he turned to Una. "Afternoon, Ma'am. General Ashcroft, first in command of Station Alpha-Bravo, on Fremont Peak. You crashed our party a few days ago. Sorry I didn't have the pleasure."

He seemed young for someone with so much authority. "What are you *doing* here, General?"

"Following orders, Ma'am. Priority One. This comes strictly from the top. Higher-ups in Langley got a hold of your photos. We're here for retrieval. Please take us to the boy, at once."

"Langley? But that's CIA--"

"Not so fast," said Chu'si, "I work here, and this is private property. We can't let you in without proper clearance. I'll have to contact the Principal. We've got rules too, you know!"

Ashcroft stared straight ahead, with eyes unmoving, like a gunslinger. He showed no signs of emotion.

Two more camo officers appeared from the third vehicle, with M-16's. It was beginning to feel like a showdown.

Una didn't like the odds.

"We're prepared to take him by force," said Ashcroft. "But I'd rather not. It's bad for PR. Please step aside. We don't need clearance. It's a matter of National Security."

"*What*? Now I've heard everything!"

They grabbed Chu'si by the arms, dragging her away.

There was no time to think. In D.C., Una had learned that every misfortune carried with it an opportunity.

"All right!" she said, as Jack's camera snapped away from a distance. "We'll cooperate. Let her go!"

Better to keep things orderly--for now. The general was used to getting his own way. She did not want to be labeled a troublemaker.

Chu'si frowned. "So much for my first--and last--job teaching summer school. Seven runaways and one threat to National Security. I probably did those kids more harm than good."

Una sighed. "Don't be so hard on yourself. We all have to choose our battles. They've won for now. But we have destiny on our side. You were right. This whole thing *is* extraordinary, but not unheard of.

"In D.C. you meet all kinds. Some into horoscopes. Some UFOs. *They* say it's part of a wave; telepathy, clairvoyance, and healing. Gifted kids popping up, in places like the U.K., Russia, and Europe. Now Arizona."

***

Army officers entered the classroom.

"Moki Basin? I'm Ashcroft. We're from the U.S. government. I guess you know why we're here?"

The boy nodded, with maturity beyond his years.

"Well, come along, son. You've got a lot of folks talking in Washington. They're mighty concerned about what's happening here. It's our job to...help you sort it all out."

Another officer helped the boy gather up his things while the general and his driver waited by the Hummers.

"Another job well done, Lieutenant. Thank your *source*, by the way--and tell 'em to keep in touch. This is far from over."

His driver nodded as they boarded the H-1. "Yes, General. Excuse me, sir, but I was just wondering...about the boy. That whole thing with the chalkboard. Pretty impressive. Could he be faking it?"

Ashcroft gazed out thoughtfully at the red desert sun.

"To most Westerners, like you and me, it's the most impenetrable language on Earth. While there may be only an eighth as many syllables, the tonal variations for each impute different meanings. A single word, *ma*, can mean linen, horse, or mother, depending on how you say it."

"But all those characters sir! Thousands! Written top to bottom, read right to left. How'd he ever master *Chinese*?"

The general cringed.

"Hell if I know. Of *course* he's faking it. But he still got the information somehow. That's what bothers me!"

13

THE SKEPTIC

Una wasted no time, proceeding to Camp Navajo, 12 miles west of Flagstaff, the next day. While she had no hopes of getting Moki released so soon, she had promised the family to plead their case just the same. Jack knew enough to get her inside the gate with a Visitor's Pass.

Beyond that, she was on her own.

Thankfully, it proved to be a busy place. No one seemed to notice her at all. Used by the National Guard for training and ammunition storage, the U.S. Army facility spanned over 44 square miles, making it the largest military installation in the state of Arizona.

"Excuse me," she said innocently to a strapping young man in uniform, "Where can I find General Ashcroft?"

The look of recognition in his eye was not reassuring. It was almost as if she had uttered a secret code. "Yes, Ma'am. I'm Corporal Biggs. He's been expecting you. Right this way."

He led her to a golf cart, driven by a second

officer.

"What the--"

"It's less conspicuous. You'll...see what I mean. Please get in."

They headed away from the cluster of buildings down a gravel road, past hundreds of earth-covered igloos, in perfect rows beneath the desert sun.

"Our premier capability," he said, "Concrete reinforced, for ammunition storage. Constant temperature and humidity make them ideal for sensitive materials."

They passed a pair of unarmed UH-60 Black Hawk helicopters, landing on open ground. Twenty ROTC (Reserve Officers' Training Corps) cadets jumped aboard with their gear.

"Training exercise with the Desert Rangers. To learn survival skills in case of chemical, biological, or nuclear attacks."

She nodded.

Next they came to a jumbled assortment of RV's and tent campers at the edge of a ponderosa pine forest, about a mile from the main gate.

"Military Campground," he said, "Maybe our best kept secret. Has everything you could hope for...darkness at night for stargazing, utter silence of the forest, and the security of being on an Army post."

Una felt confused. "Where exactly are we going?"

"It's just ahead."

But all she could see was a crude-looking

outhouse, with separate entrances for men and women. She doubted it even had running water. Exiting the golf cart, Biggs led her to a padlocked wooden door, around to the back.

As they stepped inside, closing the door, overhead lights came on automatically. Electronic panels separated to reveal the entrance to a high-tech express elevator. Its unique shape reminded her of a Tupperware sugar bowl, like an open-ended oval with another half oval on each side.

He invited her to stand beside him. She really had no choice. Reaching down, he firmly gripped a curved metal railing with both hands. "You might want to...hold on," he said.

The lights blinked, panels shut, and suddenly the floor dropped. She gasped for breath. The elevator's motion was smooth and silent, with a barely noticable surge as they slowed to a stop, moments later. She guessed the lift to be magnetic, with no need for cables.

The panels opened to simulated sunlight, so natural that she almost mistook it for the real thing. She immediately sensed electronic vibrations that gave her a slight headache. The giant tunnel before them appeared to be the work of an advanced machine, with smooth walls like polished black glass.

"How deep--" she began to say.

"About a mile," he replied.

A jeep appeared promptly before them, with a driver in black uniform. It bore a red triangular shoulder insignia with the white letter "P". Apparently young, in his mid-twenties, his head was completely shaved. The nametag read: J-31.

"Three things to remember," he said. "First, this facility is heavily monitored; video surveillance, heat sensors, motion detectors, the works. There is no way to wander far without getting caught.

"Second, do not venture anywhere that is marked OFF LIMITS. It's human nature to be curious, but don't do it. Our security guards are extremely zealous. One wrong step could land you in 'Nightmare Hall'."

He seemed to pause for effect, apparently hoping to frighten her.

"And third?" she asked.

"The 'P' is for PERICA. It means: 'large heavy knife' in South America, used for cutting vegetation, or sometimes as a weapon."

Una did not feel intimidated, in the least. "What, no blindfold?"

He smiled. "No need, Ma'am. Technically, this place doesn't exist."

***

Soon they reached their destination, a domed cement-block Command Center, complete with U.S. Flag on a white pole, and a black flag bearing the base insignia. Artificial lights approximated the feeling of midday, back on the surface. The driver escorted her inside.

"The general will see you now," a computer voice said from a lighted panel above his office door.

It opened.

Ashcroft greeted her with a cautious grin. "Crashing my party again?"

Her eyes narrowed. "Look, I don't know what kind of cloak and dagger charade you're running here, but--"

"It's no charade, I assure you. Everything you see here--and are about to see--is paid for with honest American tax dollars. TOP SECRET. Breathe one word of this when you get back, and I'll know about it."

Her blood ran cold. "I'm here about the boy. Moki, is he all--"

He activated a screen behind her. "See for yourself."

Una turned. There he was, in a lighted room with all the comforts of home; big bed, flat screen TV, microwave, personal fridge and an X-box. But without speaking to him, she had no way to read his emotional state.

"I need to--"

"Request denied," he said. "With all respect, you're not here to rescue him, or play havoc with the situation. He's in good hands. Our professional staff includes doctors from every discipline, including psychology."

"But he's--"

"Not sick? Perhaps. But the changes in his

mental acuity are undeniable. We've accessed all previous measures from educational records. None of it explains what's happening here. It goes way beyond our frame of reference. And all that stuff in Chinese? Straight from an intelligence intercept--one we damn near missed. Yet he refuses to name his source."

"His 'source'? What the hell are talking about? He's a 17-yr-old kid for cryin' out loud."

"Age has nothing to do with it. Though it could make him more vulnerable."

"To...?"

"Influence peddlers who stalk these kids online. The 'source' may have passed itself off as another player, trading game secrets to win his trust. In our experience, people do not stumble upon this sort of thing."

Her face went blank.

Ashcroft hesitated. "Maybe he knew, maybe not. At this point, it's impossible to tell."

"Knew what?"

"The *meaning* of what he wrote. It was, in fact, computer code. And pretty lethal. A specific cyber threat to the U.S. power grid--which we foiled successfully, by the way. But what if we hadn't?"

"Moki is no spy. Why can't you see that?"

"Because there are too many unknowns. Too many unanswered questions. Standard medical tests tell us nothing. Somehow, his IQ is 'off the scale' compared to results obtained only a year ago. He doesn't remember writing on the chalkboard, but he *has* made a few drawings, with symbols we don't understand."

Ashcroft showed her simple line diagrams with stick figures reminiscent of petroglyphs on the Hopi Reservation.

"There's something else, about a 'light' in the cave, that he won't talk about--maybe because it led to the loss of his friend. We're still trying to learn more. It may be the key to this whole mystery."

Una froze. That must be it. Something *happened* to him in the cave. She tried to take a mental picture. "Any clues?"

He frowned. "Not so far. For one thing, it's pitch dark. We've picked up a few anomalous readings, but that's all. We need to send a team, but that requires special training. My men don't have it. Support is on the way."

She did not know whether to believe him. Jack's archaeology expert was due in one more day. But they couldn't afford to go in blind, without a guide. They'd need Tocho. Otherwise, they might get lost, or worse, without finding any answers.

It would have to be soon.

If Ashcroft was lying, if troops were already stationed there, they could be risking their lives. *Not again.*

"Maybe I can help," she said. "According to Hopi belief, our ancestors ascended from another world, below. Many stories are not written, but passed by oral tradition from one generation to the next.

Ancient Voices still guide us. Let me consult with the Elders."

He grinned. "No offense, Ma'am, but this is the 21st century. I have to deal with the modern world. Not some imaginary past. If my superiors knew we were even *having* this conversation, it could earn me a reprimand."

Una clenched her teeth.

The general sat back, arms crossed over his chest. "So the natives are restless. I get it. Don't let 'em get out a hand. I've got a job to do. And I don't have time for pow wows."

He was getting on her nerves.

"Why, General? Why are you even here? We deserve to know *that* much, at least."

"I've already answered that. This base is TOP SECRET."

"I don't mean here below. I'm talking about *Alpha-Bravo*. Why invade the Peaks? Can't you find uranium elsewhere? Don't tell me how to 'handle' my people. We've already lost a loved one--and we're afraid of losing more. But we're *not* afraid of you! The laws of this country are meant to protect everyone. You want a fight? Be my guest."

He grinned. "Uranium? Is that what you think? No comment."

An escort appeared to usher her out.

Ashcroft raised one hand to delay them, activating a mini-holographic display of Una, hovering in midair, before her eyes. A pulsing red dot represented the GPS tracker concealed in her belt. "Give my regards to your cohorts. Trust me, they know nothing. It's useless."

Una glanced up before marching out the door. There to one side, on the wall hung an old movie poster, HOW THE WEST WAS WON, circa 1962.

"What the hell is *this*?"

"One of my favorites. Goodbye, Miss Waters."

"Winners and losers," she said. "Is *that* how you view the world? I'm talking bigger picture here...cosmic forces that shape our lives and the course of mankind. Don't you believe in anything higher than yourself?"

Rising to his feet, the general came over, standing toe-to-toe. His face became deadly serious. "I believe in *this*," he said, pointing to the Stars and Stripes on his uniform, "This We'll Defend. Good day!"

Retracing her steps, she thought about trillions of dollars from a "black budget" being spent for special projects that most people knew nothing about. She gazed up in awe at the glass-walled tunnel, its artificial daylight, and finally sighed as they stepped once more into the express elevator. Making mental notes about all she'd seen and heard--even though she might never be able to talk about any of it--Una still wondered why.

Why any government with the wherewithal to build PERICA this far from the public eye would bother with the Sacred Peaks. They weren't looking for uranium. That was a cover story. But they were after *something*. The cave's existence had apparently caught them by surprise.

That Hopi diagram *must* be the key. If only she could remember enough to write it down, get it to the Elders.

Ancient Voices might speak to them--even now.

***

Corporal Biggs transported her via golf cart once more past the Military Campground, where people roasted marshmallows around campfires bathed in moonlight. Dogs barked and children played. From a guitar rose the familiar cords of *Kumbaya*.

They passed hundreds of earth-covered igloos, in perfect rows.

Finally, exiting Camp Navajo, she rejoined Jack, still waiting outside in his car. His rapid-fire questions came as no surprise.

"How'd it go? Did you see Moki? You went off grid for a while. I completely lost track. What happened?"

"I wasn't in the camp...*exactly*," she replied.

"What do you mean?"

"One of my native scouts the other day, on horseback, was a real conspiracy buff. He had some pretty wild ideas about the U.S. military--or at least, so I *thought*. Ever hear of D-U-M-B's?"

"Well, sure. Deep Underground Military Bases. Heard about 'em for years. Rumors mostly. Never met an actual eyewitness, though. Without photos or other evidence, their existence is damn hard to prove. Is *that* where you went?"

She smiled. "It was pretty dark, most of the time. So I can't say for sure. But whatever you've heard, is probably true."

"And?"

"More to the point: I met with Ashcroft. What an *ass*! I tried to open his mind, beyond regulations and military protocols. But it was no use. He does not accept the Hopi Way."

"*And?*"

"Moki's fine. We can tell his family not to worry. But *Alpha-Bravo's* operations are considered TOP SECRET. So I'm not supposed to elaborate--unless I want to die, or disappear. Whatever! Let's just say, as far as D-U-M-B's are concerned...I'm a *believer*."

PART THREE

FOUR CORNERS

"When the blood in your veins returns to the sea, and the earth in your bones returns to the ground, perhaps then you will remember that this land does not belong to you."

--Hopi

14

BALANCE

The Hopi Tribal Council had 14 members, selected by community election or appointed by village leaders. They met in a large modern chamber with overhead lighting and elevated seats arranged on a U-shaped wooden platform. Meetings generally lasted from 7 to 9:30 PM.

Una felt fortunate to be present, but also knew that she would not be able to address them until the floor was opened to "new business"--and she had no way of knowing precisely when that would be.

Kasa urged her to be patient, but admittedly, she had been on edge since her return from Camp Navajo.

The proceedings reminded her of so many battles, large and small, fought to sustain their culture in a world marked by dramatic change. Her parents had tried to protect Hopiland against corporate greed. Though far away in D.C., periodically she kept tabs on what was happening here. Over the past decade, they had waged exhausting legal fights over land, religious rights, and water against the Navajo Nation, Big Coal and the Federal Government.

Reaching into her pocket, she drew out a folded piece of paper with the pencil diagram she had labored over so intensely the night before. She had no way of gauging its accuracy, trying to recreate from memory the original shown to her by Ashcroft.

Like many petroglyphs, from top to bottom, its symbols appeared to tell a story from past...to present...to future. Though a few seemed familiar to her untrained eye, like shapes of people or animals, most did not.

Compared to others she had seen on cliffs near Oraibi, she guessed that a few came from legends involving the Earth, with rainclouds and corn, while others depicted Sky gods in flying shields, or club-wielding figures in combat.

More disturbing were scenes of destruction, with red-tailed comets falling from the sky, ghostly-eyed spirit beings, or death, with headless forms of people upside-down, or bleeding from the mouth.

All in all, it seemed to make no sense, but she knew *better* than that.

If only Moki was here--he could attest to what he had seen with his own two eyes. They still had no word on his release.

Going into the meeting it was already clear that many locals were against the idea of cave exploration. Hopi culture frowned on digging, *period*, and viewed it akin to stirring up bones in a graveyard.

"With a majority of seven to six, the men usually get their way," said Kasa.

"But that only makes thirteen," said Una.

She nodded. "Most of the time. Big Dan 'O', wearing the white-feathered head band, is the oldest at age 79. I'm surprised to see him here. It's way past his bed time. No one's had the nerve to force him out."

Finally, gray-haired chairman Keevama nodded in her direction, as silence fell over the council chamber. "The floor is clear. I believe it is time for new--"

"Right here!" said Una, leaping to her feet. "If it please--"

"You've not been recognized--*yet*," he said, furling his silver brow. "Keep interrupting, and I'll have you escorted out of here! The council is well aware of your request. First, regarding this matter of military intrusion on Fremont Peak, resulting in a controversial death, what progress have you made toward obtaining the 'proof' needed by the district judge in Flagstaff?"

"Well, sir, I...I mean...we've not yet been able to...that is, our expert has not yet arrived to authenticate our 'findings' and...and...."

"Slow *down*, Miss Waters, this not a race."

She tried to swallow.

He raised a hand. "You must know the majority here are against entering this cave of yours, under any circumstance. Some feel it is 'taboo', considering the fates that have already befallen two of the three boys who were reckless enough to venture in there. In good conscience, we cannot sanction any effort to return, even with good intentions."

Una made a fist at her side, trying to conceal her anger at Ashcroft. The general's arrogance still wrecked havoc with her emotions. She came here determined to win approval, but also feared that any action might jeopardize Moki's release. She did not trust the man.

"Excuse me," said another male voice. "Miss Waters?"

Una turned to face him.

"Ed Sakeva. I'm confused. You *do* know that *not* every village on the r eservation chooses a seat on this council. Do you speak for Oraibi?"

He sported a modern American haircut, unlike the traditional straight "Dutch boy" bangs across the forehead worn by most of his contemporaries, meant to symbolize their face "looking through a window" for the *day of Purification*, a hallmark of Hopi lore. He was younger (she guessed forty-something) and more bold. No doubt the others considered him a bit of a hothead.

"No," she said. "I'm not here on behalf of a single village or clan. The issue before us too big. It affects all Hopi."

"How so?"

She drew a deep breath. "Besides asking the natural questions that came to mind, such as the 'where' and 'how' regarding this cave, I could not help but ask myself 'why'. *Why here? Why now?* The significance of underground spaces in Hopi lore cannot be ignored. *Achivas* represent ceremonial places to honor the Earth. Where Shamans enter to do their most sacred work. This is because according to legend, at the destruction of each age of mankind the people that were pure of heart went down into the Earth for protection with a group of beings called the *Ant People*."

"*Something* happened down there that we cannot yet explain. One of the boys saw *this*," she said, referring to her sketch of Moki's petroglyph. "You all have a copy. It means something important. What's *wrong* with all of you? Why can't you see that?"

Again, the chairman raised a hand. "Stop right there. None of us can provide an 'instant interpretation' of a penciled diagram! The petroglyph itself must be studied and authenticated before any meaning can be ascribed to it. Up to now, we've been lenient, because of your bloodline. But you're pushing too hard. Anyone can see that you've been *corrupted*, living among the white man in D.C. Be reasonable. We need clear photographs, at least."

A murmur arose from every corner of the room, and Keevama sensed that it was time to seek input from villagers in attendance. Predictably, a few complained about the 'lack of decisive action' being taken to prosecute those responsible for the boy's death at Alpha-Bravo. A few chanted for 'Hopi

Justice', even though they knew it would do no good. Not everyone welcomed or trusted Una after being gone for so many years.

After heated debate, he called upon her once more to answer them.

She turned away from council, to address the crowd. "Just to be clear, I work for the government, but I'm not here in any official capacity. I was not 'sent' by the Office of the Interior, and I do not speak for them. I came only at the request of a dear friend, because Kasa remembers my parents and how hard they once fought to protect Hopiland.

"Some of you consider me an outsider, and I don't blame you. But returning home has affected me in ways I never expected. It's made me recall a promise I made to my mother. It also makes me realize what has been missing in my life--that 'sacred center' that gives each of us direction and real purpose. And I hope to carry that with me wherever I go, when this over."

The chairman reluctantly nodded, as if little had changed. He motioned for a council vote, by a raise of hands. Una still needed a majority for permission to enter the cave. With only six women out of 14 members, it did not seem likely to happen.

Words came to her mind from Hopi elder, Kuwanyauma:

> *A new time is coming. It is up to us now,*
> *to bring wisdom and healing,*

to bring the Earth back into balance.

Suddenly, there was a commotion in the back as a chamber door burst open. It was a black man in a smoking jacket. Jack grinned. It was his old professor, the archaeology expert from North Arizona University.

"Pardon me, please. I am Jim Aguda, digger of old bones and finder of lost civilizations. My lifelong work has taken me from the pyramids of ancient Egypt to the Grand Canyon. I apologize for my late arrival. I have not yet had the privilege to examine what may prove to be a most extraordinary find, but let me offer a few words about....*silence*."

Every eye in the room turned to him with expectation.

Aguda removed his brown fedora, and bowed to the Hopi Council.

"In my experience, one encounters 'profound silence' deep within the Earth, like no other. It can be painfully oppressive to ears accustomed to the constant sounds of life in the world above. According to some, auditory 'hallucinations' may be experienced to compensate for this. In the past these were perceived as voices from the spirit world. I, for one, believe they are *real*. I listen--to learn from them."

At this point, a member of the council stirred who had long remained silent. White-haired with eyes that stared deep into one's soul, Dan "O" cleared his throat, before fixing his gaze on Una.

"Retracing the steps of one's ancestors can be perilous for one who is not prepared. On this journey, there is no place for impatience, anger, or fear. These will hinder you, as a stumbling block. Cast emotion aside. Leave it behind so that you may enter with an open heart and mind, to receive the truth.

"The noise of the white man's world has made it difficult to hear that 'still, small voice' that each of us carries within; that we first hear as a child. Reach deep inside, to hear it again--only then will you be prepared to enter the cave.

"The world is out of balance, because people make it so. Like a pair of wolves, white and black who are constant companions, you must achieve balance within yourself. A journey to 'find the truth' occurs both inside and out."

She could only smile.

"Maybe that explains it," said 'Sakeva the bold'. "Why the boys met with disaster in the cave. They were too young to understand. Not prepared. Forget what you've learned in D.C. The white man's way of conquest is not the Hopi Way."

What did Ashcroft say? According to Moki, in the cave there were "signs" and some kind of "light". For some reason, he was afraid to elaborate.

Finally, there was a vote, with hands to be counted. Old Dan "O" apparently believed in her-- and that was something she never expected. The six women were with her, of course. She made eye contact with each of them, one-by-one, to acknowledge their support. Kasa had been right all along when she wrote:

> *Men cannot fix it alone. They need*
> *to hear a woman's voice...*

And for some reason, Sakeva was with her. She grinned. Maybe he respected her decision to come back after so long, face up to her mistakes, seek answers to hard questions and accept painful answers. Or maybe he just liked anyone with enough guts to stand up to authority.

Chairman Keevama nodded at last, with approval. Many villagers rose from their seats in unity to stand behind her.

"The Hopi Council has no legal authority over Fremont Peak, but that does not matter. Your path lies far beneath it, perhaps to another world. We encourage you to seek any and all evidence that will support and authenticate this discovery. May you hear the ancient voices and learn from them--in your quest to find the truth."

With Jim Aguda on one side and Jack on the other, she turned to embrace them. Wiping away tears, Una was ready to try.

15

DEEP-SEATED

Even with Tocho's help to find the hidden cave entrance, Una wondered if it would be enough to go on. One vital source regarding Moki's odd behavior had yet to be explored: his *family*.

Up to now, she had resisted Jack's insistence, not wishing to invade their privacy. But they were running out of options. If his parents had any clue to what changed him, it might be worth the effort.

Jack's beat-up Ford Pinto slowly ascended a narrow dirt road, hundreds of feet up from the desert toward the First Mesa village of Walpi, surrounded by awesome vistas of the sky and distant horizons. Still, no words came to mind. It would be their first meeting face-to-face.

"Try to stay *neutral*," he said.

Una sighed. "What? And miss our only chance? Trust is everything! They have to believe we care!"

He cringed--because she was right.

They might be the only ones who knew the boy's state of mind. Whatever happened to him, the ancient *source* could still be waiting there below in the dark, like a snake for its next victim.

Moki's mother, Alana, petit with welcoming brown eyes, humbly greeted them at the door. Settlements here, built using hand-trimmed sandstone and earth dated back to the "Anasazi" days of the 10th century. Much like Oraibi, Walpi still lacked electrical power and running water.

Una gazed at the southwest horizon, before stepping inside. The Sacred Peaks loomed.

The modest couple seemed slow at first to open up about their son. Jack knew a few basics, thanks to a friend at the local police. Moki had some minor blots on his record, mostly for "disturbing the peace" at odd hours.

"Before joining Explorer's Club, all he ever cared about was riding his motorbike," Alana said. "A few of his friends belonged to gangs, and it worried us to no end."

She grasped hands with Cheveyo, the boy's father. "Moki seemed to have a one track mind. He watched one reality show: *Naked and Afraid.*"

Apparently his exploits with the Club changed all that. The boys soon struck out on their own, unsupervised. That somehow led to the cave. But it was hard to get specific answers.

"We've been to the school," said Una.

Alana frowned. "It was a mystery to everyone, at first. Some children do things that are odd or excessive. But he became so *distracted*. He could not get his work done. The teachers thought he might have a disorder, like ADHD. We had him tested. Results were negative."

The room fell silent.

Her eyes met Cheveyo's. "That's when they said he was 'gifted'. At first we did not understand. His mind was moving too fast for us to keep up. Suddenly he cared about new things, like astronomy or satellite communication. So hyper-focused that he became irritable and defiant, completely tuning us out. It turned our lives upside down."

"What about *Chinese*?" said Jack.

Their faces both went blank. Though in recent years, a spiritual dialogue of sorts had begun to open between Hopi Elders and the exiled leader of Tibet, they were completely unaware.

Una shook her head. "Any support, from friends, or neighbors?"

"They became like strangers," said Alana, "Suddenly, people we'd known for years would not speak to us--or even look us in the eye. Beneath their anger I think it is fear--fear that some evil has taken hold of our son. Fear that if they get too close--it may take hold of them as well.

"Moki's newfound abilities set him apart. He was isolated, shunned and abused verbally by other kids. Even special classes did not help."

"And now?"

"We wait for him to come home."

Jack leaned down, to reach for an electronic

notepad.

"No recording!!!" they both said, in a panic tone of voice.

Una tried to change the subject. "Perhaps if we could...see his room. It might shed some light. Would you mind?"

Alana led them down a short hallway. "The soldiers came from Camp Navajo. Went over it top to bottom. Took most of his things. Not that he ever had much." Tears welled up in her eyes. She turned away.

Jack leaned over close. "It's the same old story. Happened to a friend of mine, a TV news director in Virginia. Disturbing phone calls, late night visitors. A man showed up on his doorstep at 1:00 AM, a retired intelligence officer, who warned: 'They'll hit you with something deadly if necessary to keep you quiet. Most likely it'll be done by skin contact, on a door knob or steering wheel.' All because he reported a UFO."

She nodded. These folks were petrified.

Except for socks and underwear, the drawers were mostly empty. They left a few posters of rock groups on the walls, some discarded boxes in the closet--one for a new camera. Jack noticed a few DVDs, scattered on the floor. Oddly enough, only one case was empty, for the '86 movie ALIENS.

He didn't think much of it until they came across a small portrait of the Dalai Lama, taped in one corner of a bedroom mirror. A handwritten partial quote appeared on its reverse:

...one's enemy is the best teacher.

Jack thought long and hard, while Una flipped through a stack of old comic books. Suddenly it came to him, an iconic scene in which the 'creature' was hanging from a chain, completely in the open and highlighted by a beam of light, but its unusual appearance made it almost unnoticeable.

What are we missing? he thought. Moki was smart, probably smarter than his captors--smart enough to leave a clue that no one would find in a standard military sweep.

"It's here," he said. "Whatever we're looking for is hidden right in front of us, masquerading as an ordinary object."

There was a piggy bank, shaped like R2D2 on his bed stand. Even *that* was a clue...to any decent fan of science fiction.

He broke it open.

"Oops! Sorry!"

"Jack! Please! Try to be more careful. They've lost enough already. Let's not make it worse!"

He searched among the coins, to find one small black square, and retrieve it quickly, between his fingers.

The search went on.

***

With the sun at last beginning to set, Una patted him on the shoulder as Jack sifted through old textbooks for hidden pieces of paper.

She could barely contain her disappointment.

Jack understood. There was nothing more here to be gained. The return drive to Winslow would give them time to talk and plan their next move.

"What is *with* you?" she said finally, once he had started the car.

"I don't know what you mean."

"We spend half the day together, yet you barely say a word. That's not my idea of teamwork. Are we *together*, or not?"

"I had to wait, until now."

"Why?"

"Because I found something. There was a box for a high-speed camera, the kind used by explorers in low light settings, and it got me thinking--"

"Don't tell me. Jack, you can't just lift somebody's property like that. I mean, what if they found out?"

"Relax! I have standards. I'm a *journalist*, remember? I'd never do such a thing! Anyway, it was gone. They must have taken it."

"So?" she said.

He grinned, reaching into his shirt pocket. "It doesn't matter."

"Why?"

"Because all we need is *this*!"

She stared. "But...that's--"

"A flash memory card! Every image should--"
"They took it into the cave?"
"I'm *betting* on it. Let's get out of here!"

***

Volcanic hills formed a dark silhouette against the evening sky as they headed south. It would be an hour, at least, before they reached city lights. Una kept playing their visit to Walpi over in her mind.

"So, what do you think?" she said. "What is really happening? Could they be right? Is it evil?"

Winds kicked up beside them. Everything was in motion. Cloud-to-ground lightning appeared in the desert.

"No," he said calmly, "Just a monsoon."

Weather warnings boomed from the radio, turned low.

She sighed. "What about the memory card?"

Their eyes met. He paused.

Flood watches were in effect until 10 PM. Their headlights came on. Heavy rains pounded the windshield. The wipers could barely keep up.

The sky turned pitch black. There was another flash, followed by a deafening boom that forced them both down into their seats.

"I used to chase storms," he said. "The problem with lightning is that it happens only for a split second, not enough for a good long look. Photography was my answer. I'd never captured lightning. It took a few years to perfect. My goal was clear shots...with tack-sharp detail."

The car shook. Looking out her window, Una sensed this incredible feeling of *deja vu*, like she was back on Flight 564.

She knew he felt it too.

"An old Indian once told me: 'When walking in the desert, do not be looking up and around at the scenery. Watch your feet and where you are walking instead.' So I learned to keep my eyes on the storm, at all times."

He slowed down, pulling off the road.

"What are you *doing*?" she asked.

"The beams," he said pointing, "Follow them...where our route dips ahead. Notice anything?"

She strained to see through the wind and the rain. She knew about mudslides, but the terrain was too flat here. Mountains seemed far away. Yet there was *turmoil* across their path--as if the Earth itself moved. A single word formed on her lips, used by locals, "*Arroyo*."

He nodded. "Desert wash. Fifty yards across. No telling how deep. I never cross one, no matter how tempting."

Looking closer, she spied an impressive amount of debris. Logs, sand, snakes, scorpions, cactus and barbed-wire fence all floated by, with milkshake consistency.

He grinned. "If we had a choice, I'd turn around, get coffee somewhere, to wait it out and let the flood pass."

But there were no pit stops along this road.

Leaning over her seat, she reached for another bag, full of camera equipment and put out her hand.

"Good idea," he said, providing the memory card.

It didn't take long to find a match.

The first images were predictably blurred. Moving too fast, with too little light. The next few, though distorted, revealed an opening that led to a series of chambers, with dim light at the far end.

"Wait," she said, pointing. "Right there. Looks like Kwahu, holding something. What's in his hand?"

The next showed a pick being used. Close-ups revealed an odd red iridescence in the rock floor.

Yellow light filled the next, and the next after that. Where it came from, they couldn't tell, followed by more blurs, in rapid succession. The boys had small flashlights, but this was too focused, like an electrical bolt.

"It almost reminds me of lightning," said Jack.

"What's *that*?" she exclaimed as the last one came into view.

It revealed writing. Not words, but symbols, carved into stone. Just like her penciled diagram, only better.

"Bingo!" they both chimed.

When they looked up, the storm was over. No more wind. No rain. The flash flood was gone. Desert flowers filled the landscape.

"Let's get back to Winslow," he said. "On the double. I'm famished. How about you?"

Una wiped away tears of joy.

16

AFTERMATH

Southbound on State Route 87, they passed the Mogollon Rim, cliffs of desert limestone and sandstone hundreds of feet high, defining the southwestern edge of the Colorado Plateau.

"What's that?" said Una, pointing to a rusted STATE PARK sign a mile outside of Winslow.

"The ruins," said Jack, "You know, *Homol'ovi.*"

"Place of the little hills," she translated from the Hopi.

"When I was 16, I signed up for a week long dig through EarthWatch. My aunt had sent me the magazine, and since my hero at the time was Indiana Jones, I decided to give it a try. We stayed at dorms in town, riding out in vans to the dig site at 7 AM. We had a ton of rules; no one could touch anything without permission. I guess the Hopis were pretty ticked about us being there in the first place. Good grief I was bored."

She remembered it now.

The Homol'ovi cluster of archaeological sites

included seven separate pueblo ruins built by various prehistoric people, including Hopi ancestors, between 1260-1400 AD, during a drought. Though often referred to as *Anasazi*, the Navajo word for "enemies of our ancestors", present-day Hopi referred to them as the *Hisat'sinom*, meaning "long-ago people".

Jack grinned. "Some say there are powerful forces associated with ancient sites. The power released is like a flash flood. Aguda once told me the three mesas represent the stars of Orion's belt, the center of the universe. When connected to other Hopi landmarks, like Homol'ovi, they map the entire constellation."

Una nodded.

Historians speculated that when the drought ended, the land frequently flooded and the Hopis moved to Second Mesa, about 60 miles north. This agreed with oral tradition, which said they left the area when mosquitoes made their children sick. They had lobbied the Arizona parks board a few years back to remove "Ruins" from the name, as they considered the land spiritually alive.

***

Jack pulled his weary Pinto into a small gravel parking lot, filled with pick-up trucks, illuminated by a single outdoor security light. A red and white neon sign flickered "Buckhorn Cafe" intermittently above the narrow entrance. Aromas of fried food and beer wafted through the opening as they slipped inside.

"Don't be fooled," he said seated across from her in a dimly lit booth. "The steaks are to die for."

Her mouth watered. *Try our famous cheese-fries*, the menu read. It seemed like a good idea.

Three brews later, with plates half-empty, they got down to business.

"So I guess we both know it hasn't been easy," said Jack. "Living with the memory of Flight 564."

She shrugged. "I dunno. It's been a long time."

"*Bullshit*. Still sleep with the lights on?"

He had her there.

"The images from the flash drive. What's your take?"

She drew a long, cold sip. "I have none. To do that, I'd need a frame of reference."

"Okay. Well, let me tell you. It's different in the news business. People come to me with 'leads' all the time...I mean credible, eyewitness accounts that would make your toes curl. But I have to turn 'em away. Why? Because they're all talk, and no substance. Because no editor in his right mind will even take a chance without proof."

"So?"

"Whatever those kids faced in that cave, it was *real*. Just like what happened to us on that flight. Over the years, I've gathered more than a few similar tales, describing incredible encounters out here, in the desert, where you can drive for miles without seeing another soul, that defy explanation."

"Such as?"

"Mystery caves, for one. An explorer named G.E. Kincaid over a century ago claimed to have found one in the Grand Canyon containing Egyptian artifacts. Later, a Smithsonian archaeologist described an underground city with hundreds of rooms. There are even reports of black-hooded humanoids somewhere beneath the Superstition Mountains, east of Phoenix."

Una sighed.

"It gets worse," he said. "Ever wonder how many people go missing every year?"

"I give up. How many?"

"Nobody knows."

She frowned. "What do you mean?"

"A buddy of mine works for the Census Bureau. According to him, there are no reliable statistics, because there is no overall tracking system."

"That's impossible."

"Yes, that's what I thought, at first. But if you look around, adding up all the official reports from various sources, including government websites, you get something like 50 per day."

"Just Arizona, or elsewhere?"

He shook his head. "My source only had access to a state level database. But *think* of it. In police reports, news archives--disappearances happen *all the time*. Most wind up dead or reappear elsewhere. But these are different. I'm talking about people of all ages who *vanish*--never to be seen again."

"But how can that be?"

He paused, to measure his response. Una could sense wheels turning in his head. It was perhaps the moment he had been waiting for.

She would need to keep an open mind.

"Investigation reveals... a few hallmarks, they each have in common. For example, blood hounds, when used, cannot pick up a scent of the missing person. They run around in circles, or simply lay down.

"The victim is usually separated from a group, trailing or left behind for only a short distance--before they disappear, without a trace. There is no screaming or calling for help."

Una tried to understand, but had trouble.

"And now, here's the hard part, the part folks least like to talk about: *specifics*. Some children have disappeared from *inside* locked cars. In one case, a four-year-old was somehow lifted from his bed while others were home in spite of a security system--that was state of the art!"

"What happens to them?"

His eyes met the floor. "We can only guess. But we know it's a crime. And if we think for a moment, we know what happens to say, victims of human trafficking, a tragedy that occurs in countries around the world. We know there's a black market for human organs. And young people of either sex are kidnapped every day...and sold into slavery."

"But 50 per day? That's...tens of thousands per

year, just in Arizona. No way!"

Jack finished his beer.

"Believe what you want. I'm just saying there are a lot more than we think. And for some reason, no one's sounding an alarm."

Una began to shake. "Why wouldn't they?"

"You won't like the sound of this, but hear me out. Last year, the Mutual UFO Network received over 6000 reports. After investigation, nearly a third of those cases were listed as *unknowns*--cases where investigators couldn't match the sighting with natural phenomenon or anything man-made, and believed the witness to be credible. Sighting reports overall show a steady increase since 2005. I've looked at UFO hotspots according to their data. Sure enough, Colorado came up top on the list, then Nevada, Oregon and *Arizona*.

"In the summer of 1970 hundreds of UFOs were seen about 125 miles southwest of the Hopi villages near the town of Prescott, Arizona. In March, 1997 in the same vicinity a delta-winged craft perhaps a mile across with lights on its leading edges was spotted drifting silently overhead before speeding off to the south. It became known as the *Phoenix Lights*. In '98 radio talk-show host Art Bell interviewed two Hopi Elders who stated that their distant ancestors traveled to other planets. They said that during the End Times, we would be visited by 'people outside' the Earth who have advanced technology."

He was right about one thing. She didn't like it.

"We seem to take the same approach, to problems that are simply too big to solve. Problems like the War on Drugs. What if it's out of their hands? Like they really know what's happening, but feel powerless to stop it? Remember 564? When we got off the plane?"

Una closed her eyes, raising both hands to her forehead.

Complete *denial*.

After all the pilot chatter, the assessments from air traffic controllers on the ground, the acknowledgement from Air Force personnel regarding their encounter with a bona fide UFO, it was the best they could get.

"This sort of thing has happened before--with Moki, I mean. Flashes of insight that seem to come out of nowhere. There was another kid, a few years back in the Ukraine, who went missing. When they found him, he couldn't speak at first. Then he began to excel past his classmates. Later became a cosmonaut.

"We still don't know exactly what transpired. But we do know this: he was *traumatized*. And trauma is often first and foremost with any UFO encounter. The terror is enormous. People try to repress it. We both heard it from his parents. The boy felt isolated. Reluctant to tell anyone. Afraid they'd say he was too imaginative or dreaming. Yet convinced that something of profound importance had happened to him. Even now, it's expanding his consciousness, opening his mind to a whole new perspective on the universe."

She *wondered* why Jack would bring all this up now, why he kept comparing this bizarre turn of events between Moki and the mystery cave to their nightmare flight over 20 years ago. *NO*, she thought suddenly, *OH GOD, don't tell me they're connected!*

"The light in those images from the cave," he said. "Look familiar? To me, it seemed *unnatural*. Like the beams in that storm, that flickered from the object. I don't know how else to say it."

They both jumped as his phone rang.

It sounded like Jim Aguda, talking fast and loud.

"Sorry to trouble you. But I'm at wit's end. I tried to obtain a Geodetic Survey Map from the County Engineer's office, but they gave me the run around! Something about restricted air space and special permits. All because of the Grand Canyon! So I left. Drove toward Fremont Peak, to retrace your friend's route on horseback. Got pulled over by two officers in a black Humvee, who confiscated my camera. I think I'm being followed. What the hell's going on here?"

"Okay, okay, slow down, first things first. Where are you? Fine. Head west on I-40, then cut a sharp left near the historic district. Follow the tracks. That's right, Jim. East Second Street...the Santa Fe Depot and Hotel compound. Go south...past the Route 66 museum. Get out of your car...look for the train platform. Amtrak. We'll meet you at the far end.

Okay. Bring a flashlight."

He was out of his seat before the call ended.

Una ate one last fry, leaving the tip. She had no choice but to follow.

17

REASON

Una eyed twin searchlights in the rearview mirror as they pulled away from the Winslow train depot and hotel compound. It was just after dark. Jim Aguda kept his head down in the back seat until the coast was clear.

"You showed up just in time," he said. "I did not know where to turn!"

"Their car's unmarked, but the goons are in camo--sent by Ashcroft, no doubt!"

"Relax!" said Jack, "We can crash at my place. They're trying to scare us is all. Happens to me all the time. Occupational hazard!"

A few minutes later, they pulled up a winding narrow drive concealed by heavy brush to arrive at a 30's era bungalow with "battered" gable ends, white trim and shingled sidewalls.

"It's not much," he said, showing them to a rear hallway with two small bedrooms, "But I call it home. Excuse the mess!"

Like most bachelors, he seemed to live in a

perpetual state of disarray, with clothes hanging from doorknobs, dirty dishes on counter-tops.

In no time, they cleared places to sit in the living room, awaiting Jim's response to images from the flash drive. Jack poured them each a glass of wine. A lone security light cast a soft glow on outside oaks, poplars and weeping willows.

Aguda remained silent at first as they proceeded slowly through a series of nine shots, some dark, some blurred, with only a few well focused. Three showed bits and pieces of remarkable petroglyphs, etched in a flat pillar of stone. Una laid out her sketch nearby for comparison.

"I don't understand," he said. "This kind of clarity should not be possible. Ordinary flashlights are too dim."

"They used another camera," said Jack.

"No...it's *more* than that."

Una gazed at the images more closely. Illumination came from below the line of sight, but it was incredibly bright, electronic almost, reminiscent of lightning or neon. She could not imagine its source.

Aguda leaned forward, sipping from his glass. From the corner of one eye he glimpsed moon beams, entering through a far window.

"It appears to be an energy discharge. Electro-magnetic, probably. The question would be *why*. Why here? Why now? What would be the *reason*?"

The others remained silent.

"Assuming it's an ancient site, housing some monument, be it stone writing or otherwise, it may hold religious value. According to one study, sacred sites around the globe were found to have magnetic and radiation anomalies, producing a higher than average incidence of unusual light-ball phenomena or 'earth lights'.

"A telluric current is natural electricity that moves underground or through the seas. It is geomagnetically induced by changes in the Earth's magnetic field. There's evidence that ancient obelisks around the world, constructed of granite containing high concentrations of energy-responsive quartz, were designed to tap into it.

"As early as 1939, one scientist at the U.S. Navy Research Laboratories declared that the Earth is like a huge dynamo, producing 200,000 amps of natural electricity. For over a century now, there have been rumors of brilliant inventors trying to tap this power source.

"If we look at sacred tradition, myths abound regarding lightning-weapons wielded by heroes or divine messengers. Surprisingly, such 'weapons' also turn up as an instrument of healing or resurrection."

"Wait," said Jack, "Are you saying they found--"

"An anomaly, a source of energy, maybe Earth-based...maybe unknown to us--but definitely *real.*"

"And somehow, exposure to it--"

"*Changed* them," said Una, "So, *that's* what happened to Moki and Kwahu. But what about

Tocho?"

"Maybe he was too far away. Maybe he never got close enough to feel its effects."

He yawned. So did Una. In fact, their faces all showed signs of fatigue. It had been a long day. Maybe it was the drive back from First Mesa, or the rain storm, or Jim's close call at the train depot. Maybe it was the wine. In any case, they all seemed to struggle with keeping eyes open.

She stood up. "We'd better *ask* him before we risk our necks. But right now, we all need some rest. How about it?"

Jack nodded.

Soon, they were all fast asleep. The bungalow was exceedingly quiet, thanks to its distance from the road, shielded by an old row of shade trees. Ironically, Jack's selection of this place hinged upon his need for solitude away from the job. With no roadside mailbox and few visitors, he aimed to keep it that way.

A knock came on his door at 11:40 PM.

Jack did not stir from the living room sofa. It hardly seemed possible for strangers to come calling so late without warning.

Pounding rattled the walls.

"What is it?" he said finally, cracking open the door, with a baseball bat in one hand.

A sweat-covered Hopi teen in long hair and blue jeans leaned over, hands on both knees, trying to catch his breath. His motorbike leaned on its kickstand, a few feet away, still sputtering. "You

Howser? From the *Journal*? We...tried to call, but got no answer. Una here? Better come, quick! We got trouble at the Grille. Off-duty's from Camp Navajo...and there's...gonna be a *brawl*!"

She stood behind him at the door. "Damn! I was afraid of this. We've been lucky up to now. I think our luck just ran out!"

***

The *Mi Casa Bar & Grille*, just two blocks away, stayed open most summer nights until 2 AM. They had live Country music every Friday and Saturday, with Happy Hour from 5 to 7, hoping to lure the 9-to-5'ers on their daily commute. Jack had been there once or twice, but it wasn't much to his liking. Mostly bikers and Interstate truckers came for Tex-Mex, greasy burgers and cold brew. Female clientele were either too young, too old, or too full of themselves.

The teen led them to a corner table with four over-sized versions of himself, each with modified black hairstyle and tattoos in a leather vest and cut-off t-shirt. The embroidered logo on their backs read "Blood Brotherhood". Four red Harleys outside occupied their own reserved parking space. In spite of rumors to the contrary, no member had ever seen jail-time. They *did* however, all have one vital thing in common.

"Kwahu's clan," the kid whispered to Una.

She understood.

No doubt the four stiffs in camo at the bar were not regulars, had violated the Brotherhood's "space" by entering the Grille at all--and knew exactly what it meant. Few words had yet crossed the void between them.

"I hear ya'll are cousins," said one soldier, holding a beer.

"More like clones, if you ask me!" said another.

The Brotherhood nodded without saying a word.

"Real sorry for your loss, but hey, what did he expect? Nosin' around where he didn't belong? That was government property."

One brother leaped to his feet, restrained by the others. The knife blade in his hand glistened like new.

"Penny for your thoughts?" the officer grinned, reaching into his pocket for change, "Or should I say 'nickel'? Hey--found one with a buffalo! This must be your lucky day!"

The Brother's face turned beet red. "It is *you* who do not belong, invading the Sacred Peaks. Kwahu was cornered with no way to escape. All because you dig for treasure, like *thieves!*"

This time, his comrades held the officer back. Unfortunately, he was drunk and elected to pull out a gun. "Well, in case you're wondering, looks like your friend died for *nothing*. We found no crash site. No artifacts. Just a satellite glitch. The cave is empty!"

A hush fell over the bar.

"Enough!" said Una.

"Yes," spoke an older, familiar voice from a dark

corner. There, bent over with one eye closed, sat a white-haired Hopi Elder. "As children, we learn to flee men of two hearts, who say one thing but mean another. We learn the Way of Peace. Sometimes we stray from the path. I say now: ignore the white man. Hear the voice of your ancestors. Go home."

Una could not believe her eyes.

The Brother paused to consider his knife, but another took it from his hand. The younger cousin, in long hair, suddenly leaped at the officer. His gun fired. The teen fell motionless on the floor, blood pooling beneath him.

"Someone, call an ambulance!" she said, applying pressure with a rolled up table cloth. The youth squirmed, but said nothing.

Minutes later, as paramedics carried him out, the jukebox played "On the Road Again" by Willie Nelson. Jack led Una back to his car. "What was *that* all about? Crash site? Artifacts?"

Una shook her head. "I have no idea. But I *damn sure* plan to find out! Ashcroft has lots of explaining to do."

***

The next morning, just before dawn, the general enjoyed his last glimpse of starlight as his Humvee proceeded on its usual course, past earth-covered igloos down a gravel road at Camp Navajo. It was peaceful and quiet, his favorite time of day. If only he could linger here long enough to watch the sunrise.

His driver abruptly stopped.

"What is it now?" he asked.

"Sorry sir! But there's something on our path. See it there, in the beams? My god, I think it's a body!"

"Don't tell me. Another one. Passed out? We should've banned alcohol. These campers are out of control."

"No sir," the driver reported, bending over on one knee. He searched quickly for signs of injury. "At least there's no blood. Still breathing, but something's wrong. My god, sir, I think it's a *woman*!"

Una sat up in the headlights.

Ashcroft grinned. "Fancy meeting you, out here. Lost?"

She came at him, full force. "You...you...you *creep*! Ran into some of your goons last night at *Mi Casa*, like the ones at the train depot. What is wrong with you? People have a right to live without harassment."

"But I--"

"Don't pretend with me! Another boy's in the hospital, thanks to your troops! Was it your idea? To shoot and ask questions later?"

"My dear miss--"

Her eyes narrowed. "I'm not your 'dear'! All right, General. Your boy let it slip, but I want to hear it from you--the *truth*, this time. About the cave. What the hell's going on?"

He whispered privately to his driver, who remained by the vehicle.

"Miss Waters, I can see you're determined. I respect that. Follow me!"

Together they passed through brush to one side of the road, stepping onto an elevated ridge that offered a scenic view of the campgrounds. Birds sang softly as the world came to life all around them. Just beyond the horizon, red and purple hues preceded the rising sun. Under the right set of circumstances, it might even be considered romantic.

Ashcroft turned to face her with absolute sincerity. She could see it in his blue eyes. Suddenly, he was the perfect gentleman.

"Okay," he said. "You win. Let's *talk*."

18

HEART-TO-HEART

Una stood beside Ashcroft, waiting for him to go first. Row upon row of golden lights emanated from campgrounds in the lush valley below. Overnight rain still glistened from every pine tree and bush. Fog crept in from low lying hills, beyond which a red-purple haze signaled the approach of dawn.

"This is my favorite time of day," he said, "just before sunrise. When you can still see the stars. Beautiful, don't you think? Been looking at 'em all my life, but I must confess, couldn't tell one from another."

She said nothing.

"You ever follow astronomy?"

Her head shook.

"Me neither. But it seems that a number of native tribes, including the Dakota, Navajo and Hopi, having been doing it for centuries. In many cases, they believe in the same formations that we do, by different names."

"So?"

"Recently, I've learned about a few. Let me show you."

She eyed him with suspicion.

He grinned. "It matters."

She turned her gaze skyward.

"First, we have to find *Orion*, the Hunter. This time of year, he stands right about *there*, halfway between the horizon and the sky directly above your head. Locate him by his belt, a straight line of three bright stars close together."

"Got it."

"Now follow the line of his belt, moving left to right, to a bright red-orange star: Aldebaran. Fairly close to it, you should see a tight cluster of blue stars; the *Pleiades*, also called the Seven Sisters."

"Okay," she said.

"It's one of the nearest star clusters to Earth and perhaps the most beautiful to the naked eye."

"And why does it matter?"

"Because of Indian folklore. Early Dakota stories speak of them as the home of the ancestors. Navajos named them *Delyahey*, home of the Black God. And Hopis called them the *Chuhukon*, meaning 'those who cling together'."

Her mouth dropped.

And for a moment, it seemed as if there was no distance between them, and later, alone at night it would haunt her, the feeling they shared. Before she thought of the Grille...and turned away, to speak.

"Dammit, you *know* why I'm here. Last night, at

Mi Casa--"

"It's already been addressed."

"By that you mean--"

"The officer in question, a ring-leader of sorts, thought it might be fun to antagonize the locals. He was obviously wrong. That's not the way we do things. His behavior was reprehensible. He *and* his lackeys have each received a reprimand with confinement to base. They'll not trouble you again."

"Me?" she said, pointing to herself with both hands, "What's any of it got to do with *me*? Did you even speak to police? That boy's in the hospital! All because--"

He shrugged. "Things got out of hand. I know. They were in the *wrong* place at the *wrong* time. It happens."

"Yeah?" Her face puckered up like a mad dog. "Well, maybe you didn't hear the rest--or you chose to ignore it. They were harassing--"

"A biker gang. So?"

She threw up her hands. "Oooh, I swear, interrupt me like that again, and I'll, I'll--"

"Do what?" he said, glancing over the small cliff, "Push me off?"

She raised a forefinger in his face. "Those 'bikers' were cousins of Kwahu! What happened was no *accident*! Your men went there on purpose! Why? That's what I want to know. And what was he rambling about? Crash site? Artifacts? Satellite glitch? What aren't you telling me?'

Ashcroft took off his official beret, removed his overcoat and sat on a bench, apparently placed for campers to admire the view. Spectacular shades of red and orange light streaked across the sky, the first rays of morning sun. The air was beginning to heat up, and he needed to bring things down a notch.

"All right. We've been over this. Alpha-Bravo and all of its operations are considered *classified*. I'm not at liberty to--"

"Excuse me? We're way past that, General!"

He drew a deep breath. "Granted. But when it comes to facts regarding our 'mission' here, I'm still bound by strict protocols."

"What about hypotheticals?"

He grinned. She was clever and he liked that.

"Okay, let me tell you a story. We all know the history of this region is rife with certain legends, regarding 'lights' in the sky. Add to this modern tales of strange encounters by adventurers, military men, and miners. Ordinarily, of course, law enforcement would not give credence to such reports.

"But let's say that an Army Lieutenant under my command just so happens to be a former Navajo Ranger, recognized as a federal officer, trained in criminal investigation. When you ask him if the Navajo people generally believe in UFOs, he says he doesn't like the term 'belief', because it's akin to saying you believe something without evidence. His list of reported eyewitnesses include people like teachers, doctors, lawyers, casino workers, children, tribal elders, and medicine men."

Una sat down beside him.

"And let's just say that in the course of his investigations, he uncovered a Hopi legend, dating back thousands of years, one local leaders are reluctant to talk about. It describes two objects colliding high in the sky, with one crash landing, in the region of Fremont Peak.

"Speaking 'hypothetically' of course, the U.S. military would disregard such a tale, and we did, until a new spy satellite--again, *classified*--recently went into orbit. Designed to detect certain 'anomalies' based on recent intelligence regarding rogue technology being employed by enemies of the free world--like China-- we found one, right *here* in Arizona. Well, imagine our sense of alarm, fearing that infiltration was underway. That's when we realized the signal could not be new. In fact, it had to be very old, older than anyone could explain--originating from an era long before the Revolutionary War, before these United States ever came to be."

Her eyes opened wide.

"Now, as far as my men are concerned, it's still just a 'glitch' but I think we both know that isn't true. I've been around, to places that matter: Wright-Patterson, Area 51. Seeing is believing, Miss Waters. I'm sure you agree. We returned to First Mesa by the way, found the flash drive missing from the camera. Whatever you've seen, I'm sure it leaves no room for doubt."

She felt overwhelmed, trying to process it all in her mind. But none of it ruled out one possibility--that the boys might *still* be telling the truth. Her sketch, and the images of that mysterious petroglyph in the cave contained symbols like no other. The ancients would naturally record events regarding the Star People, and make it part of their history.

There was no longer any sense in attaching blame here. Events tumbling around them were set in motion long ago, before anyone alive had ever been born. There was only one choice: to see it through.

He sensed her anxiety.

"My dad was in the service. Did you know that? He tried to teach me values. I wanted to be like him. But I also had heroes."

"Like John Wayne?"

He grinned. "The poster in my office. You remembered. That means a lot to me. Yes, I loved the 'Duke' as a kid. Saw every film a dozen times. But he wasn't my favorite."

She waited. He gazed into the sun, still low, shining bright.

"Look, I don't know exactly how to say this, so I won't. My men are waiting. I have duties to perform. We've spent enough time already."

"Yes?"

He pulled out his wallet, flipping through childhood photos. Finally he stopped, held one up.

"You may recognize it. A gift from my Dad on my ninth birthday. Wore it on a trip we made, one summer to Vegas."

She stared. And that feeling of *deja vu* came over her, once again. In the photo was a boy in gray shirt, matching pants, white hat, red scarf, black gloves and silver badge.

"The Lone Ranger," she said, quivering. "So you were on--"

"Flight 564."

She froze at first, then drew a deep breath.

"I'm not your enemy, Miss Waters. Just a man serving his country."

It was time to go. And in spite of all she had gained from this maneuver, despite all she had learned about the man in charge of Camp Navajo, she could not help but feel the sting of disappointment.

The subject of Moki's release had not even come up. It would not have mattered anyway. The general was just following orders.

Her quest here, coming home, suddenly became a lot more complicated. They might not ever find what was hidden in the cave. Of course, she would still have to try. Try because her sense of loyalty to these people demanded it. Try because her mother would have expected no less.

And because the Sky People were still watching.

She smiled and stepped away.

Ashcroft turned. "And oh, Miss Waters, tell your 'friend' from the *Journal* to be discreet. Officially, this conversation never took place. If *anything* appears in print, I'll deny it. And you may face prosecution.

Consider it a breach of National Security."

"Of course," she said, "What else?"

***

Once the general's Humvee was completely out of sight, Una walked several feet along the edge of the cliff. Bending down on both knees, she leaned over, straining to see into an alcove below, concealed by natural brush.

She gave a thumbs up.

Jack leaned out, removing his headphones. He switched off the recording equipment from his backpack. "We took a hell of a chance," he said.

She nodded. "I know. Did you get it? Our conversation, I mean. Just tell me that it *worked*."

He grinned. "Every word."

19

THE RETURN

Una stared out the car window as Jack drove eastbound, 46 miles back to Winslow. Gray clouds, tinged with red reflecting upward from rocks below, hung over the landscape. Here I-40 replaced old route 66. Signs still pointed to the former Toonerville Trading Post off the Twin Arrows exit, a small zoo off Two Guns which once harbored mountain lions, and ruins for the old Meteor Crater Observatory, all lost to the ravages of time.

"Don't be so glum," he said.

She couldn't shake her sense of defeat. Instead of good news to share with Moki's family regarding his release, she had only a disturbing array of military secrets caught on tape, good to have in case they needed leverage against Ashcroft but of no practical value to anyone on the reservation.

Entering town, the old 'corner' statue from The Eagles' song "Take it Easy" appeared to their left. She studied it briefly and sighed. A fire had destroyed the building behind it in 2004, but a wall with a mural was still there. Somehow, it had survived.

But she wondered if Winslow's days might be numbered. On the surface, it appeared to be just an old railroad town with rundown gas stations, pummeled by the Interstate, bled dry by the automobile. If not for the local prison, a community college, the power plant in Joseph City, a restored hotel and fast food chains serving motorists, it might one day cease to exist.

Thus it would join the dust-covered remains of Homol'ovi to the north, a pueblo built in the 13th century, or Brigham City, established by Latter Day Saints nearly six hundred years later. Neither lasted for long.

Only time would tell.

Between the La Posada Hotel and a local diner was a small used car lot. Its lonely Navajo salesmen waved to them as Jack finally slowed to a stop outside the tall brick building where he worked.

"Wait here," he said, "I'll only be a minute."

Through glass doors, he climbed a set of steps, past a noisy printing press to the employee lounge for the *Arizona Journal*. A few staffers were busy with final preparations for the next day's edition. He nodded to a copy editor and proceeded to his personal locker. Technically the recording from Una's interview with Ashcroft needed clearance to be stashed here, but he didn't have time to explain. With any luck, they'd never have to use it anyway. Aguda's tailing episode made him paranoid. He came here mainly for peace of mind.

Jack returned to the car, cell phone in hand. "Incredible! I'll tell her right away. Thanks. I owe you one."

"Who was *that*?" she asked as he slid behind the wheel.

"A trusted source. Moki's back home. An unmarked vehicle returned him just minutes ago."

"So let's--"

"Okay, but take it easy. He may not be ready."

Eating a drive-thru burger, Una tried to figure out what it all meant. Maybe Ashcroft couldn't get much out of the boy. Or maybe he got it all, and simply didn't need him anymore. Or *maybe* she got through to him on some level, and he had a change of heart. No. That didn't seem plausible.

"What if they released him," she said, suddenly, "planning to track his movements?"

"Hoping he'd lead them--"

"To the other cave entrance!"

"Okay, but...didn't you say they went *back*?"

"To his room," she nodded, "To check the camera."

He cringed. "It's bugged. The whole house, I'll bet. We'll have to get him away. Some place neutral."

She grinned. "I'll tell him to bring his skateboard."

***

Before they could enter the house on First Mesa, Una ran up to another car parked with its motor running, out front. "Chu'si! What are doing?"

Tears flowed from her eyes. "I came as soon as I could. Just wanted to see for myself. That he was safe. I felt responsible...his test results...should've never released them. It's...*all my fault*!"

"Wait," said Una, "What's wrong? I thought he was home. I thought Moki was all--"

She held one hand up over mouth, trying not to cry. "But he's *not*! Don't you see? I was in there, trying to talk to him, and...he's not right! *Whatever* they did-- it's like he's been brainwashed, or drugged or...I don't know!"

Chu'si rolled up her window and drove away.

Una turned, but Jack was already gone. Something he had to do. He wouldn't elaborate. Suddenly, she didn't like the idea of doing this alone. *I'm no reporter*, she thought. *He'd better cut me some slack.*

Moki accompanied her to the edge of Walpi Village with his skateboard. But as it turned out, something *was* wrong. He didn't know how to use it. In fact, he couldn't recall much at all. But it was *more* than that. He tried to smile, told her he was fine, feeling better now without all the 'noise' in his head.

"What to you mean?" she asked.

"I don't know. It's like I can't think because I'm so nervous, I mean, just shaking for no reason. The doctors gave me medicine, to help me relax, but I can't rest or sleep. I still see things...but at least they're silent now. Pictures, without sound. It's still scary, but not so loud."

She'd heard about cases like this. Reaching into her pocket, she pulled out some prints they made from the flash drive. "Like *this*?"

He jumped three feet away.

It was like reports she'd read from the VA about veterans of OIF (Operation Iraqi Freedom). He seemed to exhibit helplessness, appearing variously as episodes of panic or an inability to reason, walk or even talk. The term that first came to mind was "shell-shock" but she knew it was obsolete, hailing back to World War I. Since Vietnam, the term PTSD (Post Traumatic Stress Disorder) had been used, officially accepted as a disease since 1980.

No *wonder* Chu'si was in tears! But she could not blame herself. Or even the military. Una had a sinking feeling that it all stemmed from their experience in the cave. Maybe it would pass in time. Maybe with adequate rest and the comfort of familiar surroundings, Moki would return to normal. The mathematical formulas were gone. So was the Chinese. He couldn't recall any of it.

So much for his help in finding the cave!

But maybe they could use it to their advantage, as a decoy. If he was being tracked, it might just work. But only if he agreed.

"The light," he said, to her surprise, "Like no other. It opened my mind. But I wasn't ready for it. Like a cup that's too small or a transceiver that's too weak. It was too much for me to hold. I couldn't take it. I tried. I really tried. I wanted to somehow. I wanted to bring it home, to everyone. But it was too strong or too bright and I lost my grip...and everything fell apart."

Una's questions came to mind, the ones she had planned but now felt afraid to ask. Questions regarding the cave itself, about clues that might set it apart from ordinary caves, the kind known to mortal man. Like signs of habitation. Were there any bones or other human remains? Surely none would be found in a cave once used by Hopi ancestors, hailing back not just to the Third World, but *beyond*.

And what about spirits? Not far from the Sacred Peaks were other famous landmarks with reports of paranormal activity. A popular ghost story from 1878 described an attack by Apache raiders on a Navajo encampment near the Little Colorado River, in which nearly every man, woman and child was killed. When Navajos later caught up to the raiders, exacting bloody revenge, 42 corpses were left inside a cave that was said to be cursed. Pioneers who later settled there reported hearing disembodied groans and ghostly footsteps.

Like it or not, the task of guiding them below would now fall solely upon Tocho. She only hoped that it was not too much for him to bear.

***

The scene in Oraibi rivaled that of any major event for the past thirty years. People gathered in droves around a simple two story home with a flat roof, covered in dry earth. Kasa beamed with pride, glancing out through curtains on the front picture window.

No one knew exactly how or when an official escort would arrive.

"I can't believe it," she said. "One minute, you're home, safe and sound, the next, people show up, out of nowhere. The streets are completely filled. How do they even know you are here?"

Tocho stood beside her. "Maybe the Sky People, or maybe good news just travels fast."

A strange, dust-covered car pulled up with a gust of desert wind. Out stepped Una, bidding farewell to the driver from First Mesa, who had given her a lift. Jack was expected to pick her up later.

Kasa sighed.

"Get away from there," said Ahote. "We must appear calm, as if nothing has happened. It's the only way to convince them, to leave us alone!"

Una knocked on the door.

"Too late," said Tocho.

Sukya greeted her with a smile. The two embraced at once. Always the good daughter, sensible like her mother. It seemed to be a family trait; women holding it together while the men sought adventure. So much had happened with her brother that it was easy to forget how she might be affected. When it was all over, the two of them would catch up, maybe go shopping in Flagstaff.

For some reason, Una felt safer here. Since the house was never empty, she did not believe "bugs" had been placed by men from Camp Navajo. Just to be sure, Ahote made a sweep of every room with a small metal detector. Any fears of surveillance were finally put to rest.

"I've already spoken with Moki," she said, when all were seated around a table. "His recovery is incomplete. Memory gaps make it impossible for him to help us. If we mean to enter the cave, I must ask a few questions."

Tocho frowned, "But what if--"

She clasped his hand. "This is not about blame. It was nobody's fault. We're trying to solve a mystery...about the cave itself. Its role in Hopi history. Any artifacts there could be important to support our tribal claims under law, and send the soldiers away. Protect the Peaks."

He nodded.

"Just try to recall, in your own words, what happened."

Tocho placed one hand on his forehead, eyes closed. "It was so dark, at first we couldn't see a thing. And stuffy. Not musty damp. Our clothes were wet from the rain outside, but inside, it was completely dry. More like an old attic than someone's basement."

"Go on."

"Kwahu led the group. He had this incredible

sense of direction. Said he could 'feel' his way, with or without light."

"But you had--"

"Flashlights, of course. And they worked. Massive limestone formations of every kind. Volcanic rocks and more. You can't imagine. Kwahu said caves were time traps, they could preserve and protect things like ancient art for millions of years. We were hoping to find some."

"Not gold?"

"Oh, hell no! That was for prospectors, or treasure hunters. Explorer's Club was more about uncovering ancient secrets, learning from the past. We weren't trying to get rich."

"So then--"

"It seemed like forever we stumbled in darkness, but I guess it wasn't that long. Finally, the path became smooth. We turned on our lights all at once, and there it was, some kind of carving in the walls."

"Petroglyphs?"

"No, not at first. More like shapes. Architecture, pillars and such. It reminded me of Egypt, inside the tombs. But there was something else: crack formations, and this made us all nervous. Kwahu thought they might be traces of ancient quakes. In places the floor was littered with rocks. Finally we--"

He paused, face turning red, and suddenly began to hyperventilate.

"What is it?" said Una.

"That's when...oh, god, I remember it

now...Kwahu found this huge dome-shaped cavern. It was *unbelievable*."

He fought back tears, clearing his throat.

"And Moki said we should take some photographs. That's why I brought the camera in the first place. 'Over here,' he said. But when I tried to get close, there was some kind of flash. A gleam. I can't explain it. I started clicking away. There was a pillar, with petroglyphs. He *screamed*, and everything shook. Something collapsed overhead. I panicked and...and--"

"And what?"

"I ran! I turned about face, and I *ran*!"

He was sobbing.

Una reached out, trying to console him. But it was no use.

"It's all my fault! Why Moki was messed up. Why Kwahu died--because I ran!"

She left her seat and came around to embrace him. Sukya, Kasa and Ahote followed suite. Together they tried to ease his pain. It took him a while to stop. Una knew in her heart they would have to go soon.

The source of that light in the cave would not wait forever to be found.

20

INVASION

Una climbed into Jack's car with a pout on her face. It was nearly dusk, and probably too late to venture near the Peaks.

"Where have you been?"

"You might call it...*fact-finding*. I rigged up a hunter's stand, fifty meters from Alpha-Bravo. Close enough for my telephoto lens, yet still far enough not to draw attention. I'd hoped to pick up any signs of cave-related activity. Alas, it didn't--"

"Jack! You went to *spy* on them?"

"Hell no. To keep a watchful eye. Protect the public interest. It took longer than I thought. Hence, the--"

"*Whatever*! So you got caught, and now...?"

Tocho slid in the back with his overnight bag.

"Hey! What the--?"

"Relax," she said, "He's coming with us. We have no choice. Whatever happens, he's part of it now."

The boy grinned at Jack, making faces in the rearview mirror.

His Ford Pinto meandered slowly at first, on purpose, along level dirt roads that eventually led to a steep descent, three hundred feet to the desert floor below. Dust kicked up all around them. Jack kept thinking she might change her mind and leave the boy behind.

He glanced again his rearview. Tocho was out like a light.

"It was worth it," he said.

"What do you mean?"

"My little excursion. Of course they weren't happy with me. Called me every name in the book. Security wanted to lock me away. Fortunately, I had *this*."

He held up the PRESS ID around his neck.

"Weren't you scared?"

"A little," he lied. "One minute, I was alone. The next, I was surrounded. Not just troops on the ground. Surveillance drones. It was downright creepy. But it didn't matter. Found out what we need to know."

"Which is?"

"They're on the move. Not just men, but equipment. They've widened the opening with backhoes, big enough to drive through. I'm talking support vehicles, trucks, Humvees, the works. Enough for full-scale recovery. Whatever's down there, they mean to haul it out, kit and kaboodle."

"Which means their won't *be* any artifacts."

"Are you kiddin'? There may not be a *cave*. I saw

something else, piled up there, ready for deployment."

"You don't mean--"

"TNT...and plenty of it. They'll close it up, nice and tight. You'll never set foot inside."

"Unless we go soon. How long?"

"Hard to say. 24 hours, maybe more."

She grinned to herself, glancing back at Tocho. "I guess my instincts were right. I hope you've got a good coffee pot."

"Why?"

"Aguda's waiting. It may be a long night. Looks like we need a plan!"

***

"Forget horses," said Jim, lifting his third slice of pepperoni from the box. "There's no time. Let 'em think we're just hunters who got our maps mixed up. Less suspicious that way. What season is it, anyway?"

"Desert bighorn," said Jack. "We'll find orange vests and whatever else we need a few blocks from here. *Wild Outfitters.*"

"What about guns?" said Tocho.

"*You* can be our tracker," said Una. "We'll be outgunned anyway. No sense in taking chances. I'm no hunter and neither are you."

Jack agreed. "We'll rent an ATV, go off-road. Didn't you say there was a creek? Let's follow it."

The boy perked up. "Can't miss it, in fact, it leads into--"

"That's fine, just fine--but first things first. We don't know what we're up against."

Una patted the boy's shoulder. Of course the men would take charge. But that was okay for now. His time would come. When they ran out of answers, they'd be turning to him.

***

Jack pulled up to the bungalow just after dawn, while the others were still getting dressed. He proudly displayed their ride: a Polaris Ranger Diesel 4x4 automatic, slightly used. It came standard with gun scabbard, rear rack extender, work lights and roll bar, in case of rough terrain.

"Put these on," he said, passing out orange-camo combos, with brimmed hats to block the sun, and special permits. "Good for one day only."

Una tried to conceal her discomfort. The only gun she'd ever handled was in a training facility for Federal employees, part of a self-defense course. That was bad enough. The language of big game hunting wasn't even part of her vocabulary. If stopped, she'd have to keep her mouth shut.

The ride took surprisingly less time than she expected.

Fremont Peak loomed before them like Mount Doom, though technically it was still miles away. Willow Creek popped and gurgled nearby. Aguda was the first to hop out and explore.

"The mountain is very old. I wonder if it can feel our intentions."

"What do you mean?" she asked.

"Every feature of the landscape possesses its own personality. This is true in countries around the world. I've learned to respect that. When the time comes, one thing I know. We'll not succeed unless the land *allows* it. We must enter as friends. If it even suspects otherwise, we'll be ejected for sure."

"This way," said Jack, waving his rifle.

The terrain here was primitive and difficult to penetrate with thick brush along the slope. Oak, juniper and sycamores appeared commonplace.

"Be wary of natural alcoves. They may harbor mice, scorpions or black widows."

Una found herself suddenly walking tip-toed.

There was a sound like beeping beyond a clump of trees, and everyone turned. Black choppers came swooping down from the hillsides. Men in Black Ops uniforms formed a line on the ground, marching toward them. Una saw Jack and Tocho trying desperately to hide. Aguda just stood there, helplessly looking up.

She sighed--the only woman--like Jillian on the slope of Devil's Tower in *Close Encounters*. There was no place to run.

A familiar voice came from hidden speakers, apparently among the rocks:

"To effectively guard a perimeter,

> you must make sure intruders are either kept out completely or handicapped, so security forces can reach them quickly after an alert. This usually requires a combination of audio, motion, infrared sensors and scanners. *Comprende?*"

It was Ashcroft.

> "We could arrest you right now and make all our lives difficult, with mounds of unwanted paperwork, or you can turn around and go back. It's your choice."

Jack laughed out loud.

How simple! The gig was up, and it's all they needed to know. He'd might as well say *Try harder* since that was the point. The general might be a pain in the ass, but he had a sense of humor.

***

"You know what this means," she said, once they were back on the road. "We need a better plan."

"The creek," said Tocho, "I was trying to tell you. It's how we entered the cave. Of course, we just held our breath."

Jack squirmed around in his seat. Clearly, this made him uncomfortable. He glanced over his shoulder, "Underwater?"

"Well, yeah. We'd need some stuff. But I can get what we need from Explorer's Club. Snorkels, goggles, wetsuits and flippers. If we plan it right, they'll never know."

"Know what?"

"Where we are. We could snorkel it from a distance, through the creek, beginning outside the perimeter."

Una gave him a hug.

Jack suddenly rolled his eyes. All the gun play with camo was one thing. But there was another obstacle, one he couldn't hide.

"Okay, it's like *this*," he said. "I have a thing about water. Ever since I first saw *The Abyss*, as a kid. Those *things* gave me nightmares."

Una's face went blank. How come everybody saw these but her? She needed to watch more movies.

"Oh, *I* get it," said Tocho, "Aliens? My generation's immune to all that. We don't believe in it. You want out?"

Jack sensed a challenge, and a smirk in his voice. "Thanks, but I'm a big boy now--I'll deal with it!"

***

They swung by the high school after hours. After

a janitor let them in, Tocho led the way to a special room. The door was unlocked.

"In Explorers Club we took a course; one hour classroom, three hours pool time. Learned to equalize our ears, clear our mask and use fins, with three different strokes."

"Oh...I don't know," said Jack.

"You'll *love* it," said Tocho. "There are old-growth cedar trees that have fallen in the water and been there 40 years. There's all this life clinging to it, insects and algae. All *kinds* of things."

"You'll *love* it!" echoed Una.

"Swimming sandstone eroded away by the stream. It forms this giant, swirling landscape. It's like bird watching under water, floating right past animals-- I saw a cougar once."

From a storage closet, he produced three black rubber things on hangers.

"We need *those*?"

"Oh yeah! Wet suits are imperative, winter or summer. Water temps change only a few degrees between seasons."

"You do this year round?"

He shook his head. "Not during spring runoff. Water's too fast and high. That's when we head to back country for some float time on small ponds."

"You're kidding."

He grinned. "The real beauty of nature's in the backwater, where little fish are being reared. It's so cool!"

"Ever *find* anything?" said Una.

"Oh, yeah, loads. Fishing lures, old bottles, even discarded cars--in the deeper parts. All worthless, but still fun."

Jack got more to the point. "What about ...dangers?"

He paused to think. "Sure, like drowning, I guess. You have to watch out for rocks, stumps, and logs. The current never stops. If something bad happens, you're stuck."

"Great," said Jack.

"Relax! Been at it two years. Lucky, so far. No close calls. Just stick with me, and don't be a knucklehead. It's a mountain creek; cold, wet, and miserable. Even scary at times. Not for wimps."

"You can *do* it," she said.

Jack perked up. "What? Yeah, oh sure, what the hell!"

Una returned his smile, trying not to fret. She watched him turn the snorkel over in his hand, like he was still afraid of it. *One slip up*, she thought, *that's all we need*. One slip up, and we're done for!

Jim Aguda nodded with approval.

"It all makes perfect sense. Diving and archaeology often go hand-in-hand. I've done so myself, many times.

"Just one thing. From what we've gathered so far, it will be very dark, so dark that we still don't know exactly what to expect. Most caves are inhabited by natural life forms, some of it very strange and deadly. They live without man. Once we step inside, we're invading *their* world--and they have every right to push back. Remember that!"

21

ARM-IN-ARM

U.S. Army Lieutenant Buford Shawl gunned the motor on his M9 (ACE) Armored Combat Earthmover, awaiting the go-ahead to advance through a newly created opening in the rocky slope encompassed by Alpha-Bravo. The highly mobile tractor, dozer and scraper, designed to provide combat engineer support to front-line forces, had recently returned from its service in Iraq.

His would be the first to descend a crude earth ramp down into the "pit"-- just in case the need should arise--to aid recovery of UA-492, the official Army designation for an "unknown artifact" suspected to be the source of strange readings picked up by a spy satellite not three months ago.

Little else was known about his destination, except that Black Ops recon efforts below had failed to turn up anything of value, due to extreme darkness, disorientation and equipment failures that could not be explained.

Grumblings from native tribes had caused

repeated delays, thanks to controversy surrounding the death of a Hopi teen, whose surprise appearance coincidentally revealed access to the cave. Up to that point, it had been really hard to locate. Seismic listening devices, thermal imaging, and drilling had all failed. The locals were still hopping mad. General Ashcroft had his hands full, trying to complete their mission without letting things get out of hand.

Flanked by a line of support troops, he tried to envision what they might find. Recent missions to the Middle East had revealed more than a few surprises. The Zhawar underground complex in Afghanistan, which survived both American and Soviet bombs, was said to contain a mosque, bilingual library, hospital and hotel, all connected by complex tunnels. Of course, here they were told to expect something far older, even ancient, like Egyptian tombs.

Still, better safe than sorry.

With only an hour of daylight left to them, his superiors grew tired of waiting for cover of darkness. No intruders had been detected by security sensors for at least 24 hours. Looking straight ahead, he received a thumbs up from guards at the entrance, and proceeded to ease off the brake, moving the M9 forward, when suddenly, alarms sounded.

"What the hell?" barked ground support through his headset.

"Power Failure...perimeter," said a computer voice.

"Dammit! Not another tree fall...or bighorn. All

stop. Hold position. We have to check it out."

For three minutes, there was only static, then alarms stopped.

"It's..no accident. Power surged, and went out. Like it was deliberate. WAIT. Vehicle spotted off western berm, US 89. Size: irregular, color: blue, ID...*what the--it's a freakin' church bus*, abandoned. Stand by."

Buford knew where to look. Leaping from his seat, he hit the ground running. Moments later, atop the nearest observation tower, he spotted them, through binoculars. "Command," he radio in, "Got civilians, estimated fifty or more, climbing the Inner Basin Trail. They appear to have....*sir*?"

"Yes," said a voice, "Go ahead. Report."

"Hand-held signs, in big letters."

Officers in black uniform took up defense positions, forming a line inside the compound fence, more a show of force than anything else. Their M-16's gleamed in the late day sun.

Ashcroft eyed the unfolding drama from a second floor balcony. "For god's sake! It's the *last* thing we need. A bunch a' yahoos try'in to make a difference!"

Before long, a string of Native American protestors came huffing and puffing up the nearest trail, all the way from Locket Meadow, some distance below.

The general raised a megaphone to his lips.

"ATTENTION. YOU'RE OUT OF BOUNDS. FREMONT PEAK IS OFF LIMITS. THIS FACILITY IS CLASSIFIED. THIS IS AN OFFICIAL WARNING. RETURN TO YOUR VEHICLE AT ONCE. OR FACE CRIMINAL CHARGES. BY ORDER OF THE UNITED STATES ARMY."

Many of them grinned, unphased by the empty threat. There were Hopi men and women of all ages. Someone checked the registration of the church bus. It came from the Reservation.

The protesters formed a human chain standing arm-in-arm, outside the metal fence. At first, no one spoke. But they did not seem afraid. A few, in white hair had apparently done this sort of thing before. They wore bandannas, red and white, tied around their foreheads, to signify unity. The younger ones smiled with wide-open eyes, despite the summer heat. It was nearly 90 degrees.

"How'd they get in here?" he said. "What happened?"

"Fiber optics," said a subordinate. "We think some were cut at a utility pole. It's happened to the Navy in places like Coronado and Norfolk. And an Army base in Augusta. A weak link in our system."

The general frowned, and looked away.

Hand-painted signs read "SAVE THE PEAKS".

One youth strummed a guitar while others chanted, "White men come, white men go, but we shall always be here." Ashcroft sighed. He knew from experience, that even a peaceful protest could quickly escalate to violence, with just the right spark.

"Call the Sheriff's office," he said. "Let 'em send out deputies. We'll just sit here and wait. No one's to fire. Got that? No matter what happens. Or how long it takes. We'll wait it out."

***

Ahote stood with Kasa and Sukya, holding hands to either side. Scanning the line of protesters, he saw many familiar faces. Chu'si had come with several teachers from the school. Even Kwahu's biker cousins were there.

To this day, divisions remained among his own people, thanks to the white man. The "friendlies" were those who used to hang around trading posts, their descendants now tribal leaders who argued semantics and dealt with the U.S. government.

The "hostiles" were traditionalists who owned a digging stick and lived on 5 to 10 inches of rain a year. They did not want their land mined, or modern electrical lines, and were not interested in "outside" help.

But when it came to protecting the Peaks, all agreed.

As driver of the church bus, he knew there

would be unfamiliar faces, as well. They did not discriminate, welcoming support from all who wished to participate. The Peaks were considered sacred not only to Hopi, but as many as twelve other tribes, including the Havasupai, Navajo, and Zuni. Members of each were no doubt standing here among them.

His head count before leaving Third Mesa showed 63 adults and four minors. Allowing space for extra water and signs, the bus was filled to capacity. Many more wanted to come, but the hike was too much for them. He thought of Una's parents, and the many times they had marched together in younger days, against plans of the Forest Service to allow development of a ski resort with shops, restaurants and lodges, and against the owners of Snowbowl.

In his heart he knew they were here, in spirit.

Kasa squeezed his hand. Of course, they could not stop thinking of Tocho, and his role being played out at the same time, with Una.

All of them bowed with respect to Hopi elder, Dan "O" from the Tribal Council. He came slowly toward them, using a cane on one side, supported by his daughter on the other. No one expected him to come, given the circumstances and his age. Why put himself through it?

"He would have it no other way," she smiled.

"I can speak for myself," he said.

Sukya laughed. She'd heard tales about his escapades as a young man, waging battles that often put him in jail. But it didn't change him. He never stopped fighting for what was right, or caved in to unjust demands. Though his body appeared frail, his eyesight remained clear. She could see there was passion, still burning, within.

"The caretaker of our world is Maasaw, The Fire God. In the Third World, there were flying machines called "patuwvotas", which soared through the skies. They attacked cities, causing destruction and killing people on the ground. Corruption came to them, they forgot the plan of the Creator, and war brought their world to an end.

"The Fourth World is harsh, with deserts, marshes, mountains, and rough weather. We know it is ending and even now, the Fifth World has begun.

"Nearly forty years ago, I took a Long Walk with other Native Americans, from California to Washington, D.C. It took nine months to cross the continent. Many tribes had a chance to speak, compare, and participate in traditional ceremonies. We walked with the sacred pipe. We walked to rebuild, not destroy. We walked to be heard.

"Now, here we stand, on peaks held sacred since the beginning of time. Also known as the Kachina Peaks, named for Hopi gods who live here for part of every year. According to myth, in mid-summer they fly from the top of these peaks to the Hopi mesas as clouds, bringing monsoon rains.

"We come as defenders of lands, above and below, the mountains, the rivers, the sacred spaces and places. We must stand up and speak up, together, to Defend the Sacred. *That's* why I'm here!"

***

As it grew increasingly dark, people became restless, wondering what would happen next. They came not so much with a plan as a yearning desire to be heard, to confront invaders who came like grave robbers to steal from the mountain, and profit from its plunder.

Against their better judgment, a few taunted officers standing behind the fence. The men in black uniform remained steadfast and silent, awaiting backup from the Sheriff's Office. Even when rocks came sailing overhead, they did not budge. Nor did they scan the protest line for potential targets. Any violence would be one-sided, meaning no one from Alpha-Bravo could be blamed for slapping down a few misguided protesters. Let them face the law.

At least, that's what Ashcroft thought.

Police cars arrived with lights flashing. First they strung a yellow DO NOT CROSS police line around the fence. Then officers were positioned along its length. Tooms was there, front and center.

A subtle breeze came up the side of the mountain. People could feel it, like a wave moving through them. All at once, they opened their mouths and began to chant, low at first, then slowly growing louder:

"WHITE MEN COME AND WHITE MEN GO. WE DEFEND THE SACRED."

Soon, their voices began to carry, until it was like an echo, from the Inner Basin, rising up to all the Peaks at once, as if one could hear the ancestors, all around them. Like a chorus of voices from *beyond*.

Ashcroft watched from his balcony.

As the stars came into view, he glanced upward. There was Orion, Aldebaran, and the Pleiades. He wondered where Una must be right now, and why she was not here.

Wiping sweat from his brow, he wondered if Kachinas were *up there*, right now, watching from the sky.

And the thought of it made him tremble.

22

RESPECT

From the shore's edge, Una stared down at her own reflection in the glass-like, olive-colored surface of Clear Creek Reservoir, five miles southeast of Winslow. Cream-and-rust-hued canyon walls of cross-bedded sandstone rose up behind them.

"Pretty popular with cliff jumpers and rock climbers," said Tocho. "Free soloists pick routes from the water and climb without ropes or gear. Never tried it myself, but they say the lake cushions your fall."

She dipped in a bare foot. It was cool but not cold.

"How deep?" she asked.

"Over twenty feet, in some spots. People fish here, too, mainly for trout. Stay away from the boats."

Jack struggled into his wetsuit. His midsection didn't quite jive with the fitness requirements of Explorer's Club.

"So...*why* am I doing this?"

Jim Aguda offered assistance. "Cold is a bad way

to lose energy. Heart and breathing rates go up. You must stay warm."

From the look on his face, they could tell this was not his main concern. Jack had *plenty* of concerns about water--like drowning, getting sucked under by the current, or attacked by poisonous snakes. Not to mention aliens.

"Just try to *relax*," said Jim.

Something splashed in the reeds nearby, turning his head.

"Nothing will jump at you, my friend. I swam amidst sea snakes in Niue, a Pacific Island. They may be curious, but will leave you alone."

He needed to focus.

"Okay," said Tocho, once they were all in the water. "Listen up. Holding your breath. Most people can last between 20 and 40 seconds. On average, the body 'needs' a breath every three seconds, so it means skipping breaths. Girls are usually better at it. And fitness helps. The better your circulation, the more oxygen your body can store."

"That rules *me* out," said Jack. "I've never been to a gym."

Tocho shook his head, undeterred.

"Your mask: first to put on and last to take off. Spit into it. One good spit for each window. Then rub it in. Place it on your forehead first while pulling the strap over your scalp. Lift and snuggle it onto your face while removing hair and hood from its seal. But adjust the straps first, so they're not too tight. Keep your mask on at all times."

Una noticed that many low-lying rocks were coated in graffiti. Dammed up since the 1930's, waters here backed up into the narrow canyon for several miles. With darkness closing in, it began to creep her out.

Slowly, while still listening, she decided to go under, just once, beneath the surface. Eyes closed, she drew a deep breath, and sank. The coolness of the water penetrated her hair, racing into every pore, into her ears, across her lips, attempting to breach the seals around her mask and snorkel, but failed. In a moment of stillness she opened her eyes to peer through the glass, and saw nothing.

But then something happened, she could not explain. Whether ghosts in the water were reaching out or it was just a figment of her imagination, the reservoir spoke, in a way she did not expect. From it came the distant jingle of a now defunct airline, that she first encountered in a Dallas Airport, 21 years ago:

R - E - S - P - E - C - T
Find out when you fly with me

She popped her head above water, suddenly feeling the need to escape.

"Anything else?" said Jack.

Tocho nodded, trying to wrap it up. "Clearing your snorkel. Most divers do this by blowing hard.

But there's a better way. Just before breaking the surface, blow out gently. The bubbles push the water out...with no any effort at all."

He faced empty stares.

"One more thing. An important secret: the first dip of any day, is terrible, even for experienced snorkel divers. After ten or more, your body will adjust, and it goes better. Most people don't know this and think they can't do it."

"But we only have *time* for one," said Una.

Something beeped on the shore and everyone jumped.

Jack was first out of the water. "Just my cell."

Back on dry land, Una sighed with relief. Swimming in a pool at the 'Y' was one thing. This backwater nightmare reminded her why she chose life in the big city, with plenty of street lights.

"Holy shit!" said Jack, reading a text. "You won't believe it. There's a huge protest going on...at Alpha-Bravo! Peaceful so far, but sheriff's deputies just arrived. Damn!"

Una's face lit up. "Can't you see? They're trying to help. It's a diversion. We can go to the cave right away."

"The sooner, the better!" said Jim.

Jack seemed hesitant. "But...this is breaking news! Someone should *be* there, to cover the story. Maybe I could--"

Tocho grinned.

"Don't even think about it," said Una. "We need

you right here."

They pulled away from the reservoir, heading north. Tocho rode up front with Jack, watching for desert landmarks. Deepening shadows stretched from ancient rocks and saguaros as the sun sank into the west. She could barely keep her eyes open.

"Coffee?" Jim motioned to a thermos between them.

"No thanks. It'll take at least an hour. Maybe I just need some rest."

She dozed off. Red light gave way to indigo, until finally, a thin trace on the horizon was all that remained.

Suddenly, her phone rang.

She reached down, searching a small handbag. "How's it even working?" she said, glancing out her window. "Without towers, I thought there'd be no signal."

No one said a word.

The caller's voice seemed garbled at first, broken up with static. She could barely make it out. Then, suddenly, her eyes blinked.

"*You!* But how could...I mean...*where* did you get this number?"

They could tell by the look on her face. It was Ashcroft--which, of course made it pointless to ask.

"Miss Waters," he said. "How good of you to take my call. You may know by now...we have a *situation* here, a protest staged by some of your friends. Listen to this:

"WHITE MEN COME AND WHITE MEN GO, WE DEFEND THE SACRED."

In fact, I'm disappointed not to find your smiling face among them. Unfortunately, they are also breaking the law--and refuse to leave. I can't help but wonder why."

"Maybe you should ask."

"We're way past that. It's time to break up the party. Now, we can do this the easy way, or the hard way. It all depends on you."

"Me? General, I don't see how--"

"We can play games, and waste time, or agree to work together."

She couldn't believe her ears.

"General! You surprise me. I thought you were all about *Manifest Destiny* and *Winning the West*!"

"Something tells me not *this* time, Miss Waters. I can't do it alone. Looks like we need each other--to stop this nonsense and return these people home, safely."

Una cut to the chase. "What's your proposal?"

Ashcroft paused. "We combine our efforts, in a joint search of the cave, tomorrow, in broad daylight. Invite the press. Invite anyone you like. It's the only way to solve this mystery, once and for all. Don't you agree?"

"Y-yes, of course!" she replied.

Static cut in once more, on the line, before contact was lost.

Una was so taken aback, so moved by his apparent change of heart and symbolic act of respect for Hopi beliefs, that she got choked up, wondering if there was more to him than meets the eye.

But in the back of her mind, she could not help but wonder if he was really being sincere, or whether he was in a bind, his own efforts having apparently failed. Might he now be playing the role of a clever adversary, exploiting her native insight for his own gain?

Only time would tell.

Jack breathed a sigh of relief. "Thank god! For a minute there, I thought we'd have to go through with--"

"What? Are you *kiddin'* me?" said Aguda, leaning forward. "Can't you see what's happening? It's all the more reason--we *have* to go!"

"But I--"

"Don't think for one minute they can be trusted! Throughout history, men have marched to war over sacred sites, leaving only rubble behind. It's still happening, to this day. Two standing Buddha statues, carved into a cliff in central Afghanistan in the sixth century, were destroyed by the Taliban. ISIS records the fiery destruction of ancient temples on video, like the Syrian ruins of Palmyra, for use as propaganda.

"Whether intentional or accidental, makes no difference. The end result is the same. A great historical find is *lost*. Not again. Not here. Not now.

"This one *matters*, unlike any I've ever seen before. It's hard to explain, but I feel it, deep in my bones. If Una's suspicions are correct, this site predates many of the greatest archaeological finds in Europe, or even the Middle East. It may, in fact, predate every written record we possess--including those in Sumeria or ancient Egypt. The cave acts as a kind of *time capsule*, preserving artifacts from the Third World that point to a common future, a fate we all share. We dare not lose them. We owe it to future generations, to make a stand--to do whatever we can!"

"He's right," said Una.

Jack's eyes met hers in the rearview mirror. "But...you accepted his offer!"

"Of *course* I did--and tomorrow, we'll join forces, for all the world to see. But tonight, we've got a job to do. Everything happens for a *reason*. Those boys found a secret entrance--because it was meant be. We owe it to Moki and Kwahu, to finish what they started. To prove that what happened to them was not some fantasy, but *real*. We must seize this opportunity to preserve what we find, not just for Hopi, but all of mankind."

PART FOUR

AWAKENING

"Wisdom comes only when you stop looking for it and start living the life the Creator intended for you."

--Hopi Proverb

23

ECHOES

Una was fast asleep under a bloodless sky, as moonlight covered the desert. At night, it seemed to come alive, with strange sounds. Any moment, one might detect the loud clap of a saguaro screech owl, the yelps and growls of a lonely coyote, or the sobs of a Mexican gray wolf.

Tocho peered through small binoculars out his passenger window. Some locals said these sounds were not natural at all, but the cries of restless spirits, roaming from one ghost town to another. It didn't phase him.

"What's up?" said Jack.

"Sunset Crater, a cinder cone to the north, youngest in a string of volcanoes related to the Peaks. Erupted 1000 A.D., with a blanket of ash that covered 800 square miles. Damage from hikers forced the National Park Service to close a trail leading to the crater, but a short one at the base remains. It's considered *dormant*, meaning eruption could happen again. That's somethin' I'd like to see!"

"Not tonight, I hope."

After a few miles, Jack glanced again in his rearview mirror, to check for signs of movement. Una was still out.

"This might be as good a time as any," he said. "Has anyone considered the consequences?"

Aguda looked up from his map. "Such as...?"

"Well, I mean, what if we get caught? The whole thing tomorrow would be off. No public display of unity. No healing of wounds between the two sides. It just seems like we're taking an awful risk! Look at her. She's exhausted. Snorkeling the stream at night could be dangerous. How can we protect her if something goes wrong? It...scares me."

His head shook. "She knows what's at stake. It was Tocho's idea, but she embraced it. She wants this more than anything."

Jack frowned, eyes back on the road.

A moment of silence passed.

Tocho's binoculars returned to his lap. At first, he struggled to clear his throat. "Look, maybe I'm just a kid--but she *believed* in me, when everyone else thought I was nuts. And she believed in my friends. So...I believe in *her*. She's not like most adults. She has an open mind. And besides, I think she's right. Maybe the Sky People *do* play a part in all this. Maybe they brought her here. There has to be a reason. We're so close. We *can't* turn back now!"

Jack grinned. Something about the tone of his voice, his faith in a higher power, his unwavering conviction to go on--in spite of all obstacles--reminded Jack of himself, in younger days, before he became jaded by so many disappointments, before he began to *anticipate* failure, most of the time.

It was like a breath of fresh air.

"I guess you're right. None of us would be here, without Una. She's the spark, and now, we are the flames. We've come *this* far."

Aguda reached up, patting him on the back. "Regardless of consequence. Fear or no fear--we must see it through!"

***

Una could not hear them. She found herself far away, in space and time. It was 1995, and she was only eight years old.

Familiar scenes flashed before her eyes...

> One minute, she was standing in line with her parents at Dallas-Fort Worth International.

> The next, they were on Flight 564. She gazed up in awe as they moved down the lighted center aisle.

> "*When do we sit, Papa?*" she asked.

*"Not yet. We're Economy Class.
Further back. Row 39."*

She met Ashcroft again, as
the Lone Ranger, pointing his
six-shooter. *"Better not cause
any trouble, or I'll have to
take you in."*
"Colin!" his father said, in Army
uniform, *"Never point this at anyone.
Or I'll take it away. Don't be a brat!"*

From her seat, clicking sounds
drew her gaze, until she spied Jack,
still in high school, taking pictures
with his camera.
He glanced and turned away.

She thought of Neil Armstrong
and Apollo 11's landing on the
moon: *One small step for man.*

A woman passenger remarked,
*"You heard the captain. Major
Storm. Sounds like trouble. Oh,
god! Now I'm worried."*

The entire cabin pitched, as the
plane began to shake.

Lightning flashed outside her window.

A stewardess raced by. *"The lights! Can you see them?"*

There were so many voices. First, the captain, then Air Traffic Control, then Canon Air Force Base, all chatting about a row of bright lights, hovering in the darkness, flashing in sequence from left to right, at 30,000 feet. They called it a UFO.

Another voice cut in, called Bigfoot. When asked about its size, they said, "*300 to 400 foot*". And he said, *"Holy Smoke!"*

When asked *"How fast?"* by Air Traffic Control, Bigfoot said, *"...impossible ...what does that ...what darts between 1,000 and 1,400 miles per hour?"*
And they said, *"Nothing...that we know of."*

People left their seats a few rows back, to see what they

were missing. Talk turned to
fear, some afraid to admit
what they saw.

That's when Una spotted a
familiar face in a seat across the
aisle. A face that should not be
there--because in 1995, she
wasn't born yet.
It was *Sukya*.
And she was already a teenager
--and Una knew it all *had* to be
a dream—but she asked just the
same, *"What are you doing here?"*

"*I'm bleeding,*" said Sukya, and
there was blood, trickling down
her face. "*Someone threw rocks
...and they wouldn't stop until
police came after us with clubs
...and everyone was shouting...
and I tried to get away, but
there was all this pushing, and
I fell...and I tried to get up...
but they hit me.*"

Una could hear screams. She
could see through plane
windows, and there they were,
outside somehow, protesters

waving signs, like the flight
was transported in her dream
to land at Alpha-Bravo.

"It's not their fault," she heard
one cop say. *"The violent crime
rate on Indian Reservations is
more than twice the national
average. Charges get filed in
only a few cases. Tribes say it's
second-class justice, that
encourages crime. They may
be right."*

Police did not know who to
blame, so they turned on those
nearby, pushing Hopis against
the fence, to arrest them, with
hands tied behind their backs.
"I'm innocent!" they cried, but no
one heard them.
"We'll sort it out, back in Flagstaff,"
was the only reply.

And she *tried* to wake up, to
make it Stop--all the shouting,
all the cries, all the senseless
violence, on a peak that was
long considered sacred not just
to Hopi but many tribes, a place

where peace should prevail--to
make all the voices stop
screaming inside her head.

Then, suddenly, her eyes opened...to find herself sprawled in the back seat, facing ridiculous stares from all three of her male companions. The ATV's motor was still running, pulled off to one side of the road.

"Wh-wh-what happened?" she asked.

"We were just about to ask you!" said Jack.

"A nightmare. No...*more* than that. Not just a dream...more like a *vision*. Something's gone *wrong*. There's...trouble at Alpha-Bravo!"

Tocho sighed. "What do you mean?"

"Violence. Protestors clashing with police! I've...seen it. Don't ask me how. I just know it. We've got to *do* something!"

Their faces went blank. Still in wetsuits, with their ride full of gear, there had been no time to consider another plan.

Jack went first. "In case you forgot, we're already tied up here--on a mission. I don't see how--"

"Wait," said Jim, grasping her hand. "That look in your eye. I've seen it before. You've got an idea. Spit it out!"

"Well...first, let's get back on the road!"

Jack abruptly put it in gear, kicking up gravel as they returned to the pavement.

Una hesitated. She could see he was sore,

wondering if she was out of her mind. That tends to happen when people wake up screaming in the back of your car. Perfectly understandable. But she needed his trust, and right now, it was hanging by a thread.

"Jack, you're my rock. I couldn't *do* this without you. We're more than friends. We're allies, you and me...on a kind of *crusade*. And right now, I need you more than ever." She gave him a wink.

And he grinned, in spite of himself.

"Okay! This contact of yours at the protest, who sent the text, can you still reach him?"

"I can try. What good'll it do?"

"Ashcroft is no fool. He knows we're up to something, or else we'd *be* there! We got cut off during his last call, before I could set up a time to meet. Text your friend back. Tell him to show it to Ashcroft."

"What'll I say?"

"Tell him we're on our way. It's *true*, isn't it? Not the way he expects of course. Tocho's entrance to the cave is still secret. But only on *one* condition: they let everyone go. Now. Unharmed. NO ARRESTS. Tell him I'll be there by morning. To look for me at the gate. And...Jack?"

"Yes, my *compadre*?"

"Tell him I won't be alone."

24

SKINWALKER

Jack steered his ATV off road as the land sloped up westward. The wilderness near Fremont Peak bore signs of a rich geological past which included lava flows and Ice Age glaciation. Without hiking permits they might get fined, but everyone thought it worth the risk.

He sighed as they climbed out behind heavy brush, hoping it would conceal their presence--at least until daylight.

"Relax, man," said Tocho, "No one comes here besides outlaws and runaways. You might call it *Land of the Lost.*"

Jack seemed uneasy. "Don't make jokes. Just get us to the cave and back. We can laugh later."

A full moon through broken clouds lit up the desolate landscape. Soon, they were all out of breath, except for the boy. Hiking in wetsuits along a narrow path proved to be difficult. At least they didn't have far to go.

Water gurgled nearby. "This way," said Tocho.

They paused at the creek's muddy edge to put on goggles and flippers.

Twigs cracked under the weight of something wild, making hair stand on the backs of their necks-- most likely a small predator, a bobcat or a coyote, but it could be more dangerous, like a bear or a mountain lion. The cover of night offered dreadful possibilities.

Una tried to get a grip, eyeing the water's course. It wound up and away, into the darkness, stretching out of sight.

"How far?" she asked.

"A quarter mile," said Tocho. "But it'll seem a lot longer."

Not what she wanted to hear.

Suddenly, out of nowhere came this loud, inhuman scream. They all froze, waiting for *someone* to identify it.

"Come *on*," she said, "One of you must know. I've been away for ten years. What was it?"

Tocho shook his head. "Like nothing I've ever--"

"Jack!" she whipped her head around. "Don't do this. It's not funny."

But he wasn't smiling. Slowly, he turned, full circle. There, on a rocky ledge, not fifty feet away was something on four legs, resembling a big black dog. It stared back at him with glowing red eyes.

"It's...." he tried to whisper, but choked, completely losing his voice.

Then it leaped away, into the wilderness, followed by another scream, ten times louder.

No one moved.

"Maybe a wolf," said Aguda.

"Or a *skinwalker*," Jack replied, hoarsely, trying to clear his throat. "The Navajo name is *Yee Naaldlooshii*. Literally, 'he who walks on all fours'. Said to gather in small groups in dark caves, and come out at night. Fast, agile, impossible to catch."

"They *say* to never lock eyes with it," added Tocho. "If it enters your body, you'll wither and die!"

Jack's eyes met Una's.

"Like the werewolf, from European folklore," said Aguda.

He nodded. "Yes. Originally, it referred to a kind of witch with the ability to shapeshift. But it has other meanings."

She felt a chill go up her spine.

"Look, we don't have much time. My point is, they're not just boogiemen, made up to scare children. I used to think that as a kid. Not anymore. Since the 1940's, weird shit's been happening out here. Shit the Indians never dreamed of. I've read countless reports."

"Okay," she said, "Out with it!"

"There's a place, not far from here, in Utah, known as Skinwalker Ranch. Reports include weird, beastly creatures, impossible to kill, entire pastures lit up in the middle of the night, like a football field, bright shafts of light beaming from the ground towards the sky, and, you guessed it--UFOs.

"That's *another* thing. According to Hopkins, ET's

can hide their ships in broad daylight, deflecting light to bend, making themselves invisible. Altering an abductee's vibrational frequency zaps them out of sight.

"It stems from mind control; the same trick used to 'turn people off' while others, in the same room or even the same car, are taken. It also explains why abductees report dreams with big eyes in wild animals, like a deer, owl, wolf or coyote. At least, that's what they see at first. Hypnotic regression strips away the deception. The eyes are *alien*.

"One family who lived there, saw three types of UFOs, plus other airborne lights, some of which emerged from circular doorways that appeared in midair. Once, as they approached the lights, they saw a human-like animal scramble high into a tree. They described it as tall and hairy, identical to Bigfoot."

Una frowned. "So, why *here*?"

"I don't know...maybe to stop us. According to every tale, they're not just monsters. They act with motivation."

"Consider where we are," said Aguda. "About to enter a sacred space--technically, part of the Underworld--sealed off from humanity for millenia, until three boys stumbled in there, a short time ago.

"Suppose they're *gatekeepers*. Legends around the world describe creatures below, determined to drive men away. If the petroglyph contains a warning, to keep it hidden. Some say they're biding their time, waiting to seize the Earth from human hands. To make us pay. Too many centuries of tragic human history behind us now, to turn it around. They don't *want* us to know."

She shook her head. "Because...?"

"*If* we succeed, and survive--it could mean *their* demise, for good!"

"Let's go," said Tocho, leaping into cold, restless water.

And the adults knew he was right. It was time.

Aguda swam beside him, crawling upstream. The others stayed close behind. Relying on natural light alone meant coming up to 'clear' one's snorkel more often--at least, that was Jack's excuse--but Una kept him moving. The creek flowed fast in some spots, slower in others, where it pooled around deep bends, or crept over fallen debris, like brush and tree limbs from the hillside. Bass, bluegill and catfish darted to and fro.

And that was not all. Spotlights swept across the land from black choppers overhead, repeating every hour. They could sense the beam's approach, then feel it penetrate the water's surface, ever briefly, in a bright, blinding flash, before darkness returned...again and again.

It served as a constant reminder of Alpha-Bravo's so-called 'perimeter'.

Swimming against the current did not seem hard at first. The creek was clear and cool. But climbing in and out of shallow spans, over rocks, wading through stretches of mud--not to mention creepy-crawlies like snakes and scorpions and centipedes--began to take its toll.

Una imagined herself enduring this watery obstacle course--in spite of it all--only to enter the cave's relative peace and quiet, crawl onto dry ground, remove her snorkel, and collapse. They'd brought fresh water and energy bars, of course, but not enough to sustain them for any length of time.

None, except for Aguda, had any real experience with caving, in places like Kenya, where the Shimoni caves once hid locals on the run from slave hunters, or the Chyulu Hills near Tsavo East National Park, with the deepest known lava tube in the world, accessed by staircases leading down inside.

Sufficient training to navigate the potential dangers might take years, with endless hours of 'hands on'. Few experienced cavers ever felt that *newbies* were truly ready for the 'plunge.' Tocho's brief stint with Explorer's Club amounted to little more than an intro to basics, with no time to try them out.

Jack harbored no delusions regarding his own 'fitness to the task'. Unlike most kids his age growing up, he had no attraction to water parks. Hanging out on playgrounds or visiting museums with dinosaurs was more his speed. Nature hikes lost their fervor and so he turned increasingly to books, which offered more than enough 'sense of adventure' to a boy who slept with his lights on after seeing *Fire in the Sky* in '93.

While he paused to 'clear his snorkel', Una

glanced at her watch. Just before 10 PM. Another chopper sweep was imminent. A small stabbing pain to her chest forced her to unzip the top of her wetsuit. There, inside a t-shirt breast pocket was the culprit: a mini-compact, less than two inches in diameter. When it fell from her purse in Oraibi, Tocho had misidentified it as a signal mirror, carried by explorers in case of emergency. If only it was that simple. But of course their mission here was *not* to be found.

They moved on.

Breathing through snorkels, it was impossible to speak under water. This made it hard to know if they were getting close. The original plan had been to exit the cave before dawn, around 5 AM. But they had to reach it first.

Apparently, the entrance must be submerged, making it hard to find for anyone who didn't already know where to look. Tocho knew. They had that much in their favor.

But what if they weren't alone? What if the *creature* returned, and Aguda was right? Surely, an Underworld guardian would know, and take steps to dissuade them. Maybe create an illusion, the way Jack said ET's did to abductees.

Una shivered. Either her wetsuit was not keeping her warm, or she was beginning to freak out.

How much longer? she wondered.

They must be getting close. She debated leaving Jack behind for only a moment to catch up with the others, but knew it would be a mistake. Fatigue was setting in, and loss of momentum could pull him backwards, especially where the slope became increasingly steep. In some places already, it felt less like swimming, more like climbing up falls under water.

The creek leveled off briefly before an abrupt incline that dipped inward, like an alcove, and she realized *this must be it.*

Her sense of relief was short lived.

The *skinwalker* reappeared, leaping overhead, legs spread out to both sides, balancing itself in place directly above the water. Its fierce, menacing face with red eyes, a cross between wolf and something *else*, terrifying and unworldly, came after her, with gaping jaws.

She ducked away, pushing Jack deeper. Unfortunately, this submerged his snorkel, causing him to choke and gasp for breath.

As they both tried not to drown, a sudden thought sprang to mind. What did Tocho say, earlier? *Never lock eyes with it.* Because that's what it *wanted.*

Under water, she unzipped, retrieving her mini-compact. Quickly, she tore it apart, inserting one half in each side of her goggles, facing outward.

Then, she surfaced, confronting the beast.

Throwing its hypnotic gaze toward her with all of its might, the skinwalker froze, confused and paralyzed by its own reflection.

Just then, a black hand emerged from the water,

and she realized they had formed a human chain.

Placing Jack's hand firmly in Aguda's, she held on as they pulled. With a great whoosh, she felt herself surge forward into pitch blackness as they slipped through the cave entrance, to safety.

25

JUST A FEELING

Aguda switched on a small light source, just enough for the others to get their bearings inside the cave. Here water flowed through a dark narrow channel, with no signs of green growth, before it dipped out of sight. Their attention quickly turned to a winding tunnel that went deep into the mountain.

Tocho began to strip. "No need for wetsuits. It's pretty dry in there. Temp hovers around 55. Warmer in some spots. We can leave this stuff here."

Passing a water bottle, each of them drank sparingly, enough to wash down an energy bar. Retrieving dry clothes from waterproof backpacks, they donned hiking shoes and simple caving gear. The men turned away from Una out of courtesy, but she did not expect it to last.

Aguda checked his watch: just before midnight.

Jack seemed better now, checking his phone for messages. The signal was too weak here for anything else. There would be no way to respond.

"Check this out," he said, showing his dim screen to Una. It was a text from his source at Alpha-Bravo:

> ASHCROFT PROMISED JOINT SEARCH OF CAVE. NO ONE BELIEVED IT UNTIL WE HEARD UNA'S VOICE RECORDING FROM CELL PHONE, THANK GOD. HANDCUFFS REMOVED. ALL RELEASED. PROTEST TURNED TO CANDLE LIGHT VIGIL WITH MUSIC BEFORE EVERYONE PEACEFULLY ESCORTED TO BUS. HEADED HOME AT LAST.

She pictured Sukya, and sighed with relief.

Aguda came up beside her. "We've got two, maybe three hours, tops. Turn around any later and we won't make it out before dawn."

She smiled at Tocho. "Okay, kiddo, this is your party. We're just along for the ride. Get us in and out!"

The tunnel sloped down gently, curving around to their right. Instead of heading directly toward the complex center, it seemed to lead outward, along the edge. Perhaps there was a formal gate to mark the entrance. She only hoped that Tocho could retrace his steps to the petroglyph.

They stayed close together, moving at a steady

pace.

"Don't kid yourselves," said Aguda. "The air in here is bound to be thinner. Take measured breaths. It may contain microbes. You each carry a filtered pocket mask. Don't hesitate to use it."

Jack felt for his mask, just in case. "What can we expect to find?"

"Stone Age tunnels have been uncovered across Europe, from Scotland to Turkey. Some include dwellings with apartments, stables, temples, even tombs. Others remain a mystery, stretching for many miles between, carved out of stone. Some say early man used them for protection from predators, or safe travel, sheltered from harsh weather--or even warfare.

"But if my hunch is correct, this find predates almost every known example of early civilization. That makes it unique with its own defined sense of purpose. If Hopi legends are true, it served more like a shelter to protect the human race, to ensure our survival."

"So...you don't know."

He nodded.

Before long, they approached a series of long straight vertical lines, like carved stone columns, reminiscent of a Tibetan prayer wall. Following these, they came to an arch, perhaps thirty feet high, completely sealed off with massive stone doors. They felt dwarfed standing before it, like small children.

"We're out of luck," said Jack.

"Over here!" cried Tocho. Just beyond the arch,

a jumbled pile of rocks revealed fissures and an opening in the wall above, apparently the result of an earthquake collapse. He was already climbing toward it.

It led to a flat terraced step-like pattern on the inside, which enabled them to climb down. Immediately it seemed as if they had entered an ancient city. A complex of carved rooms and connecting tunnels spread out before them, stretching as far as the eye could see.

Combined with these structures were natural cave formations, such as long, graceful curtains, fragile soda straws six feet in length, and multicolored flowstones --all produced over eons of time. Under the light, brilliant sparkles from flowstone crystals flickered across cave floors and walls.

Jack clicked away with his camera.

"Easy, my friend," said Aguda. "We have a long way to go, and that's not what we came to see. Save it for the main event."

"Any guesses, so far?"

"It reminds me of a massive cave recently discovered at Giza, beneath the shadow of the Great Pyramid. Part natural, part man-made. If these tunnels were created by water flow, they don't simply stop, since the water must have gone somewhere. If only we had satellite imagery. It would show the exact location of chambers and passageways. *C'est la vie!*"

"What's *that* mean?"

He grinned. "*Such is life!* We'll have to go step by

step!"

Tocho was getting way ahead of them. In an ordinary cave, his light would serve as guide. But here, with so many walls, it was lost in the maze. Aguda raced ahead, vowing to reign the boy in.

Jack paused, as Una came up beside him. "It's okay," she said. "We won't lose them."

"How do you know?" he sighed.

"Look down."

His light on the ground revealed two sets of tracks in red dust. A thick layer had apparently settled here over time--the natural result of stone carving under dry conditions. Exposed surfaces must have slowly crumbled.

She marveled at its color. "Maybe Tocho was right."

"About what?"

"When I tried to question him about Kwahu, about what led them to this place. He spoke of Hopi legends regarding the ancestors living beneath the Grand Canyon. In a place called *Palatkwapi*."

His eyes lit up. "The Red City of the South! Built by Star People, and said to be a temple city of wisdom--where they taught important rituals and secrets of the universe to migrating clans.

"Most everyone agrees it was *someplace* south of the Hopi Mesas. According to the Patki or Water Clan, *where* 'no one knows', exactly. But they say the city was surrounded by 'high walls,' and that its name is derived from 'a high bluff' of red stone.

"Some wonder *how* it could've been built. If construction of megalithic circles and temples occurred during the time referred to by Hopis as the First or Second Worlds--when humans had their *'crown chakra'* wide open and remained in constant touch with the Creator--the designs may have been *given* to them.

"Anyway, they *say* it was built in three sections. Completely surrounded by a high wall, the first was reserved for ceremony--maybe our best bet for any petroglyphs. The second, adjoining it, contained storage for food; and the third comprised living quarters. Underneath them all ran a river."

Una looked at him in bewilderment.

"Inquiring minds want to know, that's all. A good reporter tries to connect all the dots. Past *and* present."

"Okay," she said, peering up at stone columns all around them. "Let's follow the prints, before it's too late."

"For what?"

"I don't know. This place just feels haunted. Like any minute, ghosts from the past will appear...to chase us away. It's giving me chills. And I don't think it's safe to split up!"

Taking her by the hand, he led the way. The trail of prints wandered left, through a wide open gallery with vaulted ceilings, like a cathedral. Tocho's were smaller and wide apart, almost as if he'd been running; Aguda's more steady, slower paced, as if he was trying to take it all in.

"Over there," she said, and Jack redirected his light to one wall.

Its curved stone panels formed a geometric pattern, converging overhead. Una's heart melted. Its symmetry reminded her of balance in nature, like the wings of a butterfly, or the cross-section from a sliced piece of fruit.

Suddenly, they both froze in awe.

There, carved into stone with great skill, like two dimensional murals from an Egyptian tomb, were three diminutive, humanoid figures.

Each had an oversized head, with large eyes, reminiscent of *Akhenaten*, the father of Tutankhamen, and ancient pharaoh of the 18th Dynasty. According to myth, he descended from beings who arrived on Earth at the time of *Zep Tepi*, the fabled First Time, when gods ruled the earth.

Jack stared, at a loss for words.

Una's mind raced. Nothing had prepared her for this. So far, every structure had seemed almost generic, without writing of any kind, to connect it with any living culture. And so, she assumed it to be dead, without knowing for sure who'd built it, in spite of her hopes and dreams. *One must not assume,* she'd heard Aguda say at least a dozen times since they'd met--the mark of a good archaeologist. Their purpose here was to verify not only Moki's claims but the images recorded on his flash drive. To find corresponding, physical proof.

This was not *it,* of course, but maybe a step in the right direction. Only one explanation came to mind: *Ant People*.

Jack snapped a photo. He simply could not resist.

Moments later, they rejoined the others, without saying a word. Precious time may have already been lost. Tocho and Aguda greeted them with nods. From a simple ledge, they peered out together over a decorative wall, notched along the top. The ancient red city, divided into sectors--only a few of which they could barely see--spread out beneath a vast cavern, enveloped in darkness.

The immensity of their task was overwhelming.

Aguda patted Tocho, on the back. "It's a wonder you managed to find your way, the first time, without better equipment."

"It was mostly Kwahu. His incredible sense of direction. He seemed to 'feel' his way more than anything."

"So...which way?" said Jack. "Still remember?"

He pulled a folded piece of paper from his pocket, pointing to a curved diagram. "We find some steps off the ledge, then follow *this* passage, in a wide arc. It's joined by openings that go deeper, like the spokes of a giant wheel."

"Wait a minute. You drew a *map*?"

"Well, yeah...sort of. First rule of Explorer's Club: *Never enter the unknown without a plan to get back.*"

"Okay. So this Sacred Pillar. Where would it be?"

"Well...," said Tocho, tracing lines through a kind

of labyrinth, "About *here*, roughly. But it's not that simple."

"What do you mean?"

"It's *different* in there. More obstacles. Not dark and quiet, like out here. Humming sounds and weird sparks that come off and on...like someone forgot to shut off the power. Makes you feel *vibes*...like you're not alone. It's what scared me, so bad. It's what made me run."

Una embraced him from behind. "You've done good, so far. Don't be afraid. We're with you. Lead the way, and we'll figure it out."

She knew that trust was all important. All for one, and one for all. It held the boys together. And they needed it now. Only the bond of trust could make them strong. Help them fight fear. Without it, they would not get far.

She also knew the power of fear. Fear that kept her away for ten years. Made her avoid confronting the loss of her parents. Afraid to acknowledge the Sky People or tell any of her D.C. friends that she was even Hopi. Fear of the past held her back for so long, that she'd nearly forgotten how to live.

Fear almost prevented her from trusting Ashcroft. It was still tentative. But he'd shown more than one sign of good faith. Only time would tell if that trust endured, to become anything more. Somewhere, deep inside, she longed for the kind of trust that might heal a broken heart. Trust that would last a lifetime.

Her greatest fear now: the thought of returning *empty-handed*.

Besides, she'd already glanced at her watch. With nearly two hours elapsed since first entering the cave, they were running *out* of time--fast.

26

FOREVER

Tocho led them along the ledge to a platform with steps leading down into a broad, curved passageway. The first connecting tunnel revealed an amphitheater-like space, suggesting that it was used for large, well-organized ceremonies.

Paintings adorned its stone walls in natural colors, depicting strangely carved figures without clear facial features, holding weapon-like objects. A few were even wearing space suits.

"Not unlike beings in 10,000 year-old rock art recently discovered in a remote cave system in India," said Aguda. "Tribal villagers there have ancestral cults linked to them, known as *Rohela*, meaning 'small-sized people'. According to legend, they used to land in flying saucers. Those taken were never seen again."

As the two of them moved on, Jack lingered, camera in hand. In spite of all his instincts, he resisted the temptation to use it. Una paused to look up, standing beside him. He seemed torn.

"I keep thinking, 'What if'. *What if* we hadn't been on Flight 564? *What if* I'd forgotten to bring my camera that day? *What if* you hadn't taken that long bus ride all the way from D.C.? We wouldn't be standing here, having this conversation, right now."

"So?"

"*Someone* deemed it important to record these images for posterity, never knowing how long they would survive or how much they would mean to people like you and me, walking in here after untold centuries. I know how that feels."

Their eyes briefly met.

"After the flight, I was searched, like everyone else. Maybe they thought I looked suspicious. I don't know. Digital photography was still unknown. They confiscated my camera and all my film--well, *almost*. Right before we landed, I switched out the roll I'd been using with a fresh one, stashing the other out of sight. Anyway, it worked.

"But over the years, I'd also seen what happens to people who come forward, publicly disgraced, and so I vowed to never place myself in that kind of jeopardy, at the mercy of those who destroy others to conceal the truth.

"So I developed it in my own personal dark room, the size of a walk-in closet. I could only afford black and white, and my images were mostly blurred-- except for one. The one I saved all these years. I made a few prints, but always keep one with me as a reminder.

"And I thought I'd *still* have to keep it to myself. Because it had been so long since I came face-to-face with another passenger from that flight. Over the years, whenever I *tried* to find people, they were always gone--without a trace. And I began to wonder if *anyone* survived--until the day *you* came to Oraibi."

From his pocket he retrieved the print, holding it up.

"Whoa!" she exclaimed, jumping away.

The image it contained, of a flying disc outside the plane window, with a menacing ET face, gave her chills. It was a face she'd wrestled with in nightmares, growing up. A face she hoped to never see again.

He sighed. "It reminds me how I *felt* back then. How it changed my view of the world, and gave me a new sense of priorities. I could no longer be duped by those who try to shape public opinion, telling people what to believe, coaxing them to side with the 'majority' whether it 'feels' right or not, persecuting anyone whose values don't line up, who acts according to conscience.

"At first I was angry, then afraid. Fear held me back. I tried to play along, pretend there was nothing to countless MUFON reports. But it was impossible. *Everything* had changed. I grieved the loss of my former reality--one in which aliens and UFOs did not exist! I had to rethink the meaning of life and my view of the universe. I felt...alone.

"I considered attending UFO conferences, but chickened out. So I kept a personal journal. Writing became my way of coping. But it didn't prepare me for what happened next: TV's and radios turning themselves off and on, strange wrong-number phone calls, and fits of *knowing* things well in advance. I couldn't sleep, haunted by dreams of world disaster. I thought I would lose my mind!"

Una shook her head.

Jack tried to smile. "On the flip side, I've grown in many ways. My IQ and receptiveness to learning seem to have increased , and I'm more *in tune* to nature, myself, and other human beings."

She wondered if this was all the result of rural isolation. In many ways, her life had also changed. Insomnia, cosmic dreams, strange intuition, had all become part of her reality. But she dealt with it differently. Uneasiness created within her a need for change of scenery.

"But you never left town?"

He frowned. "I couldn't. I've seen plenty of decline, places go out, empty buildings; ice cream shops, truck stops, movie theaters--you name it. But I never gave up on the *people*. Friends I grew up with. So I stayed. I could never shake the idea that I belonged here, that I was born here for a reason. Winslow was in my *blood*. And I couldn't just throw that away."

They reentered the main passageway. Perhaps it was the density of stone walls between them, or the lack of light, that wreaked havoc with one's imagination. Or perhaps they'd lingered in the amphitheater too long. Jack and Una both suddenly experienced a moment of panic.

They could not detect any signs of Tocho or Aguda.

Their first instinct was to run. But it would serve no purpose. The cave's air quality was questionable at best. Breathing more of it could be hazardous. Plus they had only one water bottle to share between them, since Jack's had been lost in the creek. Running would get them overheated.

She kept trying to search for tracks, but the red dust was curiously absent.

The next connecting "spoke" of the complex wheel revealed nothing. A partial collapse had blocked if off with rubble, piled high a few feet inside. They only hoped their two companions were not trapped somewhere beneath it.

"We'd have heard something, right?" said Jack. "I mean, sound would've carried. They must be further ahead."

She nodded, more out of hope than certainty.

More and more, Una began to wonder if random knocks and whispers represented some kind of life force, still present. Not spirits of the dead, exactly, but something *else*. Entities residing in the mountain.

She remembered something about caves. In Arizona and New Mexico, some were considered shrines, stretching back a thousand years. Ancients like the Maya regarded them as part of a mystical underworld, outside of normal time and space. Mayan priests brought offerings to commune with deities who dwelled there.

Una turned to Jack. "Ever feel...*watched?*"

He eyed her with amazement.

For someone from D.C., she was really beginning to come around. Maybe it just took a few days back on native soil to awaken her mind and body to subtle forces. All along, he'd pegged her for someone with a powerful *aura*, that distinctive quality generated by some people more than others, surrounding them like a field, which gave them greater sensibility. (He'd dated a girl who was into Yoga once.) Maybe it was finally kicking in.

"All the time. Especially at night. It's a feeling that never leaves me, ever since 564. But, that's *not* what you mean."

"No. I mean here, now, ever since we came inside. It's like the mountain *knows*. And we only see what's allowed."

"But we're safe."

"Of *course* we are. It could have stopped us any time."

***

Not far ahead, but still out of range for sight and sound, Aguda and Tocho proceeded carefully, adhering to his map.

"It seems bigger to me now," he said. "Maybe because we brought more light. I felt so claustrophobic before, that I could hardly breathe. I still feel small, like a child in a maze, but at least I'm not alone."

Aguda grinned. "The ancients would agree with you. Caves were considered sacred, reserved for special rites and rituals, or to bury the honored dead. They were ambiguous spaces associated with gods, to be angered or pleased.

"They were also considered to be places where one could attain life-giving power over nature. They became important to community leaders, who sought prosperity and control. Land was not owned. It could only be borrowed from its *true* owners, dwelling within the earth. Without their cooperation, human enterprise was doomed to failure. Rituals invoked that power, for good or evil."

Tocho shuddered. "Do you really believe all that shit?"

He laughed. "It doesn't matter what I believe. For an archaeologist, it's about the thrill of the dig. A detective game that brings color to human actions and relationships that have been forgotten. Artifacts are the evidence. It's a brilliant hobby, vocation, and passion--one that can lead to lots of interesting places and people of all shapes, sizes and beard lengths. At least, it is for me."

"Is that why you became one?"

"Although I grew up with a love of history and the outdoors in my native Kenya, I didn't realize what I wanted to be until I was 23. That's when I first saw the necropolis at Giza, and viewed the Pyramid Texts, a collection of ancient Egyptian writings from the time of the Old Kingdom. Carved on the walls and sarcophagi of the pyramids at Saqqara, the "utterances" of the texts are meant to protect the pharaoh's remains, reanimate his body after death, and help him ascend to the heavens. They could also be used to call the gods for help.

"I was hooked. The truth they embodied would stand forever. And I wanted to be a part of it. There was more, of course. The chance for adventure, world travel, my insatiable curiosity, and the thrill of discovery. All played a part."

"I'd like that," said Tocho.

"Yes, well you might. But it's not all glamour. Archaeologists are the lowest paid of all graduates. Over 17 years, I've published hundreds of articles in professional journals, authored book chapters, and posted to online blogs--without receiving a dime. It's not about the money.

"But it *is* about finding the truth."

He nodded. "To answer all the unanswered questions...about those who came before us. A way to better understand ourselves. It's a noble quest, one that will not make you rich or famous, but it may give a you a sense of purpose. It was a choice I made thirty years ago, and I've not regretted it since."

27

ILLUSION

Aguda's light source dimmed ever so slightly as he and Tocho proceeded around another bend up ahead. They were not far away.

Una paused as a familiar sound echoed from another chamber nearby.

"What *is* that?" she asked.

"I don't know," said Jack. "Let's take a look."

Peering carefully through a narrow arch, directing his beam, he suddenly froze in awe, afraid to take another step. Thousands of narrow, pointed stalactites jutted down from a pitch black space, high above, like blood-tipped spears. The same emptiness dropped away below into a yawning, bottomless pit, with its own set of deadly stalagmites. It was like the giant mouth of an underworld monster, ready to swallow them up.

He held up his arm, to keep Una from toppling forward.

It reminded her of all the pitfalls she faced in D.C., on a daily basis--where even casual dinner party conversations could be like mine fields through which one had to navigate one's path oh-so-carefully--or risk the ramifications of a misplaced word or phrase. Politics flowed beneath the surface of everything at all times, no matter what the pretense, and she had learned that one could only let down one's guard in the safety of solitude.

"It's funny," she said. "I wish life was so simple."

"What do you mean?"

"I left the Reservation because, without my parents, I felt isolated and cut off from the world. My future was filled with uncertainty.

"I felt compelled to find answers. My parents *tried* to make things better, but their hands were tied by people in the government, far away. I had no choice but to leave. It was the only way to make a difference, to reach decision makers.

"It became clear to me, my first year in college-- or so I thought. Seduced by the modern world, with all its technology, all its promise. I wanted a 'normal' life, so I set my sights on D.C."

She paused to catch her breath.

"But I was fooling myself. We all do. Thinking we won't be judged by others who'll hold us up to a false standard and find us wanting. But in the *modern* world, it happens every day. So many different labels applied to undesirables...to make us feel better about ourselves. And they all mean the same thing: *abnormal*.

"I tried to blend in, concealing my Hopi background even from friends, afraid of the *Indian* label, afraid I'd be treated differently, like a minority or worse. All because I feared rejection.

"As it turns out, living in D.C., *normal* is pretty hard to find. With so many opposing points of view, so many flip-flops on what matters, distinctions between 'right' and 'wrong' become blurred. Relationships are superficial at best.

"By the time I received Kasa's letter, my life had become meaningless. I felt lost. I tried to cope with the stress of modern life, like everyone else: exercise, sauna, massage. New age gurus. You name it."

"But nothing worked," said Jack.

Una sighed. Carefully, she reached down without leaning forward, to pick up a small pebble beside her boot.

Their eyes met, and she smiled.

"One good thing, at least. Coming home again has enabled me to *reconnect*, remember who I am and finally accept my place in the world. My eyes have been opened. In a way, all that turmoil I endured was worth it. Maybe it was a test. To see if I'd find the courage to face my past."

She stepped away from him carefully, clinging to the arch.

"We'd better catch up," he said, "It's not safe here."

"You're right. But not for the reason you think. That sound I heard, the one that drew us here, made me realize it, just now."

"Realize what?"

She tossed her pebble high toward the middle of the space, and Jack expected it to fall, down and down, but then it *splashed*--disrupting the glass-like, mirrored reflection of perfect still water--that created the *illusion* of a bottomless pit.

"No telling how deep it is," she said. "We might've drowned."

He turned away, with a grin.

***

They found Tocho seated on the remains of a broken pedestal, holding the light up for Aguda, positioned before a giant stone carving.

It depicted a sacred female at its center, with lines extending out in all directions, to join a symbolic swirling circle. He stretched out his arms, tracing several of them with his fingers. "We must be getting closer."

"Why?" said Una. "What's it mean?"

"*Enter the world of the Spider Woman*. Not just Hopi. She is found among many tribes, including the Lakota, Zuni, and Pueblo peoples. Revered among Navajos, for teaching them how to weave. In their rugs, the 'Spider Woman's Cross' is sometimes seen as a symbol of balance."

"Right," said Jack. "To this day, a bit of spider web is rubbed into the palms of infant girls, to make them good weavers. It's considered a sacred art."

Una tried to rack her brain. "Where've I seen

this before? Of course! On a shawl worn by Kuwanyauma. It makes sense to me now. *Spider Woman* represents the world seen through a web of relationships. We're all connected. For those with eyes to see, her Web is everywhere."

"Okay," said Tocho, standing up. "So we're close. Let's get to it. Has anyone checked the clock?"

They all stopped to look at their watches. Less than forty minutes to the half-way point, otherwise known as *turn-around-time*.

"Not so fast," said Aguda. "Let's be careful. The boys made it out by sheer luck. We must do better than that. Awareness is the key. Has anyone noticed the symmetry here? The layout of this city is so...balanced. One could easily get disoriented. Cavers get lost all the time because they go too fast, without watching for landmarks, to retrace their path."

Jack perked up. "Did y-you say *l-l-lost?*"

"Or confused. Let's not forget Plato's 'Allegory of the Cave."

They all faced him with blank stares.'

"It points out the difference between *reality* and *illusion*. In the story, a group of men spend their entire lives chained to pillars inside a cave, where they can only see shadows cast by firelight onto a blank wall, but never see outside. Thus they live in a state of ignorance. When one breaks free and escapes, he returns to convey truth about the real world. Instead of expressing gratitude, they angrily reject his words and threaten to kill him. Why? Because they can't accept any interpretation of reality which is beyond their experience."

Jack rolled his eyes, "So?"

"For Plato, the philosopher is like a prisoner, who escapes and comes to realize that shadows on the wall do not make up reality at all. It *is* possible to perceive the truth *directly*, rather than mere shadows."

"How does that help?"

Aguda frowned. "Because it *cautions* us: don't be quick to judge. Whatever we find is bound to seem strange, even impossible. But we can't reject it out of hand. Reality depends on your frame of reference. We're at least twenty centuries out of step."

"And out of sync?"

"You bet. Oh...one thing I forgot to mention. Plato was trying to make a point about people in authority forcing their world view upon others. His 'Allegory' was told by Socrates, his teacher, who died unjustly."

"How?" said Una.

"Sentenced to die by the government--for corrupting the youth of Athens by introducing strange gods. It challenged their *view of reality*."

And suddenly, she wished it could all be over.

Photos of the Sacred Pillar, with its ancient petroglyph would no doubt prove their claims of Hopi ancestry, driving Ashcroft and his cronies back to their secret hideaway, beneath the desert. Tribal Council would be pleased. And her friends in Oraibi would be rewarded for all their faith and support.

At the same time, Aguda was right.

Getting lost would ruin *everything*. She could just imagine Ashcroft venturing into the cave at dawn, only to find her wandering aimlessly--in clear violation of their agreement. It would jeopardize the "spirit of cooperation" established between them earlier and destroy any trust.

Una *couldn't* let that happen.

"Okay, listen up," she said. "Forget everything else. We must find the Sacred Pillar, right away. Before it's too late."

She patted Tocho on the back.

"Don't let anyone stop you. Just go. We've got thirty minutes, until we have to turn around."

He smiled. For once, he would not just be a follower, but a leader, marching without fear into the unknown. It was the dream of everyone he knew who ever joined Explorer's Club.

But according to Aguda, the real expert, the only Archaeologist among them, their whole concept of reality might be at stake, in a world with its own frame of reference, a world of illusion.

It meant reliving a mistake from the scariest moment of his life. When a million questions seemed to go through his mind, in mere seconds, as he stared for what seemed like an eternity, before snapping his camera.

Since then, he'd replayed it over, countless times, wondering what he might do, if given a second chance.

That time was now at hand.

And Tocho was determined to try--if they had no hope of success, even if they might not survive. Because he was not afraid; of the past or its secrets regarding the destiny of man.

Plus, he needed to redeem himself. To prove that no matter what happened before, *this* time things would be different. He would not let them down, by running away. There was no time for a change of heart.

He felt ready to face the impossible.

28

REVELATION

Tocho marched boldly ahead, sweeping his light from side to side, in search of another opening. It caught him by surprise, with its ornate design: two tapering, tower-like structures, each surmounted by a cornice, joined by a less elevated section, which enclosed an archway between them.

"Wha-what the--"

"*Pylon*," said Aguda. "It mimics an ancient hieroglyph for 'horizon', which depicted two hills, 'between which the sun rose and set'. It was associated with rebirth."

Stepping through it, they immediately found themselves crossing a small foot bridge over a narrow stone-lined channel, which encircled the domed round chamber interior.

"Undoubtedly a spring once flowed here," he went on, "to represent 'waters of chaos' in the outside world, and separate the mound within, where cosmic order was renewed. This must be a temple."

They passed between tall, thick columns of a

hypostyle hall, arranged to permit an open space at its center. Tocho's light revealed elaborately carved reliefs, depicting previous eras, known to Hopis as the "Three Worlds".

Its appearance was almost Egyptian.

The first, *Tokpela*, depicted a kind of paradise, not unlike the Garden of Eden, in which humans and animals lived together in harmony--until, distracted by gossip and fighting over race, language, and religion, paradise was lost.

"The Creator told sky god Sótuknang to eliminate evil people," said Una, surprising herself, as if an old lesson suddenly sprang to mind. "Fire came from above and below, all around the earth, the waters, the air...and there was nothing left except for those who survived *here*--inside its womb."

The second, *Tokpa*, depicted people obsessed with material goods, bellicose, distrustful and uncivilized, engaging in *cannibalism*.

She cringed. "Sótuknang commanded the warrior twins to leave their polar posts without warning, and so the earth teetered off balance. Mountains plunged into seas, which overflowed the land, and as the world spun through cold and lifeless space, it froze into ice. Led to safety underground once more by *Anu Sinom*, the Ant People, righteous Hopi survived."

The third world, *Kuskurza*, showed advanced civilization, with aerial vehicles for transport and combat, *patuwvotas*, also known as "flying shields". These aircraft were akin to vimanas described in

Hindu texts, and strikingly similar to modern day UFOs.

"Sótuknang decided to destroy all those corrupted by evil thoughts, *this* time by flood. Those chosen to survive, sealed in rafts of hollow reeds, began to float upon rising waters, and sailed across the ocean, toward sunrise. Eventually, they reached the shores of North America."

"Wait a minute," said Jack. "No offense, but what about Noah's ark?"

Aguda grinned. "Most people do not realize that many versions of this tale have been told. The Sumerians, Babylonians, and Incas all speak of a Great Flood with few survivors, who 'found favor' in the eyes of God. It appears in the ancient writings of India, Malaysia and Greece. Plato described it as the 'great deluge of all'. All we know for certain is that a real cataclysm occurred, few survived, and we are their descendants."

Tocho suddenly began to shake.

"What is it?" said Una.

"I'm feelin' it again."

"*It?*" said Jack, "What do you mean?"

"I don't know...a tingling inside. It's hard to explain. I feel weird, like I'm all butterflies...like something's *wrong*. It just...makes me want to run. It's...oh my god...I can't...*stand* it!"

"Here," she said, "Take my hand."

Maybe it was the sweatiness of his palm, or something in the air. She sensed an unfamiliar vibe, like shadows moving around her, seen from the corner of one's eye, but not otherwise clearly perceived. It gave her chills.

"Maybe he's right. Anyone else? A presence, like breathing, almost. As if we're being watched. I feel it, too."

Jack shuddered. "You mean like *intuition*?"

Aguda came forth, patting them each on the back. "Relax! You're not imagining. We are standing in the temple *sanctuary*, designed to manifest divine presence. It touches the soul in ways that go beyond words. Your response is perfectly normal."

"So, what about you?"

"Mine's altogether...different."

"How so?"

"It *feels* like I've been here before. Which is impossible, because I know it's not true. But I can't shake the feeling. It's so much like other temples I *have* been in. That same atmosphere of reverence, of close proximity to a higher power, as if something--or someone--*knows* we are here."

"Woohoo!" cried Tocho. His voice seemed to echo, all around them. "Over here. I've found it!"

She gazed in disbelief, as they moved to join him at the mound center. One large pillar stood out from all the rest. Unlike other temple structures, carved mostly from sandstone, this one appeared to be solid granite.

"So *that's* it," said Jack, with both hands on his hips. "Let's get our photos and be done with it."

Aguda approached a raised platform before it, with caution.

His light glimmered from a solid, metal object there, cradled in a stone holder. To his trained Archaeological eye, it resembled not only a ceremonial Hopi rattle, but also a symbolic instrument of power identified with the tombs of Egyptian pharaohs.

"What is it?" said Una.

Almost afraid to speak out loud, he whispered, "I cannot say for sure...but I know what it *looks* like."

She blinked, as an image came to mind. "Of course. *Now* I remember. My first Bean Dance, as a child. A gift from Uncle: Chief Dancer Doll with his *rattle*. It gave the power of knowledge."

His head shook. "I was thinking of *sistrum*, a Latin word, derived from the Greek, meaning 'that which is shaken.' The Egyptian term *sekhem* means 'power,' as in the name of the Goddess Sekhmet, the Powerful One--one of the names for Isis. It was considered a magical instrument, tied to her worship in Greece and Rome.

"In the Temple of Amun-Re at Karnak, it was used to pacify the gods, held by the priestess in worship ceremonies. In funerary rituals, it also signified regeneration in the after-life."

She nodded.

"The rattle," said Jack, "How'd it work?"

"I don't know. It wasn't a toy. We didn't play with it, I mean. But rattles were used by Kachina dancers."

"In a 'Bean Dance'?"

She blinked again. "A 'coming of age' ceremony. Inititates are given the responsibility to grow beans in kivas. Days later, they return, to present new bean sprouts to the tribe. Finally, there's a procession."

"Yes!" said Aguda. "Exactly! Look, beneath our feet. The pattern, it's like a path, leading *through* the sanctuary."

Tocho's light traced out a swirling path of yellow stone, as they followed it with their eyes, to *another* arch, also accessed by a foot bridge. It's door, marked with symbolic waves, like water, stood half ajar.

He sighed. "According to Hopi tradition, at the end of each world the gods *return* to reestablish order. We're currently living in the *Fourth*."

"But the mural," said Tocho, "has only three."

"Because the last time people gathered here, the Fourth was yet to come. Behold what's written on the door. A promise from Sótuknang :

> "See, I have washed away
> even the footprints of
> your Emergence; the
> stepping-stones left for you.
> On the sea bottom lie all
> the proud cities,
> flying shields and
> worldly treasures
> corrupted with evil, and people

> who found no time to
> sing praise to the Creator.
> But the day will come,
> if you preserve the memory
> and the meaning of
> your Emergence,
> when stepping-stones will
> emerge again
> to prove the truth."

"Okay, guys," said Una, turning back to the Sacred Pillar. "Stay focused. First things first."

Tocho flipped around, searching in vain for the petroglyph. "Hey! I don't get it. Moki stood right *here*. I swear. Or was it there? Anyway, something's wrong. I...I can't find it. What happened?"

She came beside him, steeped in shadow. "Images on the flash drive were taken from a different angle. But he was definitely more centered, like *this*..."

Her feet touched the platform, and suddenly, she swayed, filled with a cosmic sense of awe: that primal, irreducible and indefinable sense of the *beyond* which some have called 'numinous'--impossible to convey to anyone who has not experienced it--and collapsed, to the ground.

An eerie *Gleam of Light* at once filled the sanctuary, radiating up from her body, like a miniature lightning display, in many colors, illuminating the Sacred Pillar. Like fire, its petroglyph shone for all to see, every detail sharply defined, in symbols familiar to anyone acquainted with Hopi mythology.

Una could hear the voice of the Ant Men, speaking plainly:

> *"Welcome.*
> *As a knock on the door,*
> *you have awakened*
> *the power within.*
> *This Opening of the Ways*
> *is meant to share*
> *the truth,*
> *good and bad, regarding*
> *the destiny of*
> *Mankind.*
> *Here the Sacred Path*
> *is laid out for those*
> *who would follow,*
> *to the ends of the Earth*
> *and beyond.*
> *May it bring you*
> *Peace."*

Looking down, she realized her hand was still touching the 'rattle'. She must have 'activated' it when she fell.

She tried to let go, but it wasn't easy. Something about it made her want to hold on. The way it made her feel: *all-knowing* and energized, in touch with reality outside herself--that words could not explain.

The petroglyph seemed *alive*, its symbols burning with fire, lifting her up, right out out of her body. No wonder Moki was never the same. Would she be? Would the epiphany of this moment change her perception of reality?

Time seemed irrelevant.

She could kneel here, communing with the gods for eternity, raptured in the glory of this feeling, because it would never end.

"Una!!!" they cried out to her, all at once.

A wave of emotion surged through her, memories of her parents, of Kasa's letter, the moment she first set foot in Oraibi after so many years, and the pair of spirit-guides who greeted her—not dogs, but *wolves*.

And incredibly, she thought of Ashcroft, not the general, but the boy, in his outfit, on the plane so many years ago. The light in his eyes, a light which seemed akin to hers, as if the two were one and the same.

The spark between them was no coincidence. More like *destiny*.

Her hand pulled away.

And in that moment, the incredible *Gleam of Light*--with all its wonder and promise of new life and hope for the future of humanity, all its power to transform one's consciousness and open the door to another dimension, where the Sky People were *real*, waiting for us to join them--went dark.

29

THE VOW

The duty officer seated at his computer console in a darkened room at Alpha-Bravo drained the last of his coffee from a mug that had gone cold, just minutes before shift's end, at 12:50 AM. An anomalous pulsing red blip appeared, unlike anything he'd ever seen. Range indicators showed it to be less than a mile away, subterranean, within the target zone.

But he had to be sure.

The technology, developed for National Defense and considered Top Secret, was first designed to detect enemy threats, specifically from weapons of mass destruction. It had also been deployed by sophisticated military satellites over places like Iran and North Korea.

His hands began to shake. An energy reading of this type went completely off the scale. Yet his equipment appeared to be in perfect working order.

Now what? he thought. *Why me?*

He began to hyperventilate. It was his first lone assignment, to fill in a few hours while his superior was catching some shut eye. Technically, it wasn't even his field of expertise.

Heart pounding, he tried to remember official protocol.

An automatic printout reminded him to report his findings at once to General Ashcroft. Briefly, he hesitated, reluctant to leave his post. The time: 12:58. *Close enough*, he thought. His shift replacement was bound to show up momentarily. Besides, he needed a breath of fresh air.

Printout in hand, he made for the nearest exit. The door opened onto a metal catwalk like a fire escape, with steps leading down to the hillside. Fortunately, he'd missed all the commotion hours before, from protesters outside the gate.

In his haste, he failed to notice a half-empty water bottle lobbed over the fence. It caught under his heel at just the right angle.

He slipped, trying to regain his grip but could not as he fell, head slamming into metal rails not once but three times before he spilled onto rocky terrain, the paper flown from his hand, drifting down and down until it dropped out of sight into a desert ravine.

Blood trickled from the gash in his forehead as the officer lay still in the darkness, beneath a moonlit sky.

***

Quickly Una retrieved dry socks from her

backpack, covering the 'rattle' artifact--to prevent further contact--and stashed it away for safekeeping. In spite of its hopeful message, the encounter left her with an impending sense of doom for the human race--or at least, almost everyone she knew. Things would get worse before they got better. It was only a matter of time.

Her companions were still reeling from the light show.

"Did we get that?" said Jack.

"And how!" Tocho replied, camera in hand. "Can't wait to--"

"Not so fast," said Aguda, moving away from them. He paused before the mystery doors, half ajar, carved with ancient words of Sotuknang.

"Forget it," said Una, "There's no time."

Suddenly, he squeezed through the opening, and was gone.

She gasped.

Tocho raced after him.

"What are they *doing*?" said Jack.

Of all the crazy stunts to pull, this one had to take the cake. He never thought Aguda--the steady, reliable, boring old instructor from his Comparative Ancient Culture days at NAU--would go off, half-cocked to explore, with them running out of time. So far, his presence had worked like a charm, interpreting what little info they had to go on. But his enthusiasm was getting out of hand.

What if we get lost? he thought, or *fail to make it out*

alive?

They simply had no choice but to follow.

Jack went first, still hoping to turn them around.

Una peeked through cautiously, hoping it was not some kind of trap. The sheer enormity of the space beyond and lack of voices ignited her worst fears. No sense in getting them *all* killed.

She found her friends standing in the midst of an ancient shipyard, with craft all around, in various stages of completion. Though consistent in size and shape with Viking longboats, the only lumber here formed tracks along the floor.

"What are they made of?" she asked.

"Totora," said Aguda, pointing to thick roped bundles, "A reed grown in South America, around Lake Titicaca, and also on Easter Island. Reed boats were constructed from early times in Peru, Bolivia, and Scandinavia."

"Are they seaworthy?" said Jack.

"No doubt! Ships made of bulrush have sailed the Pacific, the Atlantic, and the Mediterranean. Egyptians were using them as far back as 4,000 BC."

Tocho frowned. "But Noah's ark lasted for 40 days. I don't--"

"Use your imagination! The Uros are an indigenous people pre-dating the Incas who live, to this day, on man-made 'floating islands' made from totora. Each supports between three and ten houses. They also build boats for fishing and hunting seabirds."

Jack ran his hand along a thick blackened layer on its outer 'hull'.

"Water-proofing," said Aguda, "Probably some form of tar."

"I see plenty of raw materials," said Jack, "But no tools. How did they accomplish all this?"

He shrugged. "It usually takes a team of 30 to 50 people about three months to build a ship like this. The Uros say their ancestors used extended arms, hands and fingers as a basis for measurement. Your guess is as good as mine."

"This reminds me of something," said Una. "Didn't they find a ship buried in Egypt once?"

"*More* than once. In fact, a number of solar ships and boat pits have been found, buried near Egyptian sites--seven around the Great Pyramid alone. Their history and function is not precisely known. The most famous is the Khufu ship, now preserved in the Giza Solar boat museum."

"Why 'solar'?"

"A 'solar barge' is a ritual vessel to carry the resurrected king with the sun god Ra across the heavens. However, some ships bear signs of being used in water, as a funerary barge."

"Some?" said Jack.

"The Khufu ship is perhaps the best example; an intact full-size vessel that was sealed into a pit at the foot of the Great Pyramid around 2500 BC. It's described as 'a masterpiece of woodcraft' that could sail today if put into water."

She shook her head. Something was still missing. According to myth, these boats were the key to Hopi survival beyond the Great Flood.

There must be a way *out*.

"These wooden tracks in the floor...where do they go?"

Aguda's light revealed only a dead-end tunnel.

"That's not right," said Jack. "If it were a boat ramp--"

"Maybe it *is*," said Tocho, hopping onto the nearest ship. About 14 meters long and nearly complete, it supported his weight with ease. He guessed seating capacity for twenty, at least.

Suddenly, there was the rumble of ancient machinery, as Tocho began to slowly move.

"Wha-wha-what's *happening*?" he cried.

"The track," said Jack, "Look! There's a chain inside, pulling it forward."

"B-but I don't wanna die!"

"Hold on!" said Una. "Okay, everyone, let's go."

They hopped in beside him.

She glanced once more toward the Great Red City and sighed. "If only other people could see this."

"Who knows?" said Aguda. "Tomorrow may be our last chance. With government red tape--even *if* we succeed--it could take a lifetime."

Jack groaned. "What about the Kachinas? All this wisdom. All this advancement. How could they just leave?"

Aguda patted him, on the back.

"Because it had served its purpose: to ensure humanity's survival, from the Third World to the Fourth. There's so much we may never know. Who were the Ant People, exactly? How long did they live here? And where did they go? All we do know is that they withdrew their visible presence, promising to return should their help be needed."

Una grinned. "As children, we believed it was happening every year in time for the winter solstice: Kachinas descending from their 'homes' in the Sacred Peaks to our village for ceremonies, then departing again in late June. They came to give us Awareness."

Through a dark tunnel, they approached a flat wall of stone. An eerie silence enveloped them. Jack noticed it first. No one spoke. In fact, they just stared off into space. Perhaps it was overwhelming fear, regarding their fate. Maybe they were just holding their breath.

"By the way," said Una, "In case we survive, let's make a *vow*--right now, before it's too late. The *you-know-what* we found back there...must be our *secret*. We can't tell a soul. Not tomorrow. Not ever."

"Agreed," the rest of them said, all at once.

"What'll happen?" said Tocho.

"First, we join forces, tomorrow, to 'find' the Sacred Pillar with its petroglyph, and prove our claim to the judge. After that, who knows?"

As the ship seemed about to collide, they all braced for impact, hands over their eyes. A giant *whoosh* of fresh air came suddenly over them, as the moon appeared overhead, like a beacon of hope.

Then, like an old-fashioned roller coaster--not the smooth kind on air-cushioned rails, but the rickety kind, all made of wood, recalled by anyone over fifty--the bow dropped, and down they went, crashing over mountainous terrain, snapping twigs off desert brush, kicking up rocks in a cloud of dust.

The ship shuddered and threatened to fall apart.

Then, for an instant, it left the ground, suspended in mid air, as they skipped over a ravine, before finally skidding to a stop on a shallow slope of mud and sand. Birds and insects scattered.

And together they sat in sheer silence.

Then slowly, one by one, their eyes opened. Hands clasped tightly together let go. Heads raised, they each breathed a sigh of relief and took in familiar sights, like trees and grass, and sounds, like desert breeze and birdsong.

Maybe they were too stunned to speak, just returned from an alternate reality, from a journey through time to an impossible place--like Alice from the rabbit hole, or Dorothy from Oz.

Maybe they just wanted to be sure they were still alive.

Tocho was first to abandon ship,

"Last one out's a rotten egg!"

And they all laughed.

Surprisingly little remained of the ship which had

brought them here. Climbing out to stand beside it, Una, Jack, and Aguda eyed with awe the crumpled mix of ancient reeds and rope. It resembled little more than a heap of straw left by a desert whirlwind.

She suspected that this was no accident.

Perhaps it was designed for that very purpose: to deliver them safely, but leave no trace of the Third World behind.

They had emerged on the far side of Fremont Peak. Thankfully, there were no signs of military security. No cameras. No choppers sweeping by overhead. In fact, they were not far from the road.

Jack sized up their position, checking his watch. "Our ATV's thataway," he said, pointing westward. "Still three hours 'til daylight."

"Now what?" said Tocho.

"*You* go home to your family," said Una, turning to Aguda. "Would you mind? I promised to get him back safe."

He nodded. "What about--"

"We'll get some rest before hiking to Alpha-Bravo," said Jack. It should be less than an hour from here."

Minutes later, they watched the pair drive away.

***

Snuggled into her sleeping bag, Una tried to rest, with arms wrapped around her backpack. The Hopi *'Rattle'* had already changed her life forever, revealing man's destiny. Even if something happened to the cave after their search it wouldn't matter. They had proof. No doubt a great deal of study would be required to unravel the meaning of the ancient petroglyph.

Still, a nagging fear remained in the back of her mind. Great power and knowledge were not to be taken lightly. Their secret must not get out. She would sleep lightly, with one eye open--to be wary of *Skinwalkers*.

30

NEXUS

Una sat by the campfire, awaiting sunrise...with dread.

It would be a real circus at Alpha-Bravo. Jack's media contacts would all be scrambling to cover the event. People from the reservation would be there, with plenty of police, no doubt--not to mention armed soldiers in uniform.

She eyed her backpack through the tent's open flap. The powerful 'rattle' inside it was safe for now, but how long would that last? A slip of the tongue could ruin everything. It wasn't a matter of trust. She trusted them all--Aguda, Tocho, and Jack--implicitly.

But a secret of this magnitude could wear a person down.

There would be so many questions. She'd have to feign ignorance before everyone in the cave--and hope they didn't find footprints from the night before, or discover their abandoned scuba gear.

With luck, it would all end by 'finding' the *petroglyph*--proof enough to satisfy the judge, validate Hopi claims, and halt the search altogether.

But that was only one scenario.

A twig snapped beyond the brush, a few feet away.

Jack was still asleep. She wasn't about to play the helpless female. Not now, after all they'd been through.

She grabbed a metal poker from the flames.

Step by step, she made her way toward the sound, scanning for the slightest sign of movement. It was probably nothing, a curious muskrat or coyote. A Skinwalker would've screamed by now.

Carefully directing the beam of her flashlight, she crept beyond the nearest hedge, to find a familiar face.

"*How!*" said Ashcroft, with right hand raised.

"Not funny," she replied, keeping her voice to a whisper. "What're you doing here? I thought we--"

"We did. I mean, we *do*. It's just that--"

"What? What? What could you *possibly* have to say that can't wait until daylight? Wasn't that the point? A joint search, with everything out in the open--for all to see?"

"Yes, of course, but," his voice softened. "It seems we have unfinished business, you and I. Ever since that moment we shared beneath the stars at Camp Navajo, I've been, well...*torn*, between my duty and...something else."

She wanted to believe him, more than ever. It was hard to imagine he'd take the risk to be here right now unless it *really* mattered. Unless--

"I know you managed to slip into the cave."

She pulled away.

"But that's not why I'm here. In fact, everything I'm saying to you right now is strictly *off the record*. I have no intention of reporting it."

Una did not understand.

"But that's not *like* you, General. I thought this site was all important. What about your spy satellite, the energy readings, the ancient UFO? Don't tell me you've given up on all that. I'm from D.C.--where people don't forget. One mistake can mean the end of your career. I've seen it happen too many times."

He bristled at her suggestion.

"I told you, this is not official. I have no intention of shirking responsibility. My people are very good at what they do. Whatever's to be found, they'll find it, even it's only a trace. We don't mess around!"

"What then?" she said. "Explain yourself."

His demeanor changed. No longer the stiff-necked general. More like a regular Joe. He sighed and bowed his head in a way she'd never seen before--the way a *gentleman* humbles himself, before apologizing to a lady.

"Because, I've come to realize...there's a *link* at work here--between people, places, and events. It's all part of a chain that *cannot* be broken."

Some might call it *synchronicity*, once described as an "acausal connecting principle" or "meaningful coincidence"; the simultaneous occurrence of events that *appear* related, but have no *discernible* causal connection. Some use it to justify belief in the paranormal.

But that's not what Ashcroft meant at all.

He was thinking more along the lines of *nexus*: a central connection. If one happens to be at the nexus of something, it means they are right in the middle. The word came from Latin, meaning "that which ties or binds together." In this sense he was really talking about an invisible thread connecting all life, like that of the Spider-Woman, from Hopi mythology.

Una gasped.

Suddenly she understood why there was no security waiting to grab them outside the cave. Why their ATV and campsite remained untouched after several hours underground. And why, after all these years, that look in his eye never wavered, the same look that captured her heart so many years ago, meeting by chance on a plane--even though she didn't know it, and wouldn't come to realize it until 21 years later, when 'chance' brought her back to the place where her life began, for a purpose that she was only beginning to comprehend.

She also began to realize there was another *part* to this man, a part she *thought* might be there a few days ago, but was not completely sure--until now. He cared about *more* than military aspirations or government directives. He cared about *people*. And he wanted to do the right thing.

"Find any answers?" he asked.

Una trembled. She *wanted* to tell him everything, but wouldn't--not yet, not until *after* the search, when official duty had been satisfied. A whisper escaped from her lips, "Yes, but it's...complicated."

"Relax!" he said. "Flight 564 changed me, too."

At this point, he held out a simple gift, in one hand.

"What's this?"

"A token, between us."

Moonlight glistened off a delicate silver-chained necklace, with a round amulet, bearing a traditional Hopi symbol.

Her heart melted. *So he does understand.* She felt warm all over, just like that moment beneath the stars.

"I trust you recognize...?"

"Of *course*," she replied softly, gazing at its simple face, surrounded by rays, like the sun. "It's a *Corn Maiden*. Tradition says they were created in the palm of the right hand of the Great Spirit--as guides for the people on Earth."

She recalled, as a child, learning more:

> People
> were not always able
> to tell from among the many
> plants and animals
> what was good for them to eat
> --and what would harm them.
> So Corn Maidens were sent to
> give each clan a single seed of corn,

that, if properly cared for,
would feed and
sustain them.

The people
took and planted
their seeds in the ground.
Corn Maidens sang a song
that inspired love and faith.
Some began to offer water,
tending to the soil.
Slowly, the corn
grew.

Like a child,
each plant grew strong
and beautiful
with love and prayers
provided by the people.
As it grew, the people realized
how they were cared for
by the Great Spirit,
and so their faith grew, as well.
When the people had all the food
they needed,
Corn Maidens returned
to their home,
in the sky.

She wiped away tears.

Ashcroft gently clasped her hand--not as an adversary, but a friend, as one who understood perhaps at least a part of what she had endured all these years, the sleepless nights, wondering if 'it' really happened, or if it was all some kind of nightmare inflicted one night by a thunderstorm--one that would never come again, if she was lucky.

"I'm not your enemy," he said.

And she sighed. "Thank you, I...know that now."

Una was so moved that she found herself leaning over close, closer than they'd ever been before, lips parted, about to kiss--when a flock of sparrows, black-throated, white-crowned, and rufous-winged, erupted suddenly from the brush nearby into the red sky, forcing her to turn away.

When she looked back, he was gone.

***

Jack woke up to find Una by the campfire, alone.

"You okay? I thought I heard voices. Sun's coming. We'll have to get moving soon. Guess you didn't sleep much."

At first, she did not reply.

He eyed her up close. She seemed almost *spellbound*, watching sunrise.

"Is...everything all right?"

"Yes, Jack," she smiled without facing him, "Everything's fine."

PART FIVE

THE LONELY ROAD

*"We do not walk alone.
Great Being walks beside us.
Know this and be grateful."*

--Polingaysi Qoyawayma, Hopi

31

THE SEARCH

Sunlight broke through the trees at Alpha-Bravo as Una and Jack reached the gate. Local reporters from TV and Radio stations were already setting up shop with cameras and broadcast antennas. A crowd of onlookers included Hopi, Navajo, and Zuni, as well as curiosity seekers from Flagstaff and Winslow.

So far, things seemed pretty quiet, with anticipation in the air akin to that of a college sporting event, complete with tailgate gatherings around pickup trucks, colorful banners and T-shirt slogans like "Save Our Peaks" and "G.I. Joe, Time to Go!" Jack stayed with the Press while two officers escorted her inside.

"What's up?" she said to Ashcroft, trying to act casual.

He sighed.

"Funny you should ask. One of my men was found overnight, unconscious at the bottom of an exterior stairwell. He took quite a blow to the head and was rushed to the nearest medical center in

Flagstaff. We're still investigating."

She didn't know what to say.

People from the crowd began shouting questions. A line of police in riot gear stood between them and the fence. Tooms was there.

"Ignore them," said Ashcroft. "I've already issued a statement, per our agreement. They'll have to wait until we get back."

She nodded.

A young woman approached her in uniform. "Ma'am? It could get pretty rough. You'll need to be outfitted. General's orders. Please come with me."

He grinned.

"Okay," said Una, reluctantly. "But my backpack stays with me."

Jack waved at her from a distance.

Before long, she found herself standing in formation, wearing regulation combat overalls, boots, gloves and helmet, with goggles, surrounded by a military escort platoon of 22. Compared to her outing the night before, it seemed like overkill. Ashcroft was nowhere in sight.

A heavy tarp was removed from the backhoe-sized opening made earlier. Beyond it, the earth sloped downward, at an angle of thirty degrees.

"Don't be fooled," said a young soldier beside her. "It's not as smooth as it looks. Plenty of rocks and things. One of my buddies twisted his ankle so bad the first time he wound up in a cast."

"The *first* time?" she asked.

He suddenly turned away, realizing his mistake.

She decided he might be her only source. "It's okay," she whispered in his ear, "I'll never tell. Besides, I'm a little afraid. If you could stay close, I'd really appreciate it."

He blushed with pride. Her ploy seemed to be working already.

A command was given, and slowly, *Operation Underhill* began, with two lines descending the earth ramp.

"Miss Waters?" said a voice in her helmet.

It was Ashcroft.

"I'll be with you, each step of the way. Protocol demands I stay back, out of harm's way. You understand."

Not really, she thought.

The troops seemed well equipped. Besides weapons, radios, ammunition, helmets and flak jackets, they each humped a 50-pound rucksack. Sweat poured from their faces.

"No sign of booby traps, or mines!" a voice called out ahead.

She sighed. More overkill.

"In Afghanistan, we mostly found holes or natural ravines that were built over into large bunkers," the soldier said. "One we destroyed was 14 feet long, but we could only see about five feet of it. The rest was hidden...in rock."

"You must be older than you look," she replied.

He grinned.

Their path leveled off underground as the first tunnel appeared.

She could hear bits and pieces, just ahead. "Holy shit...*no way*...it's not random...whoever built this, sure knew their stuff!"

One by one, each opening was methodically explored. First, a cover team would provide exterior security; then scouts would carefully enter, scanning for danger. One revealed a deadly drop into an open crevasse, left centuries ago by an ancient quake. In larger spaces, they would first toss in ropes with grappling hooks to set off potential mines.

Of course, they would find none.

The biggest one ran 50 meters from its excavated entrance, forming a broad outer rim, with branches, ala spokes of a giant wheel, many of them collapsed, but these were smaller in circumference than the curved tunnel first encountered by Una's expedition the night before--as if they had somehow dropped *in* from above, more toward its center.

One branch displayed many compartments, presumably living quarters. Another, oddly enough, had divisions made of iron bars, reminiscent of jail cells--or at least, so they *said*. Una could not believe her ears.

It's the military mindset, she told herself. *They must be wrong.*

"Here we can't follow standard procedure," the soldier said.

"What do you mean?"

"Normally, in places like Afghanistan, once searched, most caves were destroyed by mortar fire or C-2 explosives. Here, we have to leave it intact. General's orders."

She sighed. Thank god for small favors.

Then, almost by chance, they stumbled upon a fissure in one wall that led, over crumbled debris, to an open room.

She recognized the reddish, thick columns of the hypostyle Sanctuary of *Palatkwapi*. Evidently, this irregular route formed a shortcut. *No wonder* Kwahu was able to reach the surface so quickly when he fled from the light.

Troops fanned out in both directions around the domed circular space. Their beams swept over its immaculate Egyptian-style mural of the *Three Worlds*, the dry moat beneath foot bridges that led to opposing stone arches, and its open, center space, which seemed empty by comparison.

Una noticed something odd. Some of the troops were equipped with night-vision or infrared. Was this meant to detect signs of her entry the night before? Were they looking for something out of place?

Then she realized they didn't have to. There were signs of entry all right. Plenty, in fact. Why hadn't she noticed it until now? The troops were following red footsteps from a *predawn patrol*.

As they approached the Sanctuary center, it all became clear.

She stopped and stared in disbelief.

This whole exercise was a *ruse*.

She had *intended* to lead them, if necessary. To *accidentally* 'discover' the object they supposedly all came to find: the Sacred Pillar with its Ancient Petroglyph, to prove once and for all, that the Hopi claim was true.

The night before--barely six hours ago--she'd stood on the very same spot where she stood right now.

Staring at the stone platform with its cradle, holding the Hopi rattle, before the granite pillar with its incredible prophecy regarding the destiny of mankind. She had hoped to point all this out to the soldiers, to let them share in its ancient wonder, even though the symbols had yet to be officially deciphered.

But that was impossible--because the platform and pillar were *gone*.

Not *just* gone, of course, as if by magic, but *removed*, with surgical precision. One could see where cuts had been made in the stone, then highly polished, to disguise the process. To an outsider, they would appear no different than a blank space in any other ancient monument, like Stonehenge or the Acropolis.

Una could hardly contain herself, but she dared not let it show. Ashcroft would get an earful, as soon as--*wait a minute, what did he say*? Every step of the way? Perhaps he was listening...even *now*.

"General!" she whispered with outrage, eyes

tuned to the edge of her helmet.

"Can you hear me? Because--"

"Yes, Una," he replied. "But before you go off the deep end, let's be clear--it was not me, or anyone under my command."

"What?!! But how can you--"

"Because, it's *true*. I've already confirmed it. The officer on duty, assigned to patrol the tarp-covered entrance, was accosted at approximately 2:50 AM by Elite Commandos, code-named *Ethereal,* sent directly under the auspices of Division Nine--which technically means they do not exist. No one in the government or the U.S. Military can vouch for them. But they have the respect and admiration of all who serve. That's all I can tell you. By the way, you can't pass it on--to anyone--or the penalty is *death*!"

"General, you can't be--'"

"I'm *not*," he chuckled. "Anyway, it's pointless to tell, because no one'll believe you."

"And you're telling *me*, because--"

"*We* have an understanding."

She paused. In spite of her outrage over this unexpected turn of events, she *did* trust him--with all of her heart--and had every reason to believe him.

"Una?" he said, "Are you with me?"

There was a lingering moment of silence, in which she wondered, beyond everything that was happening, if the future might hold something more for the two of them, another kind of life, in which they'd no longer be *apart*, on opposing sides in the eyes of independent observers, but teamed up *together*.

"Yes...Colin...I am."

And so it was settled, for now.

Retracing their steps at last, she removed her backpack, wrapped arms around it and sighed with relief. The Hopi "rattle" remained safe.

Suddenly, her mind raced. There was so much to be done! In less than twenty-four hours, she and her companions were scheduled to reappear before Tribal Council, to answer their "proof" demands.

That did not leave much time, but perhaps enough.

Aguda must be chomping at the bit...along with *others*, of course. A special team of experts was prepared to enter at a moment's notice, with everything they needed to authenticate the site.

Approaching the ramp, troops all around her seemed to quicken their steps. Una could not blame them. Moments, later, she felt the sun's warmth on her face--and smiled.

32

AUTHENTICITY

Jim Aguda found himself in good company, escorted by troops along with three other experts down the earth ramp into the cave site. Two were familiar names, by reputation only; Hastings, a revered paleobotanist from Boston, and Vogel, a symbologist perhaps best known for his work on Neanderthals. The third man, from Oraibi he'd seen once before, a sixth generation Hopi elder named Dan "O". With two escorts apiece, this brought the total number of participants in "Operation Validate" to twelve--a nice round number.

When it came to antiquities, of course, numbers were all important. Every piece of the past came from its own peculiar place in time. Tracking it down, however, often required a great deal of detective work.

One could not simply rely on an artifact's point of discovery--that is, its particular position in a dig or geographic locale on a map, because history had a way of displacing things. Natural forces, such as floods and hurricanes of course played a part, but there was also the unfortunate wildcard of human meddling, by way of activities like migration and warfare.

Aguda had a distinct advantage over his contemporaries, having seen the site already, but he must not admit to this, or risk being disqualified as a contributor to this exercise--a mistake that would undoubtedly haunt him to the grave.

"You came all this way from Kenya?" said Hastings. "I'd have thought Africa would contain enough wonders for a lifetime."

Clearly the man held a grudge of some kind. One could sense it in his bearing, looking down his nose as if it were a pointer.

"I live in America now," he replied.

"Of course. My mistake!"

"Let us hope you are more careful with your analysis," said Vogel, peering out beneath thick, dark brows. "Many people are counting on us to get it right."

Aguda marveled at their open animosity toward one another. Academics were usually more restrained. Perhaps their selection was part of a plan to foil this Operation, so that no consensus would be reached among them. Such a delay could jeopardize everything at stake.

"Save your breath," said Dan "O". "Oxygen below is less plentiful. Enjoy it now, while you can."

It did not take long to find their way to the

Sanctuary, following what by now had become a familiar path.

The troops provided plenty of light. Aguda knew to stay clear of the Sacred Pillar's vacancy and focus on other aspects of the site. While Hastings and Vogel at once latched on to opposite sides of the panoramic mural, he chose instead to examine Sotuknang's words carved into the huge half-opened doors beneath a stone arch. This time, he resisted the temptation to pass through them.

"A pity there aren't more artifacts," one soldier remarked.

"How's that?" said Aguda.

"I dunno. It's just that most places, when abandoned, have all kinds of junk left behind."

"Junk?"

"Sure. You know what I mean...eating utensils or day-to-day tools, even luxury items, like electronics, or fancy shoes. Funny how it all becomes less important, when your life's on the line. Either these people didn't have much to begin with, or they took it all with them."

After a while, it became deathly quiet, like the inside of a tomb--except for the sounds of cameras clicking or soldiers shuffling their feet out of boredom. They seemed content to remain here, with no need to explore any further.

Aguda felt they were cheating themselves. He knew for a fact that the great Red City of *Palatkwapi* had so much more to offer, but of course, they did not even know its name. Not yet anyway. And they might not discover it for weeks or months to come.

Suddenly, he began to wonder what happened to Dan "O". As a rule, the white-haired Hopi elder did not say much, even when asked. Still, in spite of his advanced age, the man had done well, traipsing about underground. They did not burden him with anything more on his back than spare oxygen.

Slowly, Aguda turned.

There, before the mural, Hastings appeared to be gathering minute organic samples with a dry paintbrush into a small vial. Simple tests performed on site would give a preliminary estimate to date the inscriptions, but *definitive* analysis would require access to high speed computers.

Vogel made tracings of engraved diagrams by rubbing charcoal over paper, then placed them, one by one, into a special three-ringed binder. He seemed especially pleased with his copy of a saucer-like object depicted in the skies over *Kuskurza*, the Third World.

Both techniques were considered to be non-invasive--the hallmark of serious archaeological study. The site appeared to be in safe hands, at least.

But in many ways, their hands were tied.

All the standard methods used to authenticate ancient relics did not apply here. X-ray Diffraction, Pigment Analysis and Radiocarbon Dating all required a great deal of time, with access to a professional lab. They worked best with small, hand-held, mobile objects, none of which could be found.

At least not now.

Besides, it would have only made their task more difficult.

Once upon a time, the market for Antiquities was well defined. The relative rarity of genuine relics made them scarce and expensive. But in recent years, owning and collecting historic artifacts had become a strong yearning for many. Thus forgers--many of them skillfully creating look-alike objects based on original designs from the same natural materials--had come forward, to take advantage of this world-wide hunger.

At least one sophisticated ring, including registered antique dealers, had made and sold hundreds of "ancient" artifacts over the past twenty years that were not antiquities at all. Using refined aging methods, they convinced scholars across the globe that their "discoveries" were real.

The advent of online auctions only made it worse. Thus even the serious modern collector faced a marketplace flooded with fake artifacts. They could be so convincing that they were unknowingly displayed in reputable museums--often sold for thousands of times their real value.

To give just one example, the market for Andean artifacts had changed dramatically. In the first years of eBay, the real-to-fake ratio was considered to be around 50 percent. After five years, the ratio of fake artifacts had nearly doubled, to about 95. In fact, so many "experts" had been trained using fakes that by now many of them could no longer tell a fake from a forgery.

Aguda found Dan "O" in the one place he least expected--at the Sanctuary center. He stood precisely over the spot once occupied by the platform, facing the empty space once held by the Sacred Pillar.

Approaching him, it was plain to see that the Hopi Elder was deeply moved, wiping a tear from his own eye.

"You all right?" said Aguda.

"I'll be fine," he replied. "But this Sanctuary has been decimated. Someone has taken its heart. I weep not for myself, or for those who built this place so many eons ago. I weep for the children who will never see this place, who will never know the prophecy because they cannot touch it up close."

Assisting Dan "O" away from there, the two of them walked together, hand-in-hand, to observe progress being made with the panoramic mural.

"What have you learned?" Aguda asked.

"Best guess?" said Hastings.

They both nodded.

"This *particular* work of art appears to date to a time period of 11,300 to 10,500 years ago. I do not rule out the possibility that it *may* have been carved as early as 14,800. But that's...only an estimate."

***

Outside the cave, Una went straight to Jack upon

resurfacing. She had to tell *someone* the news who'd appreciate the depth of her disappointment.

"It's just like Coyame, in '74...or the Dreamy Draw Dam, off the Squaw Peak Parkway!" he said.

"What do you mean?" she exclaimed.

"Both UFO cover-ups--*if* you can believe what they say. I've done some digging in the *Journal's* archives. It's all part of a pattern. You said it yourself. Ashcroft was looking for advanced technology. Maybe they found it."

"But he says he didn't--"

"So they went over his head--it happens. Back in '74, U.S. Air Defense radar detected a UFO heading for American airspace from the Gulf of Mexico. Moments later, it collided with a small civilian airplane and disappeared.

"The Mexican government sent a team to recover the plane--with spooky consequences. U.S. military personnel in Texas were monitoring radio traffic when the Mexicans recovered a shiny, silvery disk. But then, as they returned to base, *supposedly* they all dropped dead, exposed to something lethal...*emanating* from the craft! When satellite surveillance and jet flyovers showed that the Mexicans had died, U.S. recovery teams went in, seized the UFO and took it back to the States."

"So what's *that* got to do with Dreamy Draw?"

"Some people say it was *also* a UFO crash site. According to the story, back in '47, two men pulled alien bodies from the wreckage, storing the remains in a freezer. The Army Corps of Engineers used rock to cover it up, then built the Dam to conceal it. It's even documented in Frank Scully's 1950 book: *Behind the Flying Saucers*."

"You think they took the pillar as part of a cover-up?"

"*Somebody* did."

Una tried to get a grip.

The Hopi claim was not in jeopardy--of that she had no doubt. The Sanctuary, with its panoramic mural, depicting the *Three Worlds*, together with visions of the Ant People elsewhere, plus the inscribed words of Sotuknang, would all satisfy any requirements for site preservation.

The "search" could therefore be considered a success for the Hopi people, even though its primary target had failed to materialize. The *secret photos* however, would not be in vain, since they would be turned over to Elders behind closed doors and placed in the Hopi archives.

The prophecy would live on.

33

RELUCTANCE

The front page headline for the *Arizona Journal* read:

MILITARY ABANDONS
SACRED PEAKS

And people took notice. The story also appeared in newspaper rivals like the *Pioneer*, the *Tribune-News*, and the *Navajo-Hopi Observer*. But they didn't have a staff writer with the inside scoop, like Jack Howser.

He'd followed the entire ordeal from its inception, knowing details that would bring investigators from far and wide if they only knew, people from places like MUFON (Mutual UFO Network) and CUFOS (Center for UFO Studies), details that he could not put into print--not *yet*.

It was truly a David vs. Goliath tale, the kind that average folks love to read. The kind that inspires them to believe that with determination, belief in one self, and one's values, *anything* is possible in America-- no matter who you are or where you come from.

In a Press Release issued by the commander of Alpha-Bravo, the U.S. Army offered to provide any and all assistance needed to "secure" an ancient cave site recently found to contain Hopi artifacts. That offer was officially declined by members of the Tribal Council, citing other plans--in line with their rights under the Archaeological Resources Protection Act.

Like any small town, this was only the tip of the iceberg. The rumor mill among the breakfast crowd at *Falcon's Diner* had much more to offer. There everyone knew what was *really* happening--or thought they did.

Winslow's mixed population of about 10,000 Native Americans, Hispanics, Whites and Blacks did not expect the military to bow out gracefully. It seemed far more likely that "operations" would simply move out of sight. There were too many tales over the years of "roving patrols" at night. Too many to ignore. There *had* to be more to the story.

Jack thought so.

In an era of Facebook and Twitter, many people clamored for something old-fashioned and tangible: extra copies of the morning paper. Some news stands faced shortages before dawn.

"I wanted a piece of history for my children," said a native American woman who carefully covered her copy in plastic wrap to protect it from morning drizzle after waiting in line outside the *Journal* for nearly an hour.

Circulation officials finally closed their office

doors and posted a sign saying,

"SOLD OUT."

Of course, the papers only carried part of the story. No reporters (except Jack) were present in chambers when Una returned to the Hopi Tribal Council. She knew its 14 members were less concerned with rumors, more with "proof".

And she came prepared. Jim Aguda was there with detailed sketches of *Palatkwapi*, the Red City of the South, discovered beneath Fremont Peak. They brought enlarged photos taken by Jack and Tocho-- clear, easy-to-see images of giant stone carvings: Spider Woman, the hypostyle Sanctuary, and its Egyptian-like panoramic mural of the Three Worlds.

But they also held back, to avoid controversy. These proceedings were considered public--and Una had no intention of stirring up anger or resentment toward the U.S. military, or making claims of a government conspiracy.

Therefore, sensational images of the Sacred Pillar and its petroglyph were not shown. She did not mention the platform, its powerful Hopi Rattle, or the amazing prophetic "vision" she received from the Ant People while touching it. Her purpose here was not to ignite a firestorm. She had already decided to reveal such things to select Hopi Elders, in private--away from the public eye.

The district judge in Flagstaff would be satisfied.

Their native rights under law would be upheld. And the military "intruders" at Alpha-Bravo would be forced to abandon the Sacred Peaks, once and for all.

Una breathed a sigh of relief as they departed council chambers, with Jack, Aguda and Tocho all at her side. There were no reporters waiting with cameras and microphones to assault them. But there was a small crowd of smiling supporters from Oraibi, all waving signs.

It resembled a rally, like those thrown each fall for the boys' cross-country team at Hopi High, as they ran in ceremonial races, meant to bring blessings of the *Kachinas*, for rain and prosperity. Supporters shouted "Nahongvita!"--meaning "stay strong" or "dig deep". Families, like Kasa's and Moki's and Kwahu's, wanted to give thanks. They came to cheer and sing songs.

This tradition of running flowed from tribal scouts, like members of the Lizard clan, who were able to survive in the desert with little water.

But there were also unfamiliar faces in the crowd that day.

She had no way of knowing this, no reason to suspect strangers from a foreign land had come to witness their so-called "victory". It was not hard for them to conceal their true purpose in the midst of this celebration. Not even their nationality would give them away, not in America, the world's "melting pot", the 'land of the free' and 'home of the brave'. These observers, posing as tourists, were keenly aware that no one would notice or even care, when they whispered together--in *Chinese*.

***

General Ashcroft coordinated plans for departure, under a cloud of doubt. Not because his men harbored feelings of distrust regarding his leadership, or refused to follow orders. It was less tangible than that, more like a sense of uneasiness, as if somehow their work was incomplete.

It had happened before. Under pressure from bureaucrats to end occupation, forces would move out of a secured area, only to see it collapse into chaos.

No one expected a military coup in Arizona, but privately, a few officers wondered if secrets lay buried beneath the Peaks, secrets left behind that might prove valuable to the U.S. Military and its mission to secure the country against foreign invaders.

Experts at the Pentagon had pointed for years to links between ancient cultures around the globe, considered hostile to American interests--many which still persisted to this day. Theories abounded regarding how far these "Ancients" had actually come in establishing footholds on every continent. Theories could be dismissed, so long as no one had any proof. But a threat was a threat. Past or present. It was not only their job to find any and all that might exist, but to convince the general public otherwise.

One reason custodians at the Smithsonian cooperated with government educators to dispel any talk of Egyptian artifacts in the Grand Canyon was to make people *forget* such links were possible.

Ashcroft was reminded of this as the intercom buzzed on his desk at Alpha-Bravo. Though dismantling of the compound was underway, logistics required a series of protocols. Their task would require at least another 24 hours.

"Someone to...see you, sir," said his secretary's voice.

He paused, waiting for more.

Ordinarily, she gave specifics, such as name or rank or department of origin. It was not like her to leave him hanging.

"Yes?" he replied.

The intercom remained silent. This immediately put him on edge. The general did not fear for his safety or his command, but knew this was highly irregular. There must be a good reason.

"Very well, send them in."

As it opened, a strange individual proceeded through the door. He wore dark glasses to conceal the appearance of his eyes. His pale, white skin, devoid of any facial hair seemed almost transparent, as if he might be an *albino*.

The officer's long-sleeved gray uniform bore no lettering or insignia of any kind. A matching beret covered his bald head. Ashcroft detected no signs of recognition or respect or even acknowledgement. As a formality, he flashed an I.D. card, white and completely blank--except for an odd, three-sided holographic pyramid that seemed to rise from its center and vanish--so quickly that it must be an optical illusion. He decided not to ask any questions.

"Have a seat."

The stranger complied, sitting with perfect posture.

"I will be brief, and to the point," he said. "Your mission here is over. Take no further action except to complete withdrawal. Report to the Pentagon for reassignment."

"Understood."

Before Ashcroft could even rise to salute him, the stranger was gone.

***

Jack's phone beeped as they stood watching the crowd.

"What's up?" said Una.

He read a text message and grinned. "It's my boss at the *Journal*. Looks like I finally got a promotion! Maybe this'll be my chance to write a book...about this whole *ordeal*, I mean...well, to show what's it like to *really*--"

She frowned.

"The *abbreviated* version, of course!"

Kasa took hold of her hand, dragging them both. "Where to?" he asked.

"C'mon. I'm having a dinner party. It's time to celebrate!"

Tocho licked his lips in anticipation as they made their way up the street. In Oraibi, everything seemed close. Ahote and Sukya had already gone on ahead, to make preparations.

Una had bigger questions on her mind. She wondered what would become of *Paltakwapi*, and how its discovery would impact life on the Reservation. One could hardly compare it to Egypt's Giza Plateau, but it seemed to her every bit as important. Both sites encompassed an important beginning for mankind.

Hopis had reluctantly accepted tourism because it enabled them to survive. But they always had control, limiting people's access to certain ceremonies, forbidding the use of cameras--to preserve their way of life.

There was no telling how *this* would change things. More people and more money could bring more *trouble*.

She eyed red clouds overhead.

The Sky People who protected the Hopi for a thousand generations were still watching, providing direction.

Somehow, she thought they would *not* let that happen.

34

LOOSE ENDS

Helping herself to blue corn tamales with semi-sweet fillings that were so scrumptious she had to have two, Una recognized Moki, in tattered jeans and over-sized t-shirt, thumb-wrestling with Tocho. The boys seemed oblivious to everything around them.

"It's good to hear their laughter," said Kasa.

Sukya agreed. "Moki's back. I remember when this whole thing started. The way kids taunted him at school. 'They laugh at me because I'm different,' he said, 'I laugh at them because they're all the same.' "

Jack eyed hand-painted insignias on kitchen pots in a glass case. "So...that's the *Roadrunner* clan?"

Kasa nodded.

Una found him enjoying a ceramic bowl of Nogkwici--white corn and lamb stew with a nutty crunch. "Try the Piki bread," he said, "So thin, it melts in your mouth."

She grinned. He was preaching to the choir.

"I guess you'll be...leaving soon?"

Though he tried to pretend it was no big deal,

she sensed uncertainty in his voice. It was more like a plea to *stay*.

"Not yet. I still have unfinished business...with the Elders."

His eyes opened wide. "Of course. How could I forget? Which brings up an important question ...about the *you-know-what*, I mean--"

"Yes?" she answered abruptly, to keep him from blurting it out. Although they'd agreed not to mention the Hopi "Rattle" in public--out of fear that someone might catch on--Jack apparently couldn't help himself.

"Well, I mean, it's pretty high tech, I mean *unbelievable*. They won't let something like that go."

"By 'they' you mean--"

"Army, Navy, Air Force--my god, you *name* it! They'll study what they have and figure out something's *missing*. Who knows how long *that'll* take?"

"So?"

"So when they *do*, they'll come *looking* for it! Will it be safe here? What about your people? Will they even know what to--"

"Well, I don't--"

He placed his hand over hers. "*Exactly*. It's something to think about. That's *all* I'm saying."

Una's mind began to race. There *were* hidden places in D.C., so secure that few people even knew they *existed*. A friend of hers in particular, the woman obsessed with personal horoscopes, had the inside track to one of them. In spite of her flaky personality, she was apparently quite good at her job, and this gave her certain perks, like access to codes which enabled her to enter places beneath the capital--completely unnoticed.

"I see your point," she said. "There...*might* be a way."

"Good. Now, don't tell me. The fewer who know, the better. Besides, if there *is* a collapse of government--God forbid--and any of this should ever come out, I'd rather not face a firing squad."

"Jack!"

He laughed, toasting her with a pinkish glass of prickly pear wine. "Just kidding!"

The party took an unexpected turn as horses pulled up outside. When Kasa opened the door, two native scouts in familiar garb rushed over to Ahote. Una recognized them at once: twenty-something-year-old Pachua, filled with enthusiasm, unable to stand still, and Shilah the Navajo, somewhat older and more mature. He conversed with Ahote, keeping their voices low.

They motioned for her to join them. Jack naturally tagged along.

Ahote met her with somber eyes. "They bring disturbing news...from Mount Fremont. Reports of strange lights, less than an hour ago. Choppers, maybe. Then a sonic boom...followed by tremors. We...don't know for sure."

"We need to go," she said, "Right away."

"Wait," said Jack. "Could be dangerous. Let me

make a call. A friend of mine works for the National Weather Service in Flagstaff. He may have a clue."

Patiently, they waited. Pachua managed to stuff three tamales in his mouth. Shilah politely accepted a fresh slice of watermelon.

Someone tapped her on the shoulder. Una turned. It was Chu'si.

"Got a minute?"

"Well, I mean, sure, it's just--"

She decided to play it cool, so as not to spoil the party--or create a panic. Hopefully, it would turn out to be nothing. Final Army preparations to leave the Peaks, maybe--like demolition of Alpha-Bravo. Or something completely natural, like a minor quake. They'd seen evidence to support that idea in *Palatqwapi*. She had a few minutes to kill anyway, waiting for Jack to get off the phone.

Chu'si downed the remainder of her wine glass. She seemed anxious, almost afraid to speak.

"There's something I've been meaning to tell you."

Una sighed. They'd already covered old ground and patched things up. She could not imagine anything *else* that Chu'si might have done in the past ten years that could possibly make any difference between them.

"When you first got here, I was resentful, afraid to trust you. I thought you might have ulterior motives, trying to take advantage of us. So I did something I deeply regret. It *seems* like things have worked out pretty much, but I can't let you leave without knowing the truth."

Tears welled up in her eyes.

"And I *hate* to tell you this, because I feel in many ways that our friendship has been renewed. And *that* means a lot to me, because I *really* missed you. And I hated myself for ever hurting you the way I did. And now, I'm afraid that we'll *never* be friends, and I can't live with the thought of that!"

She threw her arms around Una, and began to cry.

Talk about bad timing.

Patting Chu'si on the back, she found *herself* crying, even though she did not know why. It was a *woman thing*.

"Okay," her friend said at last, sniffling, trying to clear her throat. "I'm just gonna say it. I was an *informant* for Ashcroft, behind your back. I thought I was being patriotic, or something. It was a *terrible* mistake--and I'm sorry!"

Una grinned at the thought.

"So, *you're* the one! I totally forgive you! Do you know how I *feel* about him? How this whole thing has changed me? You did me a favor! You are my best friend--and always will be!"

Chu'si's face lit up with elation.

Across the room, she could see Jack coming her way, with a frown. She left her friend to speak with him.

"They know about it," he said, "but have no data.

Checked all the regional monitors. There's no record of volcanic or seismic activity. *Whatever* the cause, apparently, it's *not* natural."

A sense of panic rose up inside her.

"Let's go," she said. "Right now. I'm ready."

Her friends were not surprised. They brought extra horses, just in case.

This time, she hopped into the saddle without hesitation.

"What about your meeting with the Elders?" said Jack.

"It can wait."

And so they trekked on horseback once more through the wilderness to Fremont Peak. There was little discussion, afraid of what they might find. The four horses seemed to appreciate the urgency of this trip, making better time than anyone expected--almost as if they had supernatural guidance.

It did not take long to figure out what had happened. One could still smell traces of jet fuel and see a lingering trail of twisted gray smoke against the moonlit desert sky.

Little remained of Alpha-Bravo, except for rubble and fallen pines. The heavy fence, fortified cinderblock building, and electrical wires were gone. A bulldozer had leveled the site to its original slope configuration.

But the rocks were more prominent, piled higher than before, beyond what might be considered possible with ordinary earth-movers. In fact, it appeared as if the mountainside had *collapsed*, raining tons of debris directly down to completely seal off the cave.

She gasped.

And Una knew this was no avalanche, no accidental result of misplaced explosives. It was deliberate *destruction*, meant not just to fulfill the judge's orders but to render their discovery moot, to bar anyone of ordinary means from finding *Palatkwapi*, the Red City of the South, ever again.

"That bastard!" said Pachua, waving his fist, "How could he?"

"He *couldn't*," she said, "That's how I know Ashcroft didn't do it."

"But he was in command. You can't trust the military! Bombs are their weapon of choice. No 'loose ends' left behind."

Jack shook his head.

"You're *both* right. He didn't have to. They probably went over his head. There are plenty of misguided people within our own government whose agenda could easily explain it. Truth will come to light. Their efforts to conceal it will not last forever. It's only a matter of time."

***

After returning to Oraibi, Una gathered up her backpack and a leather carrying case specially prepared for Hopi Elders. She walked through the streets alone to meet at the appointed place.

Three old men greeted her with warm hugs in a traditional adobe structure, perhaps the oldest of its kind on the entire reservation. It had multiple levels, extending down beneath the village to a secret space behind a metal door, known only to the Keepers of the Archives.

Here every conceivable artifact of ancient Hopi history that one might imagine was stored--at least all that were known prior to Una's discovery--including the red *Sacred Stone Tablet* given to them by the Great Spirit long ago. One of four, the other three, white, black, and yellow, were given to races for safekeeping in the South, in Africa, and in Tibet--just as it was told to her by *Kuwanyauma*.

Relaying their discoveries in *Palatkwapi*, Una explained their finding of the Sacred Pillar, displaying clear photos of its prophetic message carved into the Petroglyph, recounting parts of her "vision" from the Ant People--at least, what she could remember. The details seemed to fade over time.

There was no need to mention the Hopi "Rattle", with its unearthly power. No need to endanger these people or their sacred way of life. No need to make them targets of modern day operatives within the government or military, who would stop at nothing to grasp its superior technology and wield it for their own purposes against enemies across the globe.

She knew that when the time was right, a still, small voice inside her would sound the alarm--the same voice that brought her home to Oraibi.

Two of the Elders expressed eternal gratitude to Una, for hearing the cries of her ancestors. But Dan "O' long remained silent. No one could understand why he seemed so withdrawn, compared to his last appearance at Tribal Council.

Holding up the largest image of the Petroglyph beside him, Dan "O" at last cleared his throat, and they knew he was ready to speak.

"No doubt, much time and study will be needed to grasp its full meaning. What I give you now, is a rough translation:

First...

"Visitors come to Earth, long ago,
slowly transforming man,
World War comes...twice,
The Victors accept technology
in exchange for human subjects,
Through abduction and breeding,
to build a better race."

Then...

"Manipulated by fear, lust, and greed,
man sows chaos,
World War III brings Armageddon
between East and West,
Ancient messages are deciphered,

> and ghosts walk among us,
> As Star Brothers visit
> in flying shields."

Lastly...

> "In the wake of war, a
> Dragon awakes to seize dominion,
> Alerting a secret Armada
> to invade from Beyond,
> When at last the Purifier brings
> Red Dawn and Illumination,
> We walk with our Brothers...
> and rebuild the Earth."

There was a moment of silence.

"So...it's a message of hope?" said Una.

He nodded. "The last part refers to our future. We are moving into the *Fifth World*, a time when all four of the sacred powers--red, white, black and yellow-- will be *reconnected*.

"The ancient cultures are not dead. All the wisdom that has been collected, is being kept for us-- in places like this Archive--waiting to awaken in our spirits. When that happens, things long forgotten will return to us: *art*, *music*, *song* and *dance*. But the Earth will also *shake*, like it has never done before. There will be much fear--but we must not be afraid. It will a *cleansing*, to remove the spiritual sickness of generations. Thus it will also be a time for *healers*, when the wisdom to work with Mother Earth will be restored."

Una sighed. She did not understand it all, but she knew that *one* day, she would return to this place, with the Hopi "Rattle", to meet the Great Spirit. She only hoped that her loved ones would survive, to face it *together*.

35

FIELD REPORT

Una sat down in front of her laptop, fingers poised. Outside the nearest window, red dust kicked up in the streets of Oraibi. Duty required her to file an official report. Yet it hardly seemed possible.

How could anyone without a sufficient frame of reference begin to make sense of what had happened here?

Maybe *that* was the wrong question.

The Department of the Interior concerned itself with the management and conservation of federal land and natural resources. It administered programs relating to Native American territorial affairs.

So it was *really* a matter of territory. Did the Hopis have land rights or not? It seemed as if the matter was already settled.

Una sighed. Soon, she'd have to pack and head for the airport.

But not *yet*. Not before she made an effort to sum things up, while it was still fresh in her mind.

Maybe *that* was it. Here role was not to *explain*,

but simply to put it to rest. Give the bureaucrats peace of mind. And so she began:

> Field Report #117-01A
> Prepared by Agent Una Waters
>
> Issues regarding Native Rights pertaining to Fremont Peak have been officially resolved.
>
> A joint search of the recent cave discovery there, conducted by special U.S. Army forces, field experts and native representatives has yielded human evidence of ' archaelogical interest' over 100 years old, thus enabling the site to qualify for protection under the Archaelogical Resources Protection Act.
>
> In keeping with the Act, a copy of expedition findings has been provided to Hopi Elders.
>
> All U.S. Army forces, under the command of General Ashcroft have withdrawn from the temporary installation known as *Alpha-Bravo*. Army offers to

FIELD REPORT

secure the cave were declined by the Tribal Council.

"Native Rights" have been legally recognized by a federal judge in Flagstaff--a point rendered moot by a subsequent rock slide of unknown cause, sealing the cave entrance. An environmental impact study is currently planned.

Preliminary findings suggest a disconnect between the level of technology displayed in stone carvings and the historical record as it pertains to this site. Unfortunately, without access for further study, its true significance may never be understood.

Barring further authorized inquiry, this case -- File #117-01A -- is closed.

Personal note: with permission of the Secretary, a special one day "pass" to the Smithsonian has been granted to teen Hopi members of the Explorers Club, in appreciation for their assistance.

Agent Una Waters,
Native Rights Division.

Backing away from the keyboard, she paused, thinking of her friends that dark lonely night, making their "vow" to keep the Hopi "Rattle" a secret. Something deep down inside told her it was the *right* decision.

Would she ever be able to tell Ashcroft?

Yes, she decided--*but only under the right circumstance.*

Una moved to another window, eyeing the Sacred Peaks. She pictured the Sanctuary at *Palatkwapi*, its mural of the Three Worlds and doorway to the Fourth. How long would it be before events foretold by the Petroglyph--pertaining to the Fifth World--came true? Would it happen in her lifetime? And what role would the "Rattle" have to play?

She could not begin to guess.

"Need some help with that?" said Tocho, pointing to her carry-on bag. It was already packed.

She nodded. Zipping up her laptop in its carrying case, she followed him through the house, dragging her feet.

She paused to consider the photo of Tocho and his two pals, Moki and Kwahu, from Explorer's Club, realizing that it was actually a closeup from a much larger gathering. Teens beside a school van sporting the club logo waved a huge banner in the background:

FIELD REPORT

EXPLORERS *FIND* A WAY!

"Oh yeah," said Tocho, "Thanks for the pass! We're all super excited. Can't wait to get there! Road trip, here we come!"

She smiled. "You've got my number?"

He pulled up his sleeve. There it was in black magic marker, written on his forearm.

Una laughed. "That seems a bit extreme. Will it wash off?"

"Sure. I guess. In week or two."

"Ring me when you get into town."

He nodded, escorting her outside.

Sukya approached with an empty back-pack, wiping tears away from her eyes. "Wait! W-won't you be needing this?"

Una felt tears of her own, coming on. "Not right away. We don't hike many trails in D.C. Save it...for next time, or better yet, bring it when you come to visit. We'll try out a few super shopping malls!"

They hugged and cried together.

Jack waved to her from his Ford Pinto, waiting patiently. She still had plenty of time for goodbyes. He grinned, not meaning to interfere.

"To think this all started with a letter," she said to Kasa, as they embraced.

"Don't be foolish. It began the moment you were born. That light in your eyes, was always there for a *reason*. It shines on us all. The voices cried out, and you answered. I *knew* you would come back to us!"

"What about our discovery? The cave?"

"Not to worry," said Ahote, with a final embrace. "Its legacy will live on. The Elders know what to do. We will keep watch over the Peaks, for any signs of mischief. We have the law on our side. Perhaps one day soon, when the time is right, the Ant People will return, to lead us all away from the Reservation, to prepare for the Fifth World. We are not afraid!"

A huge gust of wind kicked in from the desert, rolling over the edge of Third Mesa, throwing red dust in the air. They all paused to cover their noses and eyes. For a moment, it was impossible to see anything. The ancient village of Oraibi, with its hand built stone houses and dirt roads, became almost invisible, blending in so well with the dust that it threatened to disappear.

Then, the wind became still, as they all breathed a sigh of relief.

Startled by a moving shadow, Una's eyes came into focus. She detected a familiar sight.

There, on the edge of town, appeared the pair of spirit wolves, one black, the other white, who greeted her that first day, upon arrival, at the Bus Depot.

Of course, no one else could see them.

She understood that now.

The unworldly light in their eyes did not frighten her, because she knew they came to bring her comfort.

Una blinked, and suddenly, the wolves were

replaced by her *parents*, standing there, plain as day, in the clothes she last remembered them--like the vision she had a few days before, of them together, just before the avalanche that claimed both of their lives.

A sense of well-being surged through her, from top to bottom. Every cell in her body felt energized. Her heart leaped for joy, knowing that her parents were not gone. They would always be with her now, like the Sky People who watched over her as a child.

It made her feel *loved*.

Then, just as suddenly, another gust lifted their eyes skyward, toward thick clouds drifting slowly overhead. It was a good sign, a sign the *Kachinas* were bringing rain to Oraibi, rain that would create blooms in the desert with an explosion of color and make their corn grow.

She wanted to dance.

A rain drop fell into her eye and she blinked, once again. Soon there would be a steady downpour, dancing in metal gutters and bouncing off hot pavement, with rivulets of steam rising upward.

She turned.

The wolves were gone.

"We're lucky," said Jack, suddenly beside her, with a smile on his face.

It was time to go.

"Rain'll keep the dust down for a while. C'mon...take a seat!"

36

KEEPSAKE

Una sipped coffee with Jack, seated at a small cafe overlooking the lone runway at Flagstaff Pulliam Airport. Her Western boots and blue jeans had completely lost their newness after ten days of rocky terrain on foot and horseback in the Arizona desert.

Aromas of salsa-laden Diablo burgers, hand cut fries and breakfast tacos drifted over from other tables, but she had no appetite.

With time to kill, he opened a morning paper. The news had plenty to say about fear over cyber-threats from other countries, uncertainty in the stock market, and corrupt politicians.

Yet there was no mention of Fremont's "rockslide mystery", or its devastating consequences.

Why was he not surprised?

Jack noticed her fidgeting with a simple amulet on a delicate silver chain around her neck. Though it might be a souvenir from any of the countless giftshops in Winslow, he assumed it to mean something more. Its symbolic face, with sun-like rays in all directions did not ring a bell.

"*Corn Maiden*," she replied to the look in his eyes. "Sent by the Great Spirit to guide people on Earth. It helps me now, to remember who I am."

She said no more.

So he figured there must be a long story behind it--one she cared not to tell, filled with emotion that might come spilling out, causing her to fall apart--when she very much needed to keep it together.

He let it go.

Jet sounds reverberated through the glass, growing louder each time someone opened the door. The morning sun was already heating things up. An outside thermometer read 84 degrees.

"So...it's back to 'life in the big city'," he said. "I'll bet you can't wait. Must make *this* place look like Hicksville."

Their eyes met.

"Not really," she said. "I grew *up* here, remember? To me, it'll always be home. The big city's not all it's cracked up to be!"

Silence reigned again.

She wondered if anyone in D.C. would even care to ask about her trip. They were all so self-absorbed, obsessed with politics and campaign rhetoric. Life in remote places like *Hopiland* held little meaning for them.

Jack took a refill on his coffee. Una didn't seem to notice that hers was getting cold.

"Just because you're going back doesn't *mean* we

can't stay friends. I've got contacts all over. We can still chat, from time to time. D.C.'s a real cess pool, I'm sure. Some predict dark days ahead. Hopis aren't the only ones. Ever see *Independence Day*? If aliens arrive, give me a heads up!"

Una was not amused.

"Seriously...about what happened in the cave. The "vow" I mean. You can count on me. I won't say a word."

A weak smile crossed her lips.

"By the way, don't be fooled. This airport *looks* small, but they still do everything by the book...security, the whole nine yards. The *you-know-what* would never make it past the gates. Do you have a plan to safely transport it to D.C.?"

She nodded. Tocho came to mind:

> Tooling down the road in his school minivan with its hand-painted "Explorer's Club" logo, music blaring, kids shouting as they made their way across country. Wanting to save money by sleeping on the way or eating food mostly from drive-thru's, the trip would last a couple days, maybe more. The Hopi "Rattle"— wrapped in brown paper

to prevent direct human contact--would travel with him, securely fastened beneath the driver's seat with duct tape.

She'd be waiting on his call.

Out of curiosity, Jack couldn't help but glance at her ticket, poking out of her purse. She'd be in a giant B-757 airliner, the same size as Flight 564. A weird expression came over his face.

"Hey, I thought you arrived on a *bus*. Since when do you fly?"

"I've managed to put that behind me."

"What? Fear of *planes*?"

She shook her head. "The *unknown*. I've learned a few things."

"Such as--"

"There's *someone* on the other side, for one thing. And they *know* me--better than I know myself."

He folded his newspaper, setting it aside. Big city or small didn't matter. Too many ads and too little substance. They just weren't like they used to be. Not like he remembered.

Once upon a time you could spend a lazy Sunday at home, pouring over each section. Everything was in there, from Homicides to Touchdowns, local and nationwide. One could catch up with the world over a single pot of coffee, and come out feeling pretty well informed.

Not anymore.

He took another sip. By now, his cup was getting cold, and the waitress was nowhere to be found.

He looked at his watch, and sighed. Time was running out.

"Well, at *least* the Army's gone. People are mighty happy about that. We don't much like the idea of uniformed spies watching every move we make. This used to be the Wild West. Which reminds me--"

And she knew what he was going to say.

Jack had been pretty considerate up to now, not prying into her personal life. He kept his distance, even when her behavior practically gave it away, when logic would have dictated otherwise.

Something *else* had happened to her here, something she could not have predicted or ever explain. Because it's a bit like facing the unknown.

A change of heart had taken her by surprise...opened a door that she thought might forever be closed...and filled her with impossible dreams. The dreams she once held as a little girl growing up in a big wide world. Dreams that were shattered by the loss of her parents, but now sprang anew with the help of a spark.

"The general was sort of a *cowboy*, was he not?"

She grinned.

"Some might even say *brat*."

Her smile opened wide.

"Well, you'll *probably* never see him again. I mean, what are the chances?"

As she fiddled with her necklace, by chance she felt something with her finger, flipped it around and nearly gasped. Etched on the back was a single word, *Colin*, with a number : his personal cell.

"I don't know," she said, "*Stranger things have happened!*"

THE END

ABOUT THE AUTHORS

T.J. & **M.L. Wolf** joined forces in the field of Healthcare, exploring mutual interest in the work of UFO researchers like Budd Hopkins and movie directors like Steven Spielberg. The History Channel's *Ancient Aliens* became a focal point of their quest to uncover the truth regarding humanity's purpose and how it pertains to our future. Married twenty years, they write speculative fiction and live in Boardman, Ohio with their six-pound Yorkie, who keeps the family in line.

Be sure to look for:

THE DRAGON'S GLARE

BOOK TWO

THE SURVIVAL TRILOGY

Coming to AMAZON in 2017

Made in the USA
Columbia, SC
02 November 2017